"Angelique and Carlotta, I'm seeking your help tonight. Don't be afraid to make your presence known. You do not need to be afraid. Brenda is here tonight, and so is Tina."

She stopped and moved her head back as if listening but didn't open her eyes. Brenda couldn't figure out why Susan thought she needed this elaborate setting to get Angelique or Carlotta to appear. Then she noticed the candle. For a few seconds, she saw two candles. One wavered and melted into the other. Brenda blinked and the illusion was gone. She looked around the room. If Carlotta or Angelique were there, they were hiding.

Susan's shoulders started to sag, and her head was slowly dropping to her chest. Was she falling asleep? Brenda wasn't ready to pull her hands free. Without warning, Susan jerked up and opened her eyes. Except they weren't her eyes. It wasn't her face. Something else was trying to take shape. She stared directly at Brenda. Brenda shook her head hard and shut her eyes tight, hoping all would be back to normal. But when she looked again, the eyes that were not Susan Christie's were still staring back at her. Then Susan smiled.

It was subtle at first, a slight chill in the touch of her hand. Then a jolt of ice shot through Brenda, and Susan's hand gripped hers like a vise. It frightened Brenda. She was about to yank her hand away and break the circle, but Susan's hand suddenly felt warm and soft again. Except it was slender and gray. Not Susan's.

When Brenda looked up at Susan's face, it wasn't Susan at all. The porcelain blue eyes of Carlotta were locked on her, sparkling and wet with tears.

Visit

Bella Books

at

BellaBooks.com

or call our toll-free number

1-800-729-4992

Tangled and Dark

Patty G. Henderson

Bella
BOOKS
2004

Bella Books, Inc.
P.O. Box 10543
Tallahassee, FL 32302

Printed in the United States of America on acid-free paper
First Edition

Editor: Christi Cassidy
Cover designer: Michelle Corby

ISBN 1-931513-75-9

This book is a humble homage to H. P. Lovecraft. Without his fantastic fiction, *Tangled and Dark* would not have been possible. But beyond that, this book is dedicated to my nephew, Terence, who is a bigger influence on me than he realizes, and who discovered H. P. Lovecraft at just about the same age I did.

Acknowledgments

Despite the somewhat romantic image of a writer as a solitary creator, the writer needs love and support to create a book. I couldn't have finished *Tangled and Dark* without that love and support from a special woman in my life. Michelle Corby spent hours talking, eating and breathing Brenda Strange with me. She also did the stunning cover for the book. For that, I repaid her by naming a character after her in *Tangled and Dark*.

I'd like to give special attention to Nolan Canova for allowing me to mention his Web site. Nolan is Webmaster and owner of Nolan Canova's Crazed Fan Boy. Yes, there really is a site by that name. It's a wild and crazy site for anyone who enjoys the science fiction, mystery/suspense, horror or fantasy culture and can relate to the word *fan*.

Thanks also to Will Moriaty, who writes the "La Floridiana" column for Nolan Canova's Crazed Fan Boy Web site, for letting me reference his column on Florida's sea creature sightings. Check out the archives on the Web site and read the actual reports that Brenda accessed in this book.

www.CrazedFanBoy.com

Oh yes, my doubting friends, there are places deeper than deep in the ocean. Places so tangled and dark that you'd think nothing could live there. But something does. In places cold and hidden from prying eyes, dwell others who are neither man nor fish, but something not meant to walk with us.

—*From the Depths to Madness*, 1938, by Quentin Trask

About the Author

Patty G. Henderson has been published since the early 1970s in magazines such as *Paragon* and Dale Donaldson's, *Moonbroth*. More currently, she is the editor of an online fiction magazine, *Flash Fantastic* and the author of the Brenda Strange supernatural mystery series. *The Burning of Her Sin* was the first book in the series which is set in Tampa, Florida. *Tangled and Dark* continues the Brenda Strange PI series, with a third book, *The Missing Page*, due to follow soon in 2005 by Bella Books. *Blood Scent*, an erotic vampire romance, was Henderson's first published book.

Between writing novels and writing flash fiction, Patty still works a full time job at a photography studio. Patty G. Henderson is a Tampa, Florida native, born in Ybor City, and still lives in beautiful South Tampa.

Chapter 1

Brenda flipped through the police report one more time. She had spent the better part of the chilly afternoon reading the Paula Drakes file that Kevin had faxed from his New Jersey office.

Anything to help out an old friend, Brenda thought. Kevin loved running his agency on overload. She'd agreed to help him with this case only because it was right here in her backyard.

Unfortunately, it was now the first of December. Two months since Kevin had faxed the report to her. It had taken Brenda several days to get reacquainted with the details.

After September 11, everything in everyone's life just went to hell. Both Tina and Brenda had friends in New York. Although they were okay, Tina was shaken. Since Brenda hadn't heard from Denise Miller, Paula Drakes' sister and now her client, she made the decision to leave Malfour and stay with Tina for a while. Their time together, while not under the best of circumstances, might repair their relationship. In addition, Denise Miller lived in Jersey City. Not far from Newark. Brenda thought a personal visit with her client might prove beneficial.

Brenda hadn't known Denise Miller was a nurse. Denise had volunteered to work extra shifts at whatever New York hospital needed her during the weeks after September 11. Brenda never got a chance to meet her, but at least now she understood why Denise Miller might have her hands full with other things.

The report in front of Brenda was thorough. A Detective Canello of the Tampa Police Department had written the detailed report. TPD officially closed the case but they'd left too many holes in it to satisfy Denise Miller, Paula Drakes' sister. She was paying Brenda big money because she believed someone murdered her sister. The Tampa Police Department apparently wasn't as convinced. They'd tagged it an accidental drowning.

Brenda was missing an important piece. The autopsy report. It wasn't in the file. She needed to get her hands on it. There were far too many questions and Brenda didn't like dancing in the dark with a new case. She'd been that way as a lawyer. Brenda Strange never went to court until she had every little detail clear. She still hated being unprepared and liked surprises even less.

Earlier in the week, she'd called the TPD contact Kevin had mentioned. She got Detective Lisa Chambliss's voice mail. Brenda left a message and both her home and cell numbers.

She sank farther down into the leather sofa and found herself unable to fight off that sluggish, late-afternoon kind of sleep that was creeping over her.

Brenda woke with a start. How long had she been asleep? She looked around for what had disturbed her nap. The police file lay scattered and open on the floor, the sheets of paper floating away. The windows were partly opened, but there wasn't even a hint of a breeze.

"Carlotta? Angelique?" Brenda sat up and started picking up the loose sheets. Carlotta and Angelique were ever-present at Malfour. In her bedroom, Carlotta had become a constant visitor; Brenda often found her sitting on the chair by the window. Brenda was never alone. And she liked that. She didn't want to admit it, but she'd barely had time to miss Tina. Just as well. Tina would never understand. Talking to ghosts wasn't acceptable to her lover.

Brenda often engaged in lengthy conversations with Carlotta and Angelique. She'd learned that Angelique was playful, teasing and headstrong. Carlotta was more reserved, serious and full of curiosity.

"Why do you stay here in this house when so much beauty, love and light await you on the other side?" Brenda had asked once. "You can have eternal bliss."

"How would you know?" Angelique questioned.

"I've seen it. I was almost there," Brenda said, remembering her purifying and euphoric trip through the tunnel of light after Danny Crane's bullets sent her knocking at death's door.

Neither Carlotta nor Angelique answered her now. Brenda had just placed the last sheet of the report in the file when she heard the crunch of tires on her driveway outside. From a front window, she watched a big gray sedan roll to a stop in front of the porch. Brenda kept her eye on the tall, large man who got out and walked toward the house at a leisurely pace. Paunchy belly, thinning hair and a moustache, he wore brown pants that almost matched his dark, Latin complexion and a tan sport coat. He took in everything around him. Brenda already had him pegged. She opened the door before he could knock.

"Detective, what can I do for you?"

"Do you always greet your visitors that way?" He covered his apparent surprise with a smile.

"My powers of deduction astound me sometimes."

"Well, they certainly astound me." He held out his large hand. "I'm Detective Canello, Homicide." He held up his ID and badge. "And you must be?"

"Brenda Strange." She took his hand. "Why don't you come in, please." Brenda noticed him staring at her as she directed him to the living room. She offered the big high-backed chair by the window. He didn't sit down right away.

"I know you probably hear this a million times, but do people tell you that you look just like—"

"Princess Diana. All the time, Detective."

Detective Canello decided to sit down. Brenda sat on the couch opposite him.

"This is an unofficial visit, Miss Strange. You called about Paula Drakes."

"But I was expecting Detective Lisa Chambliss."

"Yeah, well, she's tied up with paperwork. We worked on the case together."

"You wrote an in-depth report, Detective. TPD must have had their doubts when they put homicide detectives on the case." Brenda looked straight into his face. "I'm not convinced Drakes' death was an accident. Why are you? And why are you here if the case is closed?"

"She's as close to a drowning as they come. We had nothing to tell us otherwise." He met her gaze without flinching. "If you've got something to change my mind, now would be a good time to let me have it."

"What I've got is a sister who's so convinced Paula was murdered that she hired a private investigator." Brenda smiled slightly and gave him one of her most unassuming looks.

Canello shook his head. "People sometimes have trouble facing the death of their loved ones, Miss Strange. They can't accept the simple reason for the loss."

"Maybe the reason isn't so simple."

"Or maybe they just want to stir things up because they can't cope with the guilt," Canello said as he shifted in the chair. "Miss Strange, the TPD has a seventy-five percent rate for solving murder investigations. We do the job better than most."

Brenda leaned back into the couch. "Detective Canello, I'm not sticking the knife to the police department. I'm just trying to take a different angle here. I'm going to do my job and I'd like your help."

Detective Canello got up slowly. "As far as TPD is concerned, Paula Drakes is an accidental drowning. Closed. Period. If you get anything that can change that, you have the department number." He started toward the door.

Brenda followed him. "Can your department provide me with copies of the coroner's and autopsy reports? That'll be a great start."

Canello turned to her, his hand on the doorknob. "I think you're wasting your time and Drakes' sister is blowing good money for your services." He opened the door, paused and looked back at Brenda. "I'll give you a tip, Miss Strange. Why don't you give Paula Drakes' life insurance company a ring? They might need your help with their accident claim." He reached in his pocket, popped a mint in his mouth and continued down the steps.

"I'll ask for your partner next time I call, Detective." Brenda offered a half wave. Detective Canello nodded, got into his car and pulled away.

Brenda stood on her porch a moment longer, wondering why Detective Cannello had really showed up on her doorstep.

Eddy Vandermast's office was in a place called New Tampa, a flashy suburb for the high rollers of Tampa.

"Tampa for the separatists," he'd joked.

The office was part of a three-story red brick and glass professional building called Lerner Point. Vandermast and Associates occupied one third of the top floor.

Not half as excessive as Stewart Davis's Davross Industries, Lerner Point had a quiet simplicity Brenda preferred. A receptionist sat in a large foyer. Behind her, a glass wall revealed an open room with desks and offices.

Brenda shivered as she stood in front of the young woman behind the desk. It reminded her of her old office in Newark. She struggled to push the image of Danny Crane and the gun in his hand back into the basement of her memories.

"I'm Brenda Strange. Eddy is expecting me." She'd no sooner said the words than Eddy was waving frantically at her from behind the glass wall, a big smile on his face.

He met Brenda at the small glass door. "Brenda, how great to see you again." He opened the door and grabbed her arm. "Did you have trouble finding the place?"

"I've yet to get lost in Tampa, Eddy." Brenda patted her Gucci bag. "My Tampa map has been the best investment I've made aside from Malfour."

Eddy made a sweeping gesture. "Well, dear, what do you think?"

"Nice, Eddy. How many people do you have working for you?"

They walked toward an office in the back of the room.

"We've got two other certified accountants, two secretaries, one receptionist and five clerks, minus one who's out on maternity leave."

Eddy motioned Brenda into his office and closed the door. The room was almost the size of a large efficiency, with two floor-to-ceiling windows. But what really grabbed Brenda's attention were the half-dozen framed portraits lining one wall.

They were old, signed Hollywood movie star portraits.

Eddy noticed her interest. "Ah, just a small portion of my vintage Hollywood autograph collection." Looking like a kid admiring his most cherished toys, he gestured to the Alan Ladd photo. "God, weren't men beautiful back then? I keep my more valuable auto-graphed portraits at home. Why don't you come by sometime and let me show off my collection?"

"I'd love to, Eddy. These are gorgeous." Brenda eyed the rest of the elegantly framed portraits. There was Nelson Eddy, Frederick March, Robert Taylor and Ray Milland.

"Each one is an original, one of a kind. I only collect the top con-dition pieces, and they're getting scarce." Eddy moved behind his big mahogany desk. "But I know you didn't come here just to admire my wall of dead hunks." He motioned Brenda into one of the overstuffed corduroy chairs in front of the desk. Eddy leaned all the way back in his chair, clasping his hands together behind his head. "So you need bookkeeping for your teddies?"

"It looks like it. Felice at Teddies in the Park tells me she can't keep up with the supply of the Zodiac Bears. She is convinced my combination of zodiac signs and miniature teddy bears will be the next big rage in the bear-collecting world." Brenda smiled. "My supply isn't always forthcoming, though. I get easily sidetracked. Making a miniature bear takes almost as much creativity and time as making good love." She let the sheepish grin linger on her lips.

"Well, is there ever such a thing as having enough time?" Eddy rolled his eyes and laughed. "I warn you, Brenda, I'm not cheap, but since you're family—" He winked with a playful smile. "I'm going to give you a break."

"Thank you for the offer, Eddy, but your fees are not an issue."

"I wish more clients agreed so easily."

"What I want you to do is arrange for all the proceeds from my teddy bear sales to go to a legitimate, local children's charity." She was still flirting with the idea of turning over her PI monies to charity as well.

"Children?" Eddy cocked an eyebrow. "Do you have children yourself?"

"No." Brenda lowered her eyes. "I . . . uh, lost my little brother, Timmy, when we were both very young."

Because you didn't watch him, Mother.

"I'm really sorry to hear that, Brenda. I didn't know." Eddy paused. "I'll just need you to sign some papers. We can do it now, but it's quite a bit of paperwork. It'll keep you here for a while, or I can get them to you later."

"Just call me when you need me to come back." Brenda shook her thoughts away from Timmy's face.

There was more than one reason why she was there.

"Eddy, you remember at Stewart and Joan's party you told me about Joan seeing the ghost of her dead friend? That was Paula Drakes, right? The woman they found in the bay in early June?"

Eddy pondered the question, twisting his lips sideways. "Oh, yeah, Joan went through a hard time." He paused again. "It was so bad she had her shrink give her all kinds of heavy-duty drugs, which wasn't exactly smart for Joan. She couldn't keep away from the alcohol. Stewart was really worried with her mixing the two and had to finally flush the happy pills down the toilet. And this is just between you and me, but I understand she still keeps him awake all night. Can't sleep." He winked and nodded.

"She's still that distraught over her friend's death?" Brenda's mind shifted into fifth gear.

"Oh, yes."

"Must have been pretty close, Joan and Paula?"

"Are you interested in that ghost Joan has in her house, or something more mundane like Joan as a suspect? Are you on the Paula Drakes case?" Eddy had an eager look in his eyes. "Come on, Brenda, I heard all about your caper at Malfour." He got up and came around to sit on the desk next to Brenda's chair. "Do you think Paula Drakes is really haunting Joan? Is the house haunted?"

Brenda had to laugh at Eddy. "One question at a time. I don't know what Joan is seeing. I haven't talked to her yet. I'm not a ghost hunter, Eddy. What happened in Malfour was unique. I can't say it means anything special."

"Speaking of Malfour, I think that big house of yours is spooky. I don't know how you can stay there all by yourself." Eddy looked at her with a crooked grin. "By the way, how is Tina?"

Brenda fidgeted in her chair. Tina's name jumbled up her thoughts. Made scrambled eggs of her emotions.

"She calls often. I spent two and a half months in Newark with her. I just got back Sunday. She's gotten busy again with her teaching at the art institute."

Truth was, they had spoken only once since that visit. Their conversation had been tense and forced. Each one was afraid to say something that would lead them to the topic both wanted to avoid. Thanksgiving had been particularly stressful. They spent the holiday at Tina's family's house in the Bronx. Although the atmosphere was festive, she felt alone. Tina was withdrawn and aloof. Two and a half months wasn't enough time to fix the rift between them.

"She's coming down for the Christmas holidays," Brenda added quickly, "and the teddy bear show is going to keep me busy between now and Christmas. After Thanksgiving is the time everyone is looking for gifts. I have to make lots of bears." The truth was, she preferred to skip all the holiday cheer.

Sensing her discomfort, Eddy let her off the hook. "Listen, dear, I have a great idea. Why don't you come down to my condo when I have the paperwork ready for you to sign? We can have dinner and I can absolutely bore you with my autograph collection."

"I look forward to it. Got a Bette Davis you're willing to sell?" Brenda winked.

Chapter 2

Detective Canello flung his jacket over the scarred and splintered wood chair tucked behind his desk at the Tampa Police Department's Homicide Division. Across from him, Detective Lisa Chambliss didn't raise her eyes from the computer screen.

"Didn't make a good impression again, Joe?" She half smiled and kept working the keys.

"Jesus Christ, Chambliss, where are all these private dicks coming from?" He pushed back the few straggling hairs left on his head and sat down, the old chair groaning under his weight.

When Chambliss continued to ignore him, Canello started thumping his large fingers on the desk. Then he let out a whistle.

"Yep, this one's a real winner. Name's Brenda Strange. Lives in this restored Victorian out there at that rich kids' playground off the Twenty-Second Causeway." He looked sideways at Chambliss and shook his head. "This Brenda Strange is poking her nose into the Paula Drakes case."

Chambliss stopped in mid-stroke and finally looked at him. "Paula Drakes? The floater we got back in June? The case waiting for FBI clearance?"

Canello put his hands up in a shrug. "Yeah, we never got anything concrete on it. Nothing new. It's just sitting on the chief's desk." He pressed his big thumb and index finger together and leaned forward. "We're this close to passing it on to the boys in black. Hope you don't mind that I took it upon myself to check her out? Since we both worked the case together, I thought it would be okay."

He stopped and eyed Chambliss, looking for any sign of disagreement. She'd gone back to entering reports on the keyboard.

"Anyway, yeah, you should see this dame," continued Canello. "Spitting image of dearly departed Princess Di. Spooky." He shook his head again. "Creepy blue eyes, too. Odd color, kinda like those fancy English collectibles my wife has. What's the name?" He looked at Chambliss for the answer.

"Wedgwood."

He pointed a finger at her. "Yeah, that's it. Anyway, this Strange chick, she was looking at me but right through me."

"Oooh, did she freak you out, Canello?" Chambliss went back to the keyboard. "You said no perp or the hordes of hell could ever get to you."

"She gave it her best shot, but I gave it back. Anyway, she's gonna be calling on you, just so you know."

"I'm sorry, but Mrs. Davis is still in Newark. She won't be back until late tonight. Would you care to leave a message?" The tall woman in a neat blue uniform stood at the door of the palatial Davis home.

"Newark?" Brenda repeated. The word stuck in her head. After that visit to Eddy's office, she was curious about Joan and Paula's relationship. She didn't expect Joan to be where Tina was.

"Yes, ma'am. Would you like to see Mr. Stewart? He'll be in for supper this evening." The maid eyed Brenda suspiciously.

11

Brenda managed a smile. "No, no, that's okay. I'll call again. Thank you."

As she walked back to the Jag, her thoughts were still on Joan Davis. In Newark. With Tina? She was being silly, of course. Brenda couldn't allow herself to get anxious. She had no idea why Joan was in Newark. Just because Joan and Tina had hit it off with their intense passion for art didn't mean a thing. Joan Davis probably had a plethora of friends she flew all over the world to see.

Brenda headed back to Malfour determined to put that whole line of thought in the trash where it belonged. She had bigger things on her agenda. She might want to talk to Stewart after all, but a surprise visit would net better results than an announced intrusion. But not tonight. She needed to talk to Paula Drakes' sister first.

On a different front, there was the teddy bear convention just around the corner. Brenda actually finished all the teddies she'd promised Felice at Teddies in the Park and offered to help her with the display.

Brenda walked in the door to the persistent beeping of the answering machine. In the library, she saw the big number two blinking on the phone. Two messages. Her heart tumbled. She hadn't heard from Tina. And when she'd spoken with her father on Thanksgiving, he'd sounded less depressed, choosing instead to concentrate on her mother's better days from the pain of cancer. Brenda found herself wishing to speak to neither of them. She had her finger on the replay button when the phone rang. She picked up slowly.

"Brenda? Hey, it's Mark Demby."

Brenda deflated like a balloon. "Hi, Mark."

"Before you say no to me again, I'm not calling to recruit you this time. It's more of an official call."

Brenda had never met Mark Demby, head of the San Diego Central Register for Paranormal Studies. But she liked and respected him and also owed him big-time for his help on unraveling the mystery of Malfour House.

"Believe it or not, Mark, I'm still giving your invitation some thought."

"Are you serious?" he asked, laughing. "Well, I'm not going to push you." He got serious fast. "Hey, listen, Brenda, your Malfour case is causing a ripple effect in the paranormal circles. Everybody and their mother is clamoring for an exclusive."

"Consider yourself lucky. You're the only one I don't hang up on," Brenda said. "Your organization let my file leak out. It was supposed to be for your eyes only."

"You're going to make this difficult for me, right?" He exhaled into the receiver. "I'd like to send a field investigator out to you. To Malfour."

"Mark, I don't think—"

"She won't be intrusive. Put her out in the garage if you want."

Brenda shook her head and ran a hand through her hair, a habit she'd developed lately. "Mark, we . . . I, uh, I'm a very private person."

"Two weeks, Brenda. That's all I'm asking. Her name is Susan Christie. She's the best in fieldwork."

"If she's your best, why wasn't she part of your original investigation?"

Brenda swore she could hear Mark smile.

"We really could have used her, but Susan was in Europe when we did your house." He paused. "Listen, Brenda, Susan's got lots of stories to swap with you. She's been doing paranormal investigations for over ten years. You might find her quite the interesting guest."

The annoying little voice of distrust kept hanging on in her thoughts. Not of Mark, but of this total stranger walking into Malfour.

"Mark, I honestly can't afford to have my daily routine interrupted. I'm currently working on a case. I don't have to tell you I need complete privacy." She was hedging. "Why can't you take this investigation? I'd have less objections to you." She smiled into the phone.

"I wish I could. They have me tied to this desk job with a ball and chain." He paused. "Susan is the second-best choice, Brenda."

"How long exactly will she stay and what dates are we looking at here?" There was no way Brenda could say no to Mark. She owed him. She was stuck.

"You give me what's good for you and I'll take care of the rest. We want this to be convenient for you."

Brenda didn't answer.

"Listen, if it'll make you feel any better, I can send you a fax of Susan's résumé, bio, credentials and references." Mark took a deep breath and exhaled. "Brenda, I give you my word that Susan is my best field investigator. If there are any problems, I won't hesitate to pull her from the case."

"Mark, I just don't . . . ."

"It's not just the inconvenience, Brenda, is it?"

Okay, so he'd hit it on the nose. She wasn't exactly keen on someone coming into her home and poking, prodding and dissecting Carlotta and Angelique. They had their rights too.

"*Let the woman come. It might be fun,*" Angelique whispered in Brenda's ear.

"Hello? You there, Brenda?"

Brenda heard Mark's voice clearly. "I'm sorry, Mark. I apologize. I've gotten to be like a possessive hermit when it comes to Malfour. But you're a special case, I suppose. Send me what you have on your Susan Christie and I'll consider it. That's all I'm going to promise for now."

She hung up, slightly annoyed at herself for being roped into having a total stranger in Malfour.

"Angelique, I should let you play hostess when Susan Christie arrives." Brenda smiled as she spoke into thin air. She knew Angelique was listening.

The messages were still blinking on the machine. She punched the button and heard Tina's voice.

"Hey, Princess, sorry I missed you," Tina said. "I'm so excited.

14

Have I got a surprise for you. Check your fax machine. Love you, 'bye."

Brenda could hear the unmistakable excitement in Tina's words. She glanced at the fax machine. A piece of paper sat upright. Brenda reached for it as the second message played.

As Cubbie prattled on, Brenda focused on the faxed letter in her hand. Tina had been promoted to assistant art director at the institute. The letter was glowing in recommendations. Brenda read it more than once, letting the sadness and regret settle in her heart.

Tina would never leave such a prestigious and financially stable position to come back to Tampa. To Brenda. To Malfour. How could Brenda even ask such a thing of her lover? This letter, while much cause for celebration for Tina, sealed their fate as a couple. It was the crippling blow to any hope they had at saving their relationship. There was just no other way to look at it.

Fighting back tears, Brenda put the letter down and searched for a way out of the melancholy that was threatening to sneak up on her. She needed to keep busy. That's when she remembered Denise Miller, Paula Drakes' sister.

There was no doubt in Brenda's mind that Paula Drakes' sister was an opinionated woman. Brenda got an earful in one phone call. Denise Miller had remained married to the same man all her life. No children. Since she and Paula had lost both their parents, Denise, being the oldest daughter, thought it her responsibility to look after Paula.

Denise gave Brenda a list of reasons why she believed her sister couldn't have died in a diving accident. While most of them lacked solid evidence to support her beliefs, there was one that proved relevant. It was, in fact, enough to convince Brenda she had a case.

Paula had attended the Drakes' family reunion last year up in Jersey. She appeared happier than usual and opened up to her sister as she never had before. Denise said it was the first time in seven years that her sister had attended the yearly family gatherings.

"Oh, yeah," Denise added, "Paula couldn't stop talking about this special someone she'd met. The way she carried on, I was convinced she'd finally found a real relationship."

"Did she talk to you often about her relationships?"

"Oh, heavens, no. That's why I was so surprised. Every time we got to talking about personal stuff like that, she'd just clam up. And I was so happy for this bonding we were doing that I just didn't push her for more information on her Mr. Right. But I remember very clearly the only thing she was willing to talk about. This new love of hers liked to dive."

"And you found that suspicious?" Brenda asked.

"Hell, yeah, especially after they called her murder a diving accident. Paula almost drowned when she was a child. You couldn't get Paula in a pool, let alone the ocean. She was concerned that her fear of the water might ruin the relationship."

"If you want to please someone new, you might do things you wouldn't normally do," Brenda suggested. "Maybe she took diving lessons?"

"Not Paula. She said she wasn't going to go that route. She was too old and too successful to go changing her ways. She was hoping her new love would accept her just the way she was."

"Any idea why Paula would own a boat if she didn't like the water?"

"Paula never mentioned a boat."

"The police report shows a boat was recovered. It was registered to Paula."

There was hesitation on the other end, then a sigh. "I just can't imagine Paula wanting a boat." Denise sounded tired.

"Denise, did Paula ever talk about other friends to you? Any new activity or group she'd joined? Someone she might have had a problem with at La Ventanas?"

"Her restaurant? No, not that I knew of. That place was like her second home." Denise paused. "Brenda, I don't know if Kevin told

16

you about what happened to Paula's body? It really creeped us out and we're still on edge."

Brenda tried to scramble through all the notes Kevin had sent and the police report. There was nothing she would have considered "creepy."

"I don't have my notes with me. Would you mind going over it now?"

"Well, a couple of weeks after the funeral, the family crypt was vandalized. The police said there had been other cases like it at that cemetery. They were involved in ongoing investigations." She sighed into the phone. "The vault door was broken from the inside. I mean, that didn't make sense to any of us. And Paula's casket . . ." She was quiet for a moment. "It wasn't enough that they took the body."

Something cold slithered through Brenda's stomach.

"Grave robbers?" Brenda couldn't believe it. Stealing dead bodies had gone out with Mary Shelley and *Frankenstein*. "They damaged her coffin?"

"The lid was completely torn from the casket and the lining shredded. I'll never forget the sight." Denise Miller's voice quivered. "What kind of monsters would do something like that?"

Brenda didn't have an answer for her but she was very interested in finding one.

"Denise, did the police offer any explanation on how the vault door was opened from inside?"

Denise's answer was no. Evidently, the Jersey police had left her dangling in the wind. She hadn't heard from them since and kept getting the runaround when she called. Paula's body was still missing.

A nagging little voice kept circling around Brenda's head like a pesky gnat. This was something related to her case. She couldn't ignore the strong warnings.

Brenda pulled out her notebook. "Denise, do you remember the detectives who worked the case?"

Denise Miller did remember and Brenda jotted down the names.

She thanked Denise and hung up. The picture of Paula Drakes was becoming clearer. But shadows now surrounded her in death.

It was time to visit La Ventanas and talk to some of the hired help. Sometimes the people who work for you are the ones who have the most light to shed.

La Ventanas means *the windows* in Spanish. That's obviously how the restaurant got its name because it was literally wall-to-wall windows. Illuminated brightly for the evening, it sparkled like a diamond nestled among giant oaks. La Ventanas was far enough away from busy Bayshore Boulevard to be private and romantic, yet close enough to offer a panoramic view of Tampa Bay. There wasn't a bad seat in the house.

And it was a busy place. Brenda had to maneuver around the people waiting for a table. The foyer inside was carpeted in rich burgundy Berber, and wood chairs lined the walls. All the chairs were filled with hungry diners waiting to be seated.

At the podium, a young woman in a white tuxedo shirt, bow tie and black pants attempted to sort the names on her reservation list. Brenda waited patiently to be acknowledged.

The hostess finally smiled but couldn't shake the frustration from her eyes. "May I help you?"

"Hi, I'm looking for the manager."

The faint smile the girl had managed disappeared from her face. "Do you have a complaint, ma'am?"

Brenda shook her head. "No. No complaint. It's a business matter."

Relief flooded back into the young woman's face. She flashed a big smile. "You can come back tomorrow after nine in the morning. Vera should be here by then."

Brenda thanked her and shouldered her way past the growing crowd of patrons standing in the foyer. She was disappointed. She'd missed Vera, the manager, and was hungry. She'd wanted to sample the cuisine at La Ventanas. Without a reservation, Brenda figured it would be closing time by the time she put a fork to her mouth. And eating at the bar wasn't an option. She never got comfortable blending food and cigarette smoke.

Thinking of what might actually be edible in the refrigerator back at Malfour, Brenda pulled out onto Bayshore Boulevard, rolled down the windows of the Jag and inhaled deeply of the pungent aroma of Tampa Bay at low tide. At a loss for how to define it, the closest comparison she could come up with was the odor of dead water.

Brenda tossed and turned all that night. Sleep played hide-and-seek with her. At one point, after taking punches at the pillow and losing the battle, she lay quietly looking up at the ceiling, resigned and exasperated.

That's when she looked at the chair next to her bed. She wasn't alone. Carlotta sat looking intently at her, eyes a smoky clear blue, her complexion a lifeless gray.

"Carlotta." Brenda whispered her name and sat up.

"*Why are you so troubled?*" Brenda heard Carlotta's words clearly.

Suddenly feeling naked and exposed, Brenda wrapped the sheet closer around her nude body. "How long have you been watching me?"

Carlotta smiled. "*Since you snuffed out the candle.*"

Brenda ran a hand through her hair, sat up and sighed. "It's so many things. The case, my mother, Susan Christie . . ."

"*And Tina,*" Carlotta finished.

Brenda nodded. "Yes, and Tina."

She had to smile at how ridiculous this scene must look. If Tina were to walk in on Brenda talking to an empty chair, she would have walked out in frustration. That's what life at Malfour would be like if she and Tina were to live here together again.

"I can deal with everything else. I just don't know what to do about Tina."

"Party time and I wasn't invited? Aren't you keeping late hours, darling Brenda?" Angelique stood on the other side of Brenda's bed.

"Don't tease her, Angelique. Can't you see she's upset?" Carlotta scolded.

"She knows what the problem is. How to solve it is her dilemma."

Frowning, Brenda looked at Angelique. "What do you mean by that?"

"Don't listen to her, Brenda, she's just playing with you," Carlotta said, eyes warning Angelique.

"I'm really trying to help," Angelique insisted.

Brenda looked from Carlotta to Angelique and shook her head, exasperated. "Well, since I'm up and can't get back to sleep, I'm open for your thoughts."

The spectral form of Angelique moved silently, swiftly and without sound. She now stood beside Carlotta, with one arm on the chair back, gaze locked on Brenda.

"You're the private investigator, dearest Brenda. Haven't you figured it out? It's us. Get rid of Carlotta and me, and Tina and Malfour will be yours."

The thought had never made its ugly way into her mind. Brenda could never think of Malfour without Carlotta and Angelique.

"You have told us of the bliss and beauty that awaits us on the other end, yet we stay. We have given up heaven. And you, Brenda, what are you willing to give up?" Angelique's dark eyes looked sad as she waited for Brenda to answer.

"We belong here, in this house," Brenda said, holding Angelique's stare, aware that Carlotta held Angelique's hand. "It doesn't matter who I live with or what I lose. We'll be together as long as I live at Malfour."

"See, I told you." Angelique smiled down at Carlotta. *"She is a selfish old girl."*

Brenda was sure that the tinkling sound in her ears was laughter. Her two ghostly friends were tittering with delight.

Chapter 3

The next morning, Brenda showered and put on a black turtle-neck sweater, jeans and black leather ankle boots. It was a little after nine when she walked out of Malfour and headed back to La Ventanas. The sky was a crisp blue and the Tampa air had turned chilly. Brenda missed the steamy summer humidity. She wouldn't mind those eighty-degree highs all year round. But the nip in the air wasn't going to get her to put the top up on her vintage Jag. Brenda had gotten used to driving her pride and joy, a 1963 cream-color E-Type Jaguar, in Tampa's tropical temperatures. She intended to go topless till the bitter cold slinked its way down to Florida. With any luck, it would never get that frigid.

When she pulled into the parking lot, she noticed a couple of cars, parked right up front. The restaurant's glass double doors were both locked. She tapped lightly on the glass as she peered inside. La Ventanas appeared to be completely shut down. Evidently, the restaurant didn't cater to the breakfast crowd.

A tall, lean woman with fiery red hair tied up in a bun appeared from somewhere inside and looked out, a suspicious look on her face. She waved Brenda away by pointing at the small sign on the door with restaurant hours. Brenda missed it last night. La Ventanas didn't open until eleven-thirty.

Brenda smiled pleasantly and dug out one of her PI business cards. She plastered it up against the glass door. The woman narrowed her eyes as she studied the card. Nodding, she stepped back, opened one of the doors and motioned Brenda inside.

"Hi, I'm Vera Beatty. Didn't mean to keep you out, but one can never be too careful nowadays."

Brenda offered her hand. "I understand. Your hostess last night said early mornings would be the best time to catch you."

Vera Beatty wore red lipstick two shades too dark for her and a rainbow of plastic jewelry.

"You really are a private eye?" She was looking Brenda over with one arched eyebrow as she pocketed Brenda's card. "You sure don't look like one. I read all the latest mysteries, and you're definitely not a big, wise-cracking macho guy." Was it distrust that Brenda caught in her eyes or a tinge of humor?

"That's what they all say. Good for business not to be so obvious," Brenda said as she kept her smile, hoping it would help put the other woman at ease.

"Well, I'm almost afraid to ask what it is I can help you with."

"Miss Beatty—"

"Call me Vera. I don't exactly like formal."

"Vera, I'm here regarding Paula Drakes."

Vera Beatty's face fell. "Paula?" She eyed Brenda with renewed interest. "What's this about?"

"Paula Drakes did own this restaurant?"

"Sure. We were all very shocked and saddened when she died." The corners of her mouth quivered and her eyes were wet when she looked at Brenda. "I would give up my manager's position and go back waiting the tables to have Paula back with us."

"Vera, I hope you'll be able to help me with her case."

"Case?" Vera leaned closer to Brenda. "You don't think it was an accident? Is that what this is about?"

Brenda smiled. "That's what I'm trying to find out, Vera. Can you show me Paula's office?"

Vera wavered between a yes and a no. Brenda wanted to get into that office. She still couldn't believe TPD had closed this case as an accident without even investigating the possibility of foul play. The contents of Paula Drakes' office might yield up a gold mine of information.

"You can stay with me if you don't trust me." Brenda wasn't going to beg. She had other tricks up her sleeve. The next thing would be to threaten her with a search warrant. Brenda didn't think Vera Beatty was sufficiently savvy of police procedure to call her bluff.

"Well, I guess it couldn't do any harm. But you can't take anything and I don't leave the room until you do." Vera led her down a narrow hallway. "I'm ashamed to admit that we still haven't shipped some of Paula's things to her sister. Denise wanted to come and do it herself, but I just didn't think that was proper, you know?" Vera looked sideways at Brenda as they reached a door with a gold nameplate that still read: Paula Drakes, Owner and Manager. They walked into a small room with two desks, office equipment, several bookcases and several small windows. There was a pile of boxes on the floor.

"Vera, who owns the restaurant now?" If Paula Drakes had a partner, Brenda needed to know.

Vera shook her head. "It's on the auction block. We're all on pins and needles wondering if we're going to have jobs with the new owners." Vera pointed to two boxes hiding behind a desk near a window with the cheery, bright sun coming in.

Brenda walked over to the boxes. "Mind if I open these?"

Vera waved a hand at her. "Go ahead, but be careful. There are picture frames and—" She stopped. "Well, you know, just be careful." She folded her hands and just stood there, watching Brenda pry open the first box.

The word *pictures* immediately sent Brenda's heart racing. This could prove to be a very fruitful visit indeed. The first box had two books, a Wayne Dyer self-help book and another very interesting hardcover that Brenda pulled out and opened. *Married Women Who Love Other Women*, by Carren Strock. Flipping quickly through the table of contents, she saw it was exactly what the title implied. The book chronicled cases of married women who had discovered their attraction to other women.

Brenda held up the Strock book. "These were Paula's books?"

"Yeah, those were the two she was reading before . . ."

Vera paused, looked away briefly, then pointed at the book. "She was openly gay. No secrets there."

Brenda was slightly shocked. Now she knew why Paula hadn't shared her romances with her sister. Vera noticed the surprise on Brenda's face.

"Paula never flaunted her sexuality. She was a great person and the best boss . . ." She wiped away the tears from her eyes.

Brenda quickly put the books aside. "Thanks, Vera." She continued digging into the box. This revelation definitely put a different spin on the investigation. Alarms were going off right and left in Brenda's head. But right now, she had to concentrate on the boxes in front of her.

Brenda pulled out a small colorful box, three photo frames and a desk calendar. Desk calendars were always great fun. So much of a busy person's life could be figured out in scribbled dates, times and notes on the tiny little squares of a calendar.

But Brenda wanted to look at the pictures first. One frame was a five-by-seven, the others were of the four-by-six variety. The larger photo was of an attractive, older woman with several people, a plaque held proudly in her hands.

"That's Paula when she got her Restaurateur of the Year award in 'ninety-nine," Vera said, clearing her throat.

Paula Drakes looked younger than 49, the age the police report gave her. One of the smaller photos was Paula with another woman, a man and several kids. Brenda held it up to Vera.

"That's Paula with her sister, brother-in-law and their kids at the family reunion."

"When was it taken?"

"Paula took that picture at this year's reunion."

Brenda looked the photo over, finally deciding that Paula and Denise didn't look alike.

The last frame held a photograph of Paula and Joan Davis. They seemed to be at a party of some kind. It was Christmas, judging from the green velvet vest and Santa hat that Paula wore. They both smiled broadly at the camera.

Vera hovered over Brenda's shoulder. "That's Joan Davis. She was a good friend of Paula's."

Those alarm bells that had gone off before turned into sirens screeching in her brain.

Brenda asked, "Did Joan eat here often?"

Vera wrinkled her brow and twisted her mouth in thought. "No, I don't think she was ever here more than once."

"Did Paula and Joan do anything together? Paula mention her often?"

Vera broke out in a wistful smile. "Oh, sure. They did everything together."

Brenda put the pictures down and looked at Vera. "Did Paula talk about doing any diving with Joan?"

Vera shook her head. "No, she never mentioned any diving. Mostly she talked about art shows, restaurants, parties, stuff like that." Vera was still shaking her head. "I still can't believe she's gone."

Brenda wished she could pocket the photo without Vera catching her. Brenda reached for the calendar. It was a Far Side desk model, the kind with metal clasps that you could refill each year. And Paula didn't tear out the old pages.

Brenda turned the pages back to May. Before they fished Paula

Drakes out of the bay. Paula's handwriting was messy, but readable. In May, she'd had appointments with her hairdresser, dentist, accountant and wholesale food distributor. And on May 28th, there were only two words written. Boat Rally. Brenda looked at the page and filed the words and date in her head.

Brenda continued flipping back the pages and found Joan's name scribbled in each month, sometimes two or three times. Brenda also found the name of what she presumed was a florist, Roses Are Red Flowers. Once in February and again in March.

"Listen, Brenda, I really have to get back to work. How much longer will you be?"

"If you could just give me another minute to go through the other box?" Brenda gave Vera her best smile, putting everything back into the first box. "I promise I won't keep you much longer."

Vera smiled weakly and waved a hand at her in agreement. The second box contained nothing that could help Brenda. A button-down sweater, a seat cushion, and the plaque Paula Drakes had been awarded in 1999.

Brenda pulled it out and set it on the desk. "I think this plaque belongs here in the restaurant, don't you think? Maybe out in the lobby."

Vera started to shake her head, then tried to smile. "Well, I don't know. Maybe."

Brenda pulled open the tiny box last. Inside were mostly business cards and some receipts. Nothing interesting except for a business card with rainbow colors. There was an organization's name printed in raised black letters: Tampa Gay Business Owners Association. Below that was the name Manda Jones.

Brenda pulled out her planner and jotted down the name and phone number. She put everything back into the small box, sealed the last of the boxes, dusted her hands and looked up at Vera.

"Thanks for your help and cooperation, Vera."

"I'd like to say I was able to help you out. Those who loved Paula want to know what really happened, you know?"

"This will help out." Brenda put her planner back in her bag as they both walked back to the lobby. "I'd like to come back and try your food. Put my name on the reservation list for next Friday night, will you?"

"Make it seven p.m. and it's on me." Vera winked.

It was early yet, just after eleven, and Brenda was pumped up. She was tempted to dial Manda Jones but decided to wait till a bit later in the day. It was Brenda's experience that most of these associations didn't keep normal business hours and were basically staffed by volunteers. She didn't want to leave a message on a machine or voice mail.

Brenda wondered if Joan Davis was back in town. Since she was on the way back to Malfour, she decided to pay her neighbor a visit this morning before going back home. Shadows were forming around Joan Davis and her relationship with Paula Drakes. The fact that Paula Drakes was gay complicated things. It could mean nothing to the case or everything. How Joan fit in was another mystery. But Brenda was sure of one thing. Joan Davis was going to play a big part.

The same lady in blue answered the Davis door again. This time, she escorted Brenda to Joan, who greeted her with a limp wrist and fake smile.

"How good to see you again, Brenda."

Brenda doubted she meant that but followed her to the very same sunken living room she and Tina had partied in this past summer. The full-length bar was dark, the mirror on the wall behind it catching the colors of the sun that filtered through the sliding glass doors. There were several of those leather Scandinavian chairs with companion footrests, a leather retro-modern couch and new artwork on the walls. It appeared to Brenda that the Davises were serious about the art scene. Brenda never did well in her art courses, but she recognized some of the masters on Joan Davis's wall.

"Wow, you've made some changes since we were here last."

"I make changes every month, darling."

Joan pointed to one of the chairs as she sat on the one across from Brenda. Brenda decided against the footrest.

"My maid said there was a tall blonde woman looking for me. I should have guessed it was you." Joan still had the smile plastered on her face and there was a strong whiff of alcohol on her breath.

Brenda wanted to mention Newark and ask if she'd seen Tina. She struggled to push the temptation aside.

"Yes, I'd just left Eddy Vandermast's office and he told me about your . . . ghost problem. I thought I'd stop and see if I could help."

Joan put both elbows on the armrests and leaned forward. "Oh, I heard about your ghosts at Malfour too and that dreadful Cuenca family."

No doubt Tina had told her everything. Brenda didn't mind it, really, if only it wasn't Joan she was sharing it with.

Before Brenda even asked her first question, tears pooled at the corner of Joan Davis's eyes. She was drunk. Brenda was certain. Could she take the ramblings of an intoxicated woman as credible statements?

"She's here, you know. Paula won't leave me alone."

Brenda thought that was an odd phrase from a friend. "You tried talking to Paula's ghost?" she asked.

"Oh, I tried, believe me, I tried. I kept telling her to go away. She was dead and she needed to be with the dead, not with me." Joan Davis waved a hand in futility. She shook her head. "She just wouldn't listen. Wouldn't listen." She kept shaking her head. There was a strange, faraway look in her glassy eyes.

"The ghost didn't listen?"

"No, no. I tried to tell her before all that." Her words slurred and Joan stopped. She looked at Brenda and forced a tight smile. Too quick and too fake. "I mean, I told her that the first time I saw her . . . her ghost."

Brenda realized Joan was drunk and suddenly evasive. "Joan, when was the last time you saw Paula alive?"

28

Joan frowned in concentration, but Brenda didn't think she was trying very hard to remember.

"Oh, it was all so long ago. I don't know, maybe a week before they, you know, found her," Joan said. "Does it matter?"

"Well, yes, it's important I get all the facts right." Brenda flashed a semblance of a smile. "When was the last time you saw her alive? Try to remember, Joan."

Joan's eyes went totally blank. She looked at Brenda and opened her mouth but nothing came out. She fingered her wedding band nervously.

"Take your time, Joan," Brenda added, speaking in a soothing tone.

"I don't . . . know." Joan's voice was just a squeak. She cleared her throat. "We were on the boat."

"Your boat?"

"Yes, the pleasure boat, not the yacht."

"Was it at the boat rally? Memorial Day? You and Paula?"

Joan gave Brenda a puzzled look. "The boat rally? How do you know about that? And what does all this have to do with getting rid of Paula's ghost?"

It was time for Brenda to tell her the truth. "Joan, I'm not here to hunt ghosts for you." She pulled out her card and handed it to Joan. "I'm investigating Paula's murder."

Joan's gaze flew from the card to Brenda's face. She looked trapped, with more than a tinge of desperation in her eyes. "Murder? I thought Paula drowned? An accident. That's what the police told us."

"I'm not working with the police. I do need your help, though. You and Paula were good friends."

Joan's eyes narrowed and she uncrossed her legs in one swift move. "Well, I don't think I want to get involved in this. Paula's death was accidental. The police closed the file." She stared down at the floor. "I mean, yes, you're right, Paula was a very good friend and I still find it hard to talk about it, so if you'll excuse me."

She clearly wanted out of Brenda's questioning. Brenda knew she could only push her so far before Joan shut down completely.

"If you decide you want to talk about Paula, you know where I live." Brenda got up and moved to the door, but Joan grabbed her arm and stopped her.

"By the way, who hired you?" Joan stepped back and crossed her arms. "I mean, does somebody think Paula was murdered?" She failed miserably at a smile.

"I can't tell you that. Client confidentiality. I'm sure you understand." Brenda stared hard at her. "You know, Joan, if the police get enough new evidence, they might reopen the case. They could be talking to you again."

Joan held the door open for Brenda and closed it quickly behind her with a weak wave. Paula Drakes' ghost wasn't haunting Joan and Stewart's palace. Brenda was sure of that but she wasn't ready to let Joan know it. Joan had been fidgety and uncomfortable with Brenda's questions. If she and Paula had been friends, something happened along the way to cool the friendship down for Joan. She was hiding something. If Joan continued to think Paula's ghost was still haunting her house, she just might get agitated enough to break. Brenda wasn't done with Joan. She'd be back.

Chapter 4

Brenda had just taken a left turn onto Malfour Road when her cell phone rang. She flinched as her heart bumped against her chest. Her father came first to mind.

"Hello?"

"Ms. Strange, this is Detective Lisa Chambliss. My apologies for not calling you sooner. I did get your message, but we have major department overload." Her voice was professional yet light, not threatening.

"Thanks for calling, Detective Chambliss. I was beginning to wonder if your partner didn't want us to meet."

"Yeah, well, Joe is a bit of a hard-nose, but he's nothing short of thorough. Listen, I've got time for a break. I'd like your take on Paula Drakes. Care to meet for coffee?"

"I'd love to. How about the Space Age Café in Hyde Park? I don't have the address, but it's north of Howard Avenue."

"I know where it's at. Give me ten minutes," Detective Chambliss said.

Brenda's adrenaline was racing through her system. She was sorry that she hadn't jumpstarted her PI career sooner.

"How will I recognize you, Detective?"

"I'll know you."

Brenda didn't even bother to ask how. She stopped, put the Jag into reverse and headed back out.

Brenda decided on a table in the center of the café. Space Age Café was an intimate trip to the Milky Way, serving coffee for the voyage instead of Tang. It was a science fiction fan's heaven.

The walls were midnight blue with tiny stars painted everywhere. Framed photographs, drawings and star maps of everything from *Star Trek* to *Apollo 13* dotted one side of the wall. On the opposite side of the room sat a large curio cabinet filled with models and memorabilia from *Star Trek*, *Star Wars*, NASA and more. Toward the back of the café was a large-screen television where episodes of famous science fiction shows flickered continuously.

It wasn't everyone's cup of java, but Brenda felt strangely at home surrounded by the geeky décor. One evening, at the tail end of grocery shopping, she'd stopped in and found a group of Trekkies decked out in costumes. She watched fleet officers, Vulcans and Klingons down cup after cup of coffee as they recited the script verbatim. The female Borg who flirted with her shamelessly by repeating "You will be assimilated. Resistance is futile" had especially delighted Brenda. Today, Brenda was the only customer in the café. One employee was wiping down the counter. Brenda had one eye on the door and another on the *Space:1999* episode on the screen.

The woman who walked in and headed in her direction wasn't at all what Brenda had expected. The thin woman who approached her table wore a brown leather jacket, tan turtleneck and black pants with boots. She put her hand out to Brenda.

"I'm Lisa Chambliss."

Brenda stood up and shook her hand firmly. "Good to meet you. I'm Brenda." Brenda guessed her to be forty-something. An attractive forty-something.

"Well, Joe wasn't wrong," Chambliss said. The eyes that scanned Brenda were jet black. "You aren't easy to miss."

She settled into the seat across from Brenda. Brenda caught the glint of the badge on the detective's belt.

"Listen, Brenda, call me Lisa or Chambliss, whatever you prefer. Rick always did, which brings me to my first question. What happened to him? Did Kevin pull him off the case?" She eased back in the chair, not taking her dark eyes off Brenda. "I figured something got him sidetracked, or you and I wouldn't be meeting."

"Apparently, he suffered a heart attack and couldn't keep up. Kevin roped me into taking the case for him." Brenda smiled, trying hard not to stare at the golden highlights jumping off of Lisa's auburn hair. The pixie hairdo made her high cheekbones more pronounced, and Brenda thought her too pale for Florida.

A young girl in all black attire came to the table and asked for their order. Without hesitation, Lisa ordered a double espresso. Brenda opted for a cappuccino.

Chambliss's stare was back on Brenda immediately. Her hands were folded together on the table as she played with the napkin the waitress had placed there.

"Now, Brenda, tell me why you think we should reopen the Paula Drakes case?" There was a slight upward curve to her mouth. It had been there since she walked in. It reminded Brenda of some of the pictures of Buddha statues from her Buddhist studies.

"I don't want to tell you how to run your department, Lisa. I just need your help with my investigation." The cappuccino maker whirred into action behind them.

Lisa Chambliss leaned forward. "I'm a lot more open than Joe is regarding Paula Drakes, but I can't just hand police data over to you or any private investigator unless . . ." She paused as the waitress brought the drinks and misplaced them on the table.

Brenda reached for the cappuccino and slid the aromatic espresso toward Lisa Chambliss, who grabbed the hot cup without using the handle and took a swig of the deep, dark espresso.

She peered at Brenda over the rim of the cup. "Unless I'm pretty damn sure I'm going to get something solid back."

Brenda inhaled the heady scent of the detective's espresso and the leather from her jacket. Sensuous. Brenda took a sip from her cappuccino and quickly licked the froth from her upper lip. She smiled.

"I've done a bit of the legwork for TPD already, you know. Your department didn't dig deep enough into Paula Drakes' personal life. Not only have I spoken with the manager at Paula's restaurant, but I also have other leads to follow up. Care to swap?"

At last Chambliss broke a smile. The corners of her mouth creased in dimples. "What is it you need, Brenda?"

"The autopsy report. Plus the records of everything taken from the crime scene."

"And in return?" Lisa was looking straight into her eyes.

"In return, you get every piece of evidence I get my hands on."

Chambliss started shaking her head. "That's not enough." She downed the last drop of espresso in one gulp. "I want your word that if you find something that belongs to TPD, you turn it over immediately without any Nancy Drew heroics. At that point, you let us slap a murder tag on it and take over the case."

Brenda had no intention of handing her case over to the Tampa Police Department, but she might hand it over to Lisa Chambliss. She liked her. There was a certain dark magnetism surrounding the detective.

"Nancy Drew?" Brenda smiled. "Well, at least you didn't call me Jessica Fletcher. Now I have to wonder, Detective, did you offer Rick the same options? I hope this isn't about my being a female PI. I'd like to think you're an equal-opportunity kind of woman and not as sexist as that comment sounded."

The words just tumbled out of Brenda's mouth. She certainly didn't want to alienate Lisa Chambliss. She needed a contact at TPD, but she also wasn't going to play the gender inequality game either. Chambliss just sat there with that perfect little curl on her mouth.

"Detective," Brenda continued, "both our careers are dedicated to bringing the guilty to justice. Righting wrongs. We're on the same team, right?" she added with a smile.

Lisa stood up and started fishing in her jacket for money.

Brenda objected. "Oh, no. This is on me."

Lisa Chambliss pulled out three one-dollar bills and set them on the table. "I'll get back with you, Brenda."

Without looking back, she walked out of Space Age Café. Brenda muttered a curse under her breath. She couldn't gauge whether the meeting had gone well or if her outburst blew it.

She finished her cappuccino and dropped a five-dollar bill on top of the money Lisa Chambliss had left.

Malfour House was alive with the flickering of candlelight. Brenda had stacked fresh wood in both the library and living room fireplaces. There was a cold front working its way down from Canada and already chilly drafts were collecting in the dark corners of Malfour.

The teddy bear convention in Orlando was this weekend. Felice would be at her door bright and early tomorrow morning. Felice had warned Brenda that the perfect setup took time to get right. Most vendors were there hours in advance of the show opening, some arriving Friday evening.

Brenda went upstairs to the bedroom where her large suitcase sat open on the bed. She'd always made a habit of double-checking all her luggage once before leaving.

The Saggy bears, her Zodiac bear for Sagittarius, were boxed in a separate carry-on case. Felice had the rest of the bears and would be bringing them with her. Brenda sorted through her travel garments, which included corduroy slacks, sweaters, jeans, socks, shoes and an extra pillow. In her travel bag, she'd packed toothbrush, toothpaste, floss, hairbrush and makeup.

Brenda snapped the large suitcase shut and reached for the garment bag beside it. The approaching cold front gave her the perfect opportunity to show off her new camel-hair jacket. Zipping up the garment bag, Brenda grabbed both pieces of luggage and headed downstairs.

She set both bags in the hallway next to the living room. She stood perfectly still, exhaling slowly as she listened to the crackling in the fireplace. The tiny dancing flames from the candles quivered and sparkled before her.

A sense of well-being flowed through Brenda. In the large living room, she sat down on the velvet Victorian couch facing the fireplace.

A log tumbled and bright flames rose up, escaping into the chimney. Brenda inhaled the scent of the lavender candles that mingled with the strong smell of smoldering firewood.

She let the experience wash over her and closed her eyes. Everything here was as it should be. Malfour House spoke to her of thanks. The house was now as splendid as it had been when built in 1899. It didn't matter that Brenda needed a few modern conveniences like a state-of-the-art kitchen.

And within this sea of bliss, the Paula Drakes case reared its ugly head. Brenda opened her eyes and caught her breath.

The case had become a persistent voice in her head. There was some new information she had gathered, but so much more that was missing. She'd tried Manda Jones at the Tampa Gay Business Association and gotten an answering machine. Too bad, because Brenda had wanted to talk to her before she left for the weekend. Manda Jones and Paula Drakes would have to wait.

The cool, deep water rippling through its scales felt good. The surface of the water was so far above that it seemed like a tiny little star of light shifting back and forth.

Higher and higher it swam, darting from the depths of the

Atlantic into the thick, murky waters of the Gulf of Mexico. It remembered the first trip above. It had seemed endless and its muscles, now accustomed to water, burned with pain each time it set foot on land. But with each visit to the surface, the muscle soreness abated, the effort required of it less traumatic.

The memories of its existence on solid dirt had faded to a mere whisper in its reptilian brain. There was only one source of emotion that it fed upon, the reason it risked its life and the only desire it could not release from its past. Vengeance.

Wide, webbed hands broke the surface, and it continued swimming at a frantic pace toward the Tampa Bay, under the darkness of the sleeping moon, to a house it had become familiar with.

The phone ringing in her head jerked Brenda out of sleep. She swallowed hard to send her heart back into her chest. The alarm clock told her it was four o'clock in the morning. She yanked the phone off the cradle.

"Brenda! Brenda, it's Stewart. I'm so sorry for waking you."

His voice was frantic. Brenda wiped the strands of hair off her face and thanked God it wasn't her father's voice.

"Stewart, slow down. What's wrong?"

"Can you come over? I know it's late, but please. It's Joan." He sighed heavily. "She wants to see you."

Brenda certainly didn't think she'd be visiting Joan so soon. Something was up and she wasn't going to bitch about being woken at an ungodly time of the morning, two hours before she would be on her way to the convention in Orlando. This was part of the job of being a private investigator. You didn't get to pick the hours you wanted to work.

"Give me about ten minutes to get dressed and I'll be there, Stewart."

When Brenda got to the Davises' palatial home, a very distraught Stewart led her up to their bedroom. The place was like a European hotel. Joan Davis sat curled up on a king-size bed, the comforter and sheets scattered on the floor. Her arms were tightly wrapped around her knees.

Stewart whispered, "She woke up screaming and wouldn't tell me anything until you got here." He nodded toward his wife.

Brenda sat on the bed next to Joan, who looked disheveled. Her curtain of blonde hair was plastered to her head, eyes bulging with fear.

"Brenda, thank God you've come." Joan clutched Brenda's arm. "She was here." Joan shook her head. "I thought she was gone. She's come back to haunt me again." Joan started biting her hand. She looked at Brenda. "She was right over there." She pointed with a shaking hand toward the master bathroom.

Stewart came over to stand next to Brenda. He looked back at the bathroom. "I didn't clean the mess up this time." He shook his head and lowered his voice. "I think we might have a leak. I don't know. I've already had it checked out once."

Brenda got up and went toward the bathroom. On the hardwood floor, between the bed and the bathroom door, were two puddles. It looked like water. She bent down and sniffed. Smelled a bit like the bay. She carefully dipped her index finger into it and brought it gingerly up to her nose. Seaweed, she thought.

She noticed that there were two sets of puddles, each with smaller wet spots only inches apart. They looked like footprints.

Brenda kept her voice low. "Stewart, you say this has happened before?"

"I usually take care of this, but Joan was frantic tonight. She didn't want me to touch anything until you got here." He pointed weakly to the puddles, then put both hands on his hips. "It's just water. I actually tasted it. A bit salty, but just water."

"Salty?" More like seawater, Brenda thought. She arched an eyebrow. "Your roof wouldn't be leaking salty water."

Stewart shook his head. "I've had one roofing company check everything out. They couldn't find a leak."

"Have you checked for any breaking and entering? Does anyone on your household staff have a key to the house?"

"Only Wilson has a key."

"Who's Wilson?"

"He's manager of the staff. He lives in the cottage out back. But why would he want to do something like this? He's been with us for ten years. It doesn't make any sense." Stewart ran a hand through his unkempt hair.

"Can't you two believe me?" Joan Davis jumped from the bed and wrapped her silk gown tight around her waist. "It's seawater. Why don't you believe me? It's Paula." She came and stood between Stewart and Brenda, looking helplessly at Brenda. "I thought you were going to help? You should know. You understand, don't you?" She began to pull at Brenda's jacket.

Stewart pulled her away and managed to get her back into bed and calmed down. He led Brenda downstairs.

"Stewart, I'm going away for the weekend, but if I were you, I'd start by asking your Wilson some questions and then getting Joan a new doctor."

He almost smiled. "She's been through a lot since her friend died. I just don't know what to do. The doctors seem to think all this will blow over."

"Yeah," Brenda replied, "but you've still got seawater in your house."

Chapter 5

The annual Teddy Bear Grand Show was a much needed diversion for Brenda. The show traveled each year to whatever city in the U.S. that won the bid to host the event. Orlando and the Magic Kingdom won the most votes this year.

The Lake Grand Hotel was smack in the middle of Theme Park Central. You didn't have to crane your neck far to catch the blue turrets and gables of that famous castle looming over the perfectly trimmed trees of the Lake Grand's grounds.

Teddy bear artists from all over the world converged in the huge ballroom of the hotel for a weekend of teddy bear heaven.

Felice and Brenda spent all of Saturday morning unpacking. They draped blue velvet over the display tables and arranged a row of clear Lucite three-tiered shelves where they placed the bears Felice brought with her. On two separate square boxes, Felice draped pale blue satin fabric and set Brenda's Zodiac bears.

Brenda was on a high all weekend, hobnobbing with renowned

teddy bear artists she'd only read about in *Teddy Bear Gazette*—Sylvia Martin, Doreen Williamson and Yolanda Cruthers, who were the premier creators of miniature bears in the country. It was like a dream world where only teddy bears mattered. Everyone she met was enthusiastic and only too willing to share favorite secrets of making teddy bears.

They sold six Saggies. Felice introduced Brenda to each of the buyers. Brenda felt uncomfortable with the hustling aspect of bear-making, but as the weekend wore on, she grew to enjoy the contact with Felice's customers.

When she and Felice found time to stop for food, they spent their meals talking about upholstery fabrics, the state of the industry and whether teddy bears were still the favorite toy of children, or investments for adults.

As exhilarating as it was, Brenda was exhausted by Sunday. Malfour was forever in her thoughts, and the case kept grabbing for attention too. And those saltwater footprints bothered her.

But Felice was so pumped up, she kept talking all the way back to Tampa. The show had gone well for her. She made new contacts and swore up and down that the Zodiac Bears could topple the monopoly Tiny Bear Kingdom had on the miniature bear cottage industry.

Felice said suddenly, "So, we haven't discussed what you're planning about setting up shop." She glanced at Brenda. "I mean, about getting an office for your private eye business."

Brenda, lulled by the sound of Felice's chatting, was caught off guard by the question. She grinned at her. "Funny you should ask. I've thought about it but haven't really had the chance to look. You have something in mind?"

Truth was, Brenda had thought about it plenty. She wasn't about to allow total strangers to invade the sacredness of Malfour. But the nature of the business was courting people with problems. Strangers. She had to find a place to meet clients.

"Well, yeah. I've got the perfect setup for you if you're interested.

Teddies in the Park doesn't take up the entire house. I have at least three rooms out back you could convert into a nice office space. The whole house was fully remodeled when I bought it, so you wouldn't have to worry about doing any work to it." She shot a quick look at Brenda. "There's even a rear entrance. *Voilà*, your own office."

By the time Brenda got back to Malfour and unpacked, she'd made the decision to share space with Felice and Teddies in the Park. They'd stopped by there first, and Brenda found the three rooms more than adequate. Felice had been right, there was little to do. The rooms were clean, painted a deep beige with just a hint of rose.

But Brenda was already looking at her new office in a different color. Having flirted with feng shui for a short time, she knew that the cooler hues of blue and green held the power to relax when used as part of a paint scheme in a room. In her line of business, cooler heads were better than hot ones. Now all she needed was furniture, computers and a secretary.

There were two calls on the answering machine and a business card tucked under her door. Brenda took a quick look at the card and recognized the name of Phillip Brown in raised black letters. The gallery name, Le Galleria, was splashed in the center of the card, in script letters. Philip Brown had written a short note that said, "Please call regarding Tina Marchanti's sculptures."

Brenda stashed it in her bag and listened to the messages. Manda Jones and Eddy had left messages. Eddy had all the paperwork ready for her to sign. He offered a seductive dinner at his place and a short course in autograph collecting. Brenda smiled as she listened to Manda Jones's message. The woman's voice was hesitant. Admittedly, Brenda hadn't given her much when she'd left her message, only that she was looking into Paula Drakes' accident. Manda did leave best times to catch her. It looked like it was shaping up to be a busy week.

Brenda propped open the PowerBook and signed on. An e-mail

from Mark Demby was in her mailbox. Brenda could feel the knots tighten in her stomach. The e-mail was regarding Susan Christie, of course. According to Mark, she would be available for five days only and those would have to be this coming week. Christie had accepted a position at Woodlyn College in Washington State with the starting date of January 2. Seems they wanted her at the college by mid December for orientation.

"Good grief," Brenda muttered. She reached for the desk calendar and continued reading. A smiley icon followed Mark's next sentence. *We've already booked her flight and got the tickets.*

Brenda couldn't suppress a smile. Mark was really pushing his luck. He knew it. She settled back and visualized the mess December had the potential to become. It could have been worse. Susan Christie could have stayed the full two weeks. Brenda would take the small blessings.

Tina was flying in on the twelfth and her parents, being as upwardly mobile as always, never gave her a date of arrival. Last she heard from her dad, he and her mother would be in Tampa "for the holidays." They could show up at her door anytime in December. Her family enjoyed Christmas but had never celebrated much at Thanksgiving. Sometimes, when the rare invitation came from one of her aunts or uncles for a Thanksgiving dinner, they would go because the Stranges always accepted family invitations. But her mother never once cooked a turkey with all the trimmings. That was one of the reasons she'd felt odd at Tina's family's this year.

She sent a quick response to Mark Demby, lamenting the fact that it wasn't he who was coming for an inconvenient visit. She smiled and clicked the "send now" key.

Chapter 6

Brenda sat eyeing the stack of hot blueberry pancakes smothered in syrup that Cubbie had placed in front of her. The Gulfbreeze had become Brenda's breakfast stop whenever she was up and out early. It was a cool Monday morning with the rising sun painting the sky in soft pastels as it worked its way up the horizon.

Cubbie made sure Brenda got her favorite seat in the restaurant. If you were lucky enough to get to the Gulfbreeze at the right time, the place offered one of the most picturesque, panoramic views of Tampa across the Port of Tampa.

"You gonna eat those or just contemplate eating them?" Cubbie settled herself in the chair beside Brenda, plopping her order pad on the table. She looked at Brenda and shook her head. " 'Cause if you're not going to eat 'em, I will. I'm on break and I haven't had any breakfast this morning."

"God, Cubbie, it's just so beautiful." Brenda couldn't tear herself away from the picture-postcard scene unfolding through the window. "I never get bored of the view."

Cubbie snorted. "Try working here for thirty years."

Brenda laughed and cut into the pancakes, stuffing a big bite into her mouth. She swallowed quickly. "Think you'd miss it if you didn't work here, then?" She wiped a dribble of syrup off her chin. "I'm offering you a job, Cubbie. Come work for me." She put her fork down, took a gulp of hot coffee and waited for Cubbie's reaction.

"And I thought you were serious when you said you had somethin' important to tell me this morning." Cubbie was eyeing her suspiciously, one eyebrow arched.

"I am serious, Cubbie. Now c'mon, hear me out. I just rented office space in Hyde Park for my new private investigation business." Brenda took another bite of the pancakes. "I want you to be my secretary." She said it with her mouth full.

Cubbie was never at a loss for words, but her face was in shock. "Are you okay, sugar? You don't have the flu, do you?" She tried to reach for Brenda's forehead.

"No, I'm not sick." Brenda pushed her away.

Cubbie shook her head and laughed. "Well, you gotta be somethin', honey, if you want me to work in your office. Look at me, Brenda." She waved a hand down the length of her body. "I'm a waitress, baby, and before that I cleaned offices, not worked in one."

"I'm serious, Cubbie. You're exactly what I want. Besides, I wouldn't trust anyone else." Brenda took Cubbie's hand. "Come on, Cubbie, I need you. It would mean forty thousand a year. That's more money than you make here." She gave Cubbie her chin-down, eyes-begging look.

Cubbie was flustered. She just sat there shaking her head. "Honey, all I know is waiting tables. I can't answer phones and all that other stuff secretaries do."

Brenda wasn't going to let her off the hook so easy. She was pretty sure the problem was that Cubbie didn't think herself good enough. But the sparkle in her eyes belied her interest.

"I need you, Cubbie. Don't you want a change of scenery?" Brenda flashed an innocent smile and pleaded with her eyes.

"You're not going to change my mind with those looks of yours," Cubbie warned Brenda.

"I don't want just any secretary, Cubbie, I want you. You deal with people everyday. You're one hell of a waitress. Your customers love you." Brenda looked at Cubbie's very skeptical face. "Look, if you don't work out at the office and the Gulfbreeze won't give you your job back, I'll pay you to do stuff around Malfour."

"Oh, Benny and Myrtle would give me my old job back, but . . ." Cubbie hesitated.

"Well, then, that's it. Give your two weeks' notice tomorrow, and I'll call you for your start date." Brenda scooped up the last piece of blueberry pancake. She could see a question forming on Cubbie's face.

"You think I could wear my hats to work?" Cubbie looked like a chubby little girl asking for something she didn't think she'd get.

Brenda laughed louder than she had in some time. "Lesson number one, don't push your luck with your new boss."

Cubbie hadn't exactly said yes, but Brenda was pretty damned sure she'd be her secretary. It wasn't going to take serious thought in deciding to let Cubbie wear her Chicago Cubs caps. Although the image of a chubby, middle-aged woman with a baseball cap for every outfit wasn't quite what Brenda imagined in her office, Cubbie would certainly be a colorful character. Right now, Brenda craved color in her life.

With Cubbie in the office, Brenda wouldn't be tied down there. She just didn't relish being away from Malfour. Going back to even the semblance of a real job sent shivers through her. The scars from the massacre Danny Crane caused were permanent. Working full time in an office environment could open up those scars.

Cubbie would probably be bored, coming from such a hectic,

people-oriented job at the Gulfbreeze, but Brenda planned on presenting her with lots of incentives, like a television. Cubbie was a soap opera freak. She hoped it would be enough to keep her friend happy.

Brenda had inked a full day in her planner. Phil Brown's card lay on the dash of her Jag. She intended to stop at Le Galleria. Tina hadn't said anything about her sculptures at the gallery the last time they talked. Brenda wasn't sure what his visit meant.

Even though she was dying to get back to Stewart, she decided to concentrate on catching up with Manda Jones instead. Brenda left the Gulfbreeze and headed to Dale Mabry and Kennedy. Right now, what she needed was a more complete picture of Paula Drakes. She'd heard from her sister, coworker, and dubious friend Joan Davis. She wondered what Manda Jones would prove to be.

The Tampa Gay Business Association occupied a small office in a strip mall off Kennedy Boulevard. There was one window with open shades and a mint-green door. Brenda walked into a cramped reception area with a few chrome and print office chairs and several partitions. A bulletin board full of flyers and business cards all vied for her attention. Gay tours, cruises, plumbers and political clubs all clamored for the limited gay and lesbian dollar.

A short, very brown woman with close-cropped hair came from behind one of the partitions and stopped in her tracks. She stared at Brenda.

"Hi. I'm Brenda Strange. I'm looking for Manda Jones."

The woman finally found a smile and extended a hand toward Brenda. "I'm Manda." She motioned Brenda back toward her space and invited her to have a seat. She sat down at her desk, her eyes fixed on Brenda.

"Wow, Brenda, I'm sorry for staring, but you really look like—"

"Princess Diana, I know." Brenda cut her short. She took out the wallet with her PI license and the cheap badge Kevin had gotten her back in Jersey. "I'm investigating Paula Drakes' death. I found your business card in her belongings at La Ventanas. Did you two know each other personally or professionally?"

47

Manda Jones smiled wider. "Well, I got your message, but you never said anything about investigating Paula." She lost her smile and looked seriously at Brenda. "Paula and I were good friends. She was a good person." She shook her head slightly. "I suspected the way she died. Are you investigating her accident?"

"Not exactly," Brenda said. "I don't think Paula's death was an accident. I'm working on getting proof of that. What made you suspicious?"

"Hell, that girl never went near the water. She wouldn't set even one toe in it. She and I attended all the Pride picnics at Desoto Beach and she never once went for a swim." She continued shaking her head. "That's why I couldn't understand why she got mixed up with Joan Davis."

"Joan Davis?" Brenda arched an eyebrow. The look of distaste on Manda's face told Brenda that Joan wasn't on this woman's faves list.

"Yeah. Joan Davis was bad news. Paula didn't belong with her kind, if you know what I mean." Manda gave Brenda a knowing look. "She's a rich bitch that only knows how to use people for her own satisfaction."

Brenda pulled her notepad out of her bag and started writing. A small smile tugged at the corners of her mouth. She wondered if Manda Jones felt that way about all rich women.

"Joan and Paula had an affair?"

"Well, it was just an affair for Joan Davis, but Paula fell in love with her. Paula was an attractive woman. She could pretty much have anyone she wanted. Except one."

"Joan Davis."

"She fell so much in love with that woman she couldn't see straight."

"Let me guess," Brenda said. "She drove all her friends crazy talking about her?" She remembered the first months of her relationship with Tina. The memory hadn't faded.

"You got it. I think it might have even cost her some friends."

"Must not have been true-blue friends. Or maybe jealous?" Brenda's inner voice was screaming for more, but she told herself to

48

be patient, something she had struggled with all through her lawyer days. Manda clearly wanted to talk.

"Well, Paula was a real socialite in the lesbian community locally. She broke a few hearts herself. There was a young girl, Steffi Vargas, who really got hung up on Paula."

Brenda asked her to spell the name and wrote it down quickly, then asked, "Did they remain friends?"

"Yeah, if you want to call it that. It was a one-sided thing, you know. Paula laid it all out and up front for Steffi. Steffi got hurt but continued a friendship with Paula. By all accounts, it remained a pretty volatile relationship."

"Do you think she was capable of killing Paula Drakes?"

Manda shook her head slowly and pursed her lips. "I'm not a detective, but from personal knowledge, Steffi's the hotheaded type. She acts before she thinks. I don't believe she could have plotted to murder Paula."

"Do you have any way of getting in touch with Steffi?"

"No, but she works at Studio Ten. It's a portrait studio in Carrollwood. They're listed in the phone book."

Brenda noted the name of the studio in her notebook. "What about Joan Davis?" Brenda asked. "Did you ever meet her?"

Manda made a noise with her lips. "Yeah, and I'm sorry I ever did. She came with Paula to one of the Pride picnics. All she could do was brag about her boats and her yacht. I tried to convince Paula to dump her." Manda stopped and smiled apologetically. "Hey, look, Brenda, I don't know you. I'm very open about who I am and my lifestyle and I just assume it's cool with everyone. Some straight women don't understand—"

"I understand," Brenda added quickly. She was rarely picked up on gaydar and her sexual preference wasn't something she openly discussed with strangers. "Manda, do you have any idea if Stewart, Joan's husband, knew about her affair with Paula?" It's the question she'd been bursting to ask. Nothing like a jealous husband to commit a crime of passion and then try to pass it off as an accident.

"I'm sorry, I really don't know. I could never get Paula to quit

49

seeing her. After Joan gave her that boat, our friendship got even more distant. She finally stopped talking to me about Joan so I wouldn't give her any more grief over it."

Brenda's heart was acting like a jumping bean. "Joan gave Paula a boat?"

"Some kind of love, huh? You don't give a woman afraid of the water a boat." The pain contorted Manda's face in anger.

That solved the mystery of Paula Drakes' boat.

"Manda, do you think Paula would have gone out diving by herself?"

"Hell, no." The anger was still hot in her voice.

"When was the last time you saw Paula?"

"Early May. She canceled a picnic some friends of ours invited us to."

"Did she say why?"

Manda shook her head. "Nope. I figured it must be Joan."

Brenda jotted down the date and put away the notepad.

"Hey, I'm sorry I couldn't be of more help," Manda said.

"You've been more help than you think." Brenda got up to leave.

Manda came around to stand next to her, a very determined look in her big brown eyes. "Listen, I hope you find out what really happened to Paula."

"I've got a lot of people who want the same thing."

When Brenda got back in her Jag, she sat behind the wheel for a moment, letting the conversation with Manda Jones sink in. Her suspect list had grown, but worse than that, the picture of Joan Davis that Manda had painted made her stomach queasy. She shuddered involuntarily when she thought of the times Joan and Tina had spent together. What if her gut feelings were on target? Joan had focused hungry eyes directly on Tina. It was now quite obvious that Joan's sexual appetite didn't discriminate between male and female.

The sick feeling seeped into her system and sat there. Like bad cholesterol. It made Brenda feel dirty. But she couldn't let those destructive thoughts overwhelm her or she would never get through her busy day. Le Galleria and Phil Brown were next on her list. She gripped the polished wood steering wheel, started up the Jag and slipped out onto Kennedy Boulevard.

Brenda was thankful for the heavy traffic. It allowed her to put aside her nasty thoughts and concentrate on her driving. She worked her way through downtown Tampa, past the Ice Palace, home of Tampa's ice hockey team, the Tampa Bay Lightning, and continued on toward the narrow red brick streets of Tampa's historic Ybor City.

Now it was frustration more than anything else that nagged her. Once again, Stewart Davis, head of Davross Industries and one of the richest men in Tampa, was a suspect in one of her cases. It was getting embarrassing. For Pete's sake, the Davises were her neighbors. While not guilty of any wrongdoing, Stewart had been involved in shady real estate dealings that had almost threatened Malfour House.

But this time, it was the murder and not the real estate cookie jar that he might have his hand stuck in. The image of a neon triangle kept flashing off in Brenda's head. What if Stewart had found out about his wife and Paula Drakes? He had motive and he had the means. The Davises owned at least two boats. By his own admission, he had a passion for diving. He could have killed Paula then dumped her in the bay to make it look like an accident. But on a more sordid note, what if Stewart Davis got off on lesbian sex? Maybe he not only knew about Joan and Paula, but also took part in their little trysts?

Phil Brown's Le Galleria was on Seventh Avenue, Ybor's main drag. In its heyday, Ybor City had been the hub of all activity in Old Tampa. The Spanish and Italian population gave it an Old World flavor. Shops, restaurants, cigar factories and exclusive clubs thrived until the late 1950s and early '60's. Urban development and Ybor residents' migration to the suburbs turned out the lights for the glory days of Ybor City.

Ybor was currently undergoing major rejuvenation. After being designated a historic district, old lady Ybor got a facelift. Some of the older, crumbling buildings suddenly came back to life with new renovations. An eclectic mix of the contemporary and the historic was creating excitement again, with art galleries, movie theaters and exclusive shops bringing in new tourists. Unfortunately, the City of Tampa granted too many liquor licenses in an effort to pump up the nightlife. This led to drunken violence, muggings and unsavory characters loitering in the streets, leaving Ybor City to the young and more reckless after hours.

As she drove slowly down Seventh, Brenda noticed the large trucks parked on corners. They were stringing Christmas lights and artificial wreaths with large Styrofoam candy canes along the three-globe light fixtures, trademarks of Ybor City, that ran down the length of the street.

Brenda looked at the business card on her dashboard. Le Galleria was a small storefront snuggled between a Jason's Coffeehouse and a vintage jewelry and fashion store. She got lucky and snagged a coveted parking space on the avenue, just a few storefronts away.

Brenda plunked two quarters in the parking meter and started toward the art gallery. The name *Le Galleria* was painted in black and gold script on the large window. *Philip Brown, Owner and Director* appeared in smaller black letters on the glass panes of the door.

Brenda was dazzled by the oversized, brilliant paintings on the tall panels of the gallery. The canvases depicted splashy scenes of dark-skinned people in chunky forms indulging in picnics, dancing and street scenes. Scattered around the gallery were sculptures and glass pieces.

Brenda scanned the sculptures in the gallery and finally spotted one of Tina's up against the back wall. It was the one Tina called *Winged Scandal*, the half female, half bird of prey, a baby in its beak.

She hadn't seen anyone since walking in, so she headed toward the back, where she distinctly heard the muffled sound of conversation from somewhere behind the wall. A doorway led to a darkened hallway. Brenda figured the gallery office lay beyond.

She stiffened as she recognized Joan Davis's voice. The other voice was a man's. He spoke in lower, more restrained tones. Brenda's ears perked up as she tiptoed closer to the doorway.

"Does Stewart suspect anything?"

"How am I supposed to know, Phil?" Joan sounded upset.

"He is your husband." His voice was distracted, distant, as if he were busy with something else while he talked.

"Stop that and listen to me." Joan was borderline hysterical. "I'm scared. And you should be too."

"You're going fucking loony." He didn't sound worried.

Brenda was plastered against the wall like a coat of paint. Her heart was beating so hard she was afraid it would give her away. She worked her way closer to the doorway, short of poking her head through. Then her cell phone went off.

Joan and the man must have heard it. There was movement from behind the wall. The cell phone rang again, more like an alarm going off in the deathly quiet gallery. Brenda dug the cell phone out from her bag and had it in her hand when a tall man came through the doorway. He was well built with dark, curly hair and moustache. Joan Davis stood frozen next to him, a scowl directed at Brenda. Her shiny wall of hair draped one side of her face and spilled over her shoulders.

Brenda held out a hand and Phil Brown shook it with hesitation.

"Hi, I'm Brenda Strange."

"Phil Brown." He looked her up and down.

Brenda smiled as the cell phone rang again. "If you'll excuse me." She pressed the "end" button and stuck the phone back in the bag, not before noticing it had been Lisa Chambliss on the other end. She kept her smile and turned back to Phil and Joan.

"I'm sorry about the interruption." Brenda didn't want them to suspect her of eavesdropping. That wouldn't be a good start for a meeting with Phil Brown. "There wasn't anyone in the gallery. I was working my way back to your office." Brenda stopped and looked at Joan. "Joan, what a surprise. I hope you're feeling a bit better than the last time I saw you?"

The air turned frigid between them. Joan didn't smile at all, but instead looked at Phil before answering. "Yes, I am feeling better. I do apologize for that little fiasco." She fidgeted, her eyes darting back and forth to Phil. "I have nightmares and they get me stressed out."

Brenda nodded her head. "Paula Drakes still around?"

She didn't give Joan time to answer, turning her gaze and smile to Phil Brown. "Phil, you left your card on my door."

Phil Brown wore a turtleneck sweater, khaki pants and suede loafers. He looked admiringly at her, a slight smile pulling at his mouth. "Well, Brenda, good to meet you. Tina didn't tell me how beautiful you were."

He wanted Brenda to gush over his compliment. She knew his type. She had him pegged already. Unfortunately for him, she wouldn't be a new filly in his stable. But by the vibes Brenda was picking up, she was willing to bet Joan Davis was.

He put his hands into his pockets. "I've sold one of Tina's pieces. Before she left, she requested that any money made from sales of her work should come to you. I wanted to deliver the check personally." He kept smiling. "I have it back in the office. I'll get it for you." He turned and started through the doorway. "You should be very proud of Tina. It was a sweet sale. Big patron."

He disappeared, leaving Joan Davis wringing her hands, as if she wasn't quite sure what to do with them. She finally crossed her arms.

"I'm so happy for Tina," Joan said, avoiding Brenda's stare. "It's not often that sculptures sell at that price." She was trying to steer Brenda away from Paula Drakes.

Brenda smiled, going along with her game for now. She looked at the *Winged Scandal* piece and then back at Joan, hitting Joan with her most intimidating glare. "Which was the sculpture that sold?"

"Oh, it was that Gorgon piece. A head bust, I think."

It was the piece Tina had started during the summer at Malfour. The memory of her hands working at the clay was still vivid in Brenda's heart.

"That is a great work. Tina put a lot into it while she was at Malfour."

Philip Brown walked back into the room and handed Brenda a

check. "Tina's making quite a name for herself in Tampa," he said. "I hope she gets in some new work for us." Phil grinned.

Brenda looked briefly at the $10,000 check, folded it in two and tucked it inside her jacket. Tina's work always paid off big when it sold. She really was proud of her.

She smiled at Phil. "I'm sure she'll want to thank you personally when she gets back."

Phil Brown never lost his smile as he tugged lightly on Joan's arm. "It's been a pleasure to meet you, Brenda, but if you'll excuse us, Joan has been a dear this morning in helping me out with inventory, and we've got so much more to do. Please take your time and look around the gallery if you'd like."

The thought of escaping Brenda's stare seemed to brighten Joan's mood. She flashed her big row of white teeth and faked a wave. "Good to see you, Brenda."

Brenda had no intention of sticking around Le Galleria. She was out the door in seconds and on the phone dialing Lisa Chambliss.

Chapter 7

"Brenda, none of this is solid evidence." Lisa Chambliss sat on the softest, creamiest white leather sofa she'd ever put her bottom to. The woman sitting beside her didn't seem to hear or even acknowledge her presence.

Brenda Strange sat leafing through the Paula Drakes file Lisa had brought. Lisa took the moment to observe the tall, elegant PI. Her long hands handled the papers gently, carefully placing each sheet behind the other methodically. The intensity on the strong-boned face showed Brenda's complete focus on her work.

Lisa looked again briefly at the list Brenda had prepared for her. There wasn't much more than hearsay from Paula Drakes' friends and family, and a freaky leaky roof at a neurotic woman's home. What was she supposed to do with this? She flicked at the sheet with her finger.

"Let's get down to gut feelings, Brenda. Talk to me about Stewart and Joan Davis."

Brenda Strange's piercing porcelain blue eyes shifted to meet Lisa's. The contrast of the blazing red sateen lounging suit Brenda wore and the intensity of the blue eyes startled Lisa for just a flitting second. She smiled.

Brenda held up the copy of the black-and-white photo of Paula Drakes' neck and back. The actual report clipped underneath the photo was thick with black marker. Only the official seal of the Hillsborough County Medical Examiner's office and the name Randall Tateman, Chief Medical Examiner, was legible.

"Who went heavy on the black? These are abnormal marks on Paula's neck and upper back. They look like open wounds." Brenda's eyes went back to the photo.

"They aren't wounds."

Brenda shook her head and smiled, her gaze falling back on Lisa. "Is your department trying to cover something up? This isn't going to work if I don't have access to the same facts you do, Lisa."

Lisa was already skating on thin ice by letting Brenda see the report. The case was marked for Special Eyes Only. Had she made a mistake by indulging her greedy little ego? She was against the FBI's taking the case from TPD. Her department deserved to investigate it. The only reason she encouraged Brenda was because she had a gut feeling that Chief Hull was waiting for just the right bit of evidence to reopen the case and give the finger to the FBI. But should some private investigator with a freshly inked license have full access to the files on the slim chance she could get them that kind of information?

"You a James Bond fan, Brenda?"

"I never considered a male chauvinist to be very entertaining."

"*For Your Eyes Only*, one of my favorites," Lisa continued. "Those files are for your eyes only. The case is pretty much in the FBI's in-basket. It's going to be out of our hands unless I can convince the chief otherwise."

"So will I have to find your medical examiner and get the answer to my question, or will you tell me why"—Brenda paused and looked hard at the photo—"why Randall Tateman's comments were blocked from this report?"

Lisa twisted on the couch to face Brenda. She studied the blonde woman's eyes, arched eyebrows and questioning smile. "You know, Brenda, you don't look like any private investigator I've ever dealt with. You really should be doing work in Hollywood or something. I bet they need Princess Diana doubles."

Brenda shook her head slowly. "You're not getting off the hook that easy, Detective."

"Lisa. Remember?"

"Lisa, why are the FBI getting involved in an accidental drowning? Tell me what these marks are on Paula Drakes' body."

"Well, I'd tell you to sit down, but you already are." Lisa exhaled slowly. "What you've got there is the doctored, unofficial report the chief released for public eyes. The real deal is locked in his office." She paused. "When I read Randall's findings, I went to him personally. It wasn't the kind of stuff we usually deal with. I needed to be sure."

Brenda put down the file. "I have a feeling it's exactly the kind of 'stuff' I can help you with."

Lisa noticed the strange intensity glowing in Brenda's eyes. "Those lacerations on her neck . . . They aren't what they appear to be. The M.E.'s official word is that those things . . ." Lisa paused and pointed to the photo. "Those marks are gills. Gills, as in fish. We both know that can't be right."

Brenda's eyebrows lifted. "Or do we?"

Lisa straightened up and cast an unbelieving look at Brenda. "You don't believe that crap, do you? That's *X-Files*, you know."

"Look at what the medical examiner says about the lungs. Mass decomposition." Brenda held up the report.

"Brenda, the entire body was decomposed."

"No, there was complete atrophy of the lungs. There are legends of amphibious races in literature, so it isn't that far-fetched," Brenda replied.

Lisa put up her hands in protest. "Oh no, Brenda, I don't talk mumbo jumbo. I need facts. Hard, cold details I can touch, smell and taste."

Brenda didn't blink. Her whole body was perfectly still. Lisa raised her hand and waved it in front of Brenda.

"Brenda, do you understand why this is FBI stuff? TPD doesn't know what to do with it. Where to go." She looked at Brenda for some sort of response.

Brenda sat immobile, as if frozen in a daze, oblivious to everything around her. Lisa fidgeted on the couch, scanning the room. The candles flickered straight and bright; not a whisper of a breeze passed through the house. The temperature had dropped considerably. Lisa noticed Brenda still had that faraway look in her eyes. The place was creeping her out. She never liked these old houses. Too much history squeezed into too few rooms.

"Brenda? You okay?" Lisa touched Brenda's arm.

Brenda's eyes focused back on Lisa with a bright eagerness in them.

"Lisa, do you know that Paula Drakes' body is missing? Her sister said the Jersey police think grave robbers desecrated the grave."

Lisa looked her over, not liking what Brenda was implying. "Hey, I don't know if I'm hearing you right, here. I never took you for the wacky type. I suppose you think that Paula Drakes is up and around frightening her murderers?" Lisa felt the warmth crawl back through her system. She wanted to laugh, but it just didn't seem the thing to do. Brenda, next to her, didn't seem to mind the cold in the room at all. She just sat there, with her piercing blue eyes, waiting for Lisa to say something.

Brenda finally put away the photo and files and leaned back on the couch, her gaze still digging into Lisa. "I don't have any of that hard evidence you seem to need to touch, smell and see yet, Lisa, but I can tell you that I don't believe Paula Drakes died as the result of an accident. You and Canello wrote the report." Brenda tapped the file. "Paula sustained a mortal blow to her head with a blunt object—"

"She could have gotten that anywhere on the bottom of the deep blue sea," interrupted Lisa. "Brenda, she committed the big no-no in diving. She went into the bay without a diving buddy."

"I don't buy that. She wasn't out alone. She didn't go diving. I mean, follow the report, Lisa. The diving tank was full. When Paula hit the water, she didn't need air anymore. She was dead. It's all here. Her lungs and larynx were free of water."

Lisa smiled and shook her head. Brenda wasn't even flinching. "Ninety-five percent of the time, Brenda, you can't prove a murder out of a floater that's been in the water for any length of time. Hell, we can't even get close to a time of death. It's only a guess. All we could give Paula was a legal time of death and that was when we pulled her out of the water and pronounced her dead."

"Yes, but the M.E. estimates time of death approximately three days before you scooped her out of the water. That would put her murder at or around the last weekend in May." Brenda picked up the folder again and leafed deftly through the report pages. She pulled a sheet out and shoved it into Lisa's face.

"This is your handwriting, right?"

Lisa took it and couldn't suppress admiration for Brenda's dogged persistence. She read her own description of Paula Drakes' body on the beach.

Brenda continued, "Your words tell me that Paula Drakes wore a diving suit of polyurethane with an aluminum tank and a diving mask. Her head was cracked open and parts of her body had been a tasty treat for fish."

"Yeah, I wrote this. What are you getting at?"

"She didn't have flippers."

Lisa shook her head and couldn't understand the smile Brenda had on her lips. "Where are you trying to take me, Brenda?"

"I don't know that much about diving, Lisa, but I do know that anyone taking a dive in the middle of the Gulf of Mexico will want a good pair of flippers."

"Maybe fish like rubber fins for dessert?" Lisa realized it was a rather flippant answer, but the truth was that Brenda was right. "She could have lost them somewhere in the bottom of the bay."

"Come on, Lisa. Paula Drakes was murdered somewhere else, possibly on a boat, decked out in diving gear to make it appear she went for a dive, then dumped like bait into the gulf."

Lisa looked long at the woman next to her. It was a complex scenario for the murderer to stage, but not completely far-fetched. She wished she could convince Chief Hull to reopen the case, but wasn't sure Brenda Strange, a PI with little experience, was the trigger that could make him change his mind.

Lisa patted the soft leather seat next to her. "Listen, Brenda. Let me take this report you were kind enough to print out for me to Chief Hull and see if we can't keep this case on his desk a bit longer. You know, tie it up with lots of red tape."

She stood up and watched Brenda unfold herself from the couch. At five feet seven, Lisa was tall, but Brenda seemed to tower over her.

"Just how tall are you, Brenda?"

"Five feet nine in my bare feet."

"I bet you had trouble in school."

"Only from the boys." There was an odd smile on Brenda's face, and her eyes were ice-blue. There was almost a shy sensuality about the tall, slim woman.

Lisa felt the air grow cold again. She was uncomfortable with the temperature changes in the house. She started for the door.

"Keep that cell phone on, and call me when you get something. I'll try my charms on Chief Hull."

As she walked to her car, Lisa shivered. It was colder in that house than the evening chill outside.

"Next time, can you please wait until my guest has left before you talk my ear off?" Brenda held the martini glass to her lips, barely able to control the smile. The Belvedere went down her throat with the bite she'd come to expect from the premium Polish vodka.

She sat with both feet propped and crossed on the guest-room sofa. Carlotta stood at one end and Angelique was draped elegantly over the top of the other end. Brenda had called Eddy after Lisa Chambliss left and arranged to meet at his place for dinner and to sign the papers. She'd also have to remember to make sleeping arrangements for Susan Christie. She'd be arriving Thursday.

"We were so excited for you. You rarely have such lovely company. Plus, you like the policewoman," Carlotta said.

"And she likes you." Angelique's playful voice teased.

"Stop it, you two." Brenda couldn't believe she was sitting here carrying on like a schoolgirl with two ghosts. "It's more likely she thinks I'm a candidate for the loony bin. I couldn't concentrate with you two rattling in my ear."

"We're sorry, Brenda, if we made it hard for you."

"Speak for yourself, Carlotta. I'm not the least bit sorry. Our girl here is as slow as a turtle with its head tucked away when it comes to romance," Angelique pronounced.

Even though they lacked the substance of flesh and blood, Carlotta's eyes expressed concern when she looked at Brenda.

"Angelique, your sharp tongue has hurt Brenda." She reached over with a pale, gray hand as if to touch Brenda's cheek, but pulled back. Her hand would go right through anything solid. *"Brenda, forget Angelique's insensitivity. There are more anxious things we must share with you tonight than the frivolities of the heart."*

Brenda nodded slowly in agreement, disturbed at the serious sound of Carlotta's voice and the sinking feeling in her own heart. She sat up on the couch and looked at Carlotta. The woman's face was an even darker shade of gray. Like ashes.

"Brenda, there is a darkness gathering at Malfour. Can't you feel it? Look at the wallpaper. The colors are deeper. The floors are becoming dull in corners. A great sadness is coming."

The alarm bells in Brenda's head started banging. She *had* noticed the oppressive feel within Malfour. The air was thick.

"Tell me what you mean, Carlotta. I can't see what you do. It's hard enough learning how to handle some of the things I do feel and see."

"*Of course you do, Brenda. You must understand that this house has been changed forever. You have consumed Malfour, loved it and given birth to a new home,*" Carlotta said, almost in a whisper.

"*Yes. Feel it in your heart and in your soul. You are Malfour. It now breathes through you. As do we,*" Angelique said.

"Carlotta, this sadness you speak of, is it my mother?"

"*We don't have those answers. We were hoping that you did. All we can sense are the faint cries of the wind on this side. And death is laughing.*"

Chapter 8

"Periwinkle? What kind of name for a color is that?" Cubbie stood in the new offices of Strange Investigations, her new workplace. She eyed the trendy new color, a mix of blue and purple, with distaste. "Sugar, this doesn't look like any serious private-eye business I've ever seen." She plopped down in one of the off-white leather chairs.

"And which movies are you using as comparisons, Cubbie?" Brenda teased.

"C'mon, everyone knows that a true-blue, pardon the pun, PI office is usually tiny and cramped with old furniture and bottles of booze on a paper-strewn desk." Cubbie had a big smile on her round face. Today, she wore a navy blue Chicago Bears football team cap, navy sweater and black pants with suede black boots.

Brenda went over and patted the boots. "I hope you didn't spend too much money shopping for your new business attire." She laughed. "It looks good, Cubbie. I mean, you've even color-coordinated the hat. There's still hope for you."

In the reception area, in addition to the desk, there were two leather chairs, a small round coffee table of rattan and a large bookcase that ran across the opposite wall. It was filled with her law books and volumes on broad subjects from psychology to pathology, all from her own library.

"Sugar, this looks more like some highfalutin doctor's office than a detective's. All you need is a television with those health tapes that never quit running."

"Let me guess, you overdosed on Yosemite Sam. By the way, it's private investigator, not detective," Brenda admonished. "And speaking of television . . ." She disappeared into one of the two rooms behind the desk. Cubbie started after her. "You stay put," Brenda warned. "I've got a surprise."

When she reappeared, she was lugging a sleek white television.

Cubbie's face broke out into a big grin. "Oh my word, honey, you didn't have to do that for me."

"Yes, I did." Brenda hefted it up on the desk. Cubbie's desk. "You're going to get very bored around here. It's a far cry from the hectic pace of the Gulfbreeze. I figured your favorite soaps would keep you occupied in between the one or two phone calls you might get a month."

Brenda smiled and patted the television set, happy with the look on Cubbie's face. She looked more like a little girl than a big and beautiful woman. She glowed like most kids with a new toy.

"Go ahead," Brenda said. "Turn it on. It's fifteen inches and color. And we've got a cable hookup right next to your desk."

"You know, this could be dangerous. You might never get work out of me." Cubbie fumbled with the cord as she plugged it into the wall, then screwed the cable wire to the back.

"Okay, now come see my office." Brenda had to pull Cubbie away from the television.

The room was small, but there was a medium-size mahogany desk, Brenda's laptop, two small chairs and a small bookcase.

"Impressive, but why these aluminum chairs that look like they came from a bankrupt nineteen-fifties restaurant?"

Brenda couldn't contain her laughter. She reached around Cubbie and pulled the office door shut. Cubbie's mouth dropped open.

It was a full glass door, framed in mahogany, the glass that frosty type with a pebbled finish, like a football. Cubbie ran her hand over the tiny bumps in the glass.

"Well I'll be. This door is just like the ones in those classic black-and-white detective movies from the forties."

"And by the way, Cubbie, those chairs are twentieth-century modern. The latest in decorating fashion," Brenda said, still smiling.

"I don't care what they are, they look like they're fit for interrogation." Cubbie turned and looked at Brenda, shaking her head in puzzled amusement. "You have a strange way of making your clients feel at home." She walked away, shaking her head of curly red hair and hat. She plopped herself down behind her desk, turning her chair around and around. "At least you got me a comfy chair." She put both her chubby hands on the desk and looked at Brenda. "Okay, boss, I'm here to work. Where do I start?"

Brenda pointed to the second room behind them, where she'd hidden the television set. "That room is the file room. You should have more than enough filing cabinets for starters. There's also a coffee maker and small refrigerator."

"Refrigerator? Got sodas too?"

"Yes, you can have drinks, but they have to share space with other"—Brenda paused—"ah . . . other things once in a while."

"Oh, boy, comin' from you, Brenda Strange, that is one itch this gal isn't going to scratch. I don't even want to know. Just give me fair warnin' when you've got something funky in there, okay?" Cubbie patted her heart. "I've got a weak ticker, you know. Those spooky folks at that old rooster's house or whatever it was you dragged me to in West Tampa nearly gave me a stroke."

Brenda disappeared into her office, grabbed the Paula Drakes case file and came back to Cubbie.

"I didn't drag you, you invited yourself, remember? You introduced me to your two friends that were part of that voodoo or Santeria or whatever that crazy religion is." She pulled up one of the chairs and propped her feet up on Cubbie's desk. "Before you zone out on *All My Children*, you've got to clock in." She pulled out a sheet from the file and slipped it on the desk. "These are the names of people involved in the Paula Drakes case. You may be taking phone calls from any of them. All the files of my current cases will always be in my office, hopefully on my desk." Brenda held up the Paula Drakes file. "This is what's hot now. Paula Drakes. They found her body floating in the bay. TPD thinks it was an accident. Drakes' sister doesn't think so, and neither do I."

"You mean you think you can find something the police missed?"

"Not missed, just didn't look for. As you would phrase it, chew on this." Brenda went on, "Promiscuous wife of very wealthy man, bored with her marriage, gets reckless with one of her affairs. Playing both sides of the fence . . ."

"You mean she liked the fairer sex?" Cubbie's face was a question.

Brenda couldn't control her smile. "Yes, that's right. This woman falls in love with her and wants more from the relationship. Meanwhile, the husband finds out about the relationship and, in a fit of jealousy, kills the lover and creates an impressive scenario to make the murder look like an accident."

"That's it?" Cubbie asked. "I gotta tell you, and I hope you don't get offended, but it's a cliché plot. I mean, even the soaps do it to death." Cubbie caught herself and laughed, one hand on her mouth. "No pun intended."

"Okay," Brenda said, "suppose we make it a bit more interesting. What if the wife wanted out of the affair? Too much heat in the kitchen, so to speak, and spills everything to the husband. Together they commit the murder."

That scenario had occurred to her earlier, and it sounded good now talking it out with Cubbie.

"We're not done, though. Add into this poisonous mix a jilted girlfriend, one who can't handle rejection. She murders her ex and stages it to look like an accident."

"So you've got two, possibly three suspects?"

"Definitely possible." Brenda mulled it over. "Each of the suspects had plenty of motive, assuming the husband knew about the affair. Two have clear opportunity."

"And the other?"

"The 'other' is my project for the day." Brenda got up, collected the file and started back to her office. "I'll be out of the office for most of the day. You've got my cell number if something comes up."

Studio Ten was a small custom photography studio and onsite lab. Unfortunately for Brenda, Steffi Vargas no longer worked there. According to the lab manager, she'd quit right after the Memorial Day holiday without giving notice, cleared out her work area and left. It smelled like guilt to Brenda.

Brenda called Manda Jones in the hopes she might know where to find Steffi. An address or phone number. Anything. Manda gave her the names of roommates Steffi lived with. It was going to be a lucky day for Brenda, because she found them in the phone book. And it listed the address. It was in an older part of Tampa.

Brenda put away the map as she downshifted to first and parked her Jag on the curb. The street sign read Mohawkee Avenue. She looked again at the address she'd written in her notepad and back at the two-story house in need of TLC. The screen door hung off the hinges; yard work didn't seem to be in the budget or the roommates' favorite pastime.

Brenda walked up to the door, peeled back the screen and

68

knocked. The door was so dirty that her knuckles came back smudged with black.

A tall, stocky young woman with a mullet haircut, flannel shirt and jeans opened the door. She didn't smile. "Yeah, can I help you?"

Brenda had her PI license in her hand. "I'm Brenda Strange. I'm looking for Steffi Vargas."

The woman made an unfriendly sound and frowned. "Yeah, you and everybody else. Does she owe you money or worse?"

"No, nothing like that. I'm investigating the death of Paula Drakes. Is Steffi in?"

The woman hesitated, took another look at the license and stepped back, waving Brenda in. She ushered Brenda into a large living room.

"Debbie, honey, we've got company," the woman called up the stairs that snaked behind a wall to Brenda's left. She wiped her hands on her jeans and held one out to Brenda. "I'm Abby. Sorry about the messy house. We're renovating it ourselves. You wanna have a seat?" She pointed Brenda toward a big couch with a colorful throw patterned with seashells and fish.

Brenda couldn't help noticing the abundance of green in the house. There were plants everywhere. Some were natural, others silk. Three cats sashayed across the room, one orange tabby taking a disinterested look Brenda's way, then scampering away.

When Brenda sat down, she sank so deep into the couch, she almost grabbed for a pillow. They definitely needed more than just a throw for this couch. A big fireplace faced her, with angels and goddess figurines haphazardly placed atop the mantel.

A big hulk of a woman came suddenly pounding down the stairs. Her dark hair was short, and she wore tasteful makeup and a long velvet dress.

"Hi, I'm Debbie." She smiled at Brenda but shot a questioning look at Abby.

"Uh, Brenda's a private eye. She's looking for Steff."

Brenda got the impression that Debbie was head of this household.

Debbie and Abby sat side by side on the small loveseat next to Brenda. *They are definitely a couple*, thought Brenda.

"Yeah, well, we'd like to know where Steff is too, Brenda. She's gone. Took off in a cab with all her belongings about six months or so ago and we haven't seen or heard from her since. Left all those bills that keep coming in," Debbie said, pointing to a big stack of envelopes on a small end table.

"She just up and moved? No advance notice?"

"Oh yeah, she told us she was moving out, but we didn't expect her to one day just pack up and leave."

"Did she find another place in Tampa?"

"Nope. Said she was moving back home," Debbie said.

"And 'back home' would be where?"

"Don't really know. She talked very little about herself. I think she said something about Mobile, Alabama, or something like that."

Brenda had her notebook out. "Did Steffi have any close friends? Someone she might have confided in? People she hung out with?"

"Nah." Debbie waved a big hand in the air. "She was a loner. There was only Paula. She was obsessed with that woman. Paula was old enough to be her mother."

"Yeah, we figured she had a mother fixation," Abby said as she looked first at Debbie, then at Brenda.

"Did you two notice any bizarre behavior on Steffi's part before or after Paula's death? Did she say anything that might have been an indication she could have harmed Paula?"

Abby and Debbie looked at each other and shook their heads.

"Steffi was a hothead," Debbie said. "She was always pissed off at something or someone. She did go a little wild when Paula dumped her. But she'd just left when they dragged Paula's body out of the bay."

Brenda's ears perked up. "How wild?"

"Well, she ranted and raved about getting the bitch who ruined her relationship with Paula."

Abby interrupted with a snort. "Yeah, as if she needed any help. She blew that on her own. She smothered Paula."

"Yeah, and she just hounded Paula until Paula agreed to remain at least friends."

Brenda stopped writing. "Would you consider her a stalker?"

"No," Debbie said, shaking her head. "Not a stalker, but a big, gooey pest. I mean, she had this really sick idea that friendship meant Paula still loved her and they would end up back together again."

"So do you think Steffi followed Paula without Paula's being aware of it?"

"Sometimes. Yeah, I think she did." Debbie sounded sure.

"I think she definitely did," Abby added. "She'd run out of here with her camera, all in a heated rush. Never said where she was going. We just got used to her crazy ways. As long as she paid her room and board, it wasn't any of our business what she did out there."

"So she rented a room from you? May I check it out?"

"Sorry, the room's already rented out," Debbie replied quickly. "Besides, she didn't leave anything but those bills."

Brenda put away her pad. "Do you mind if I take them?" She pointed to the big stack. "The police might be able to locate her through her creditors."

Hell, it sounded good to Brenda, and it was true, in a way.

Lisa could help if Steffi Vargas's Social Security number was in any of those bills. The real tracking down was going to be her own adventure and hers alone.

"Be my guest. Take them all. We're getting tired of the bill collectors calling every night." Debbie hastily scooped up the wad of letters and handed them over.

Brenda thanked them and was halfway to the door before Debbie stopped her and scurried to her side.

"Say, Brenda, do you think Steffi took out Paula?"

Brenda shook her head. "That's where I'm hoping Steffi can help me out. By the way, how close were you two and Steffi? Were you friends before she moved in?"

"Not friends," Debbie said quickly. "We posted a notice at one of the local bars for the room rental. She came calling."

"Did you check her references? Anyone I might talk to here in Tampa?" Brenda was hopeful.

Abby and Debbie both shook their heads. "We're new to this rental thing, you know. We just made sure she had a job and made enough money to pay us," Debbie said.

"Sorry we couldn't help," Abby added.

"Thank you both for your time." Brenda fished out her card holder and handed Debbie one of the cards. "Don't hesitate to call if anything comes up."

The day had left her drained. She'd officially opened Strange Investigations, gotten Cubbie settled in her new job with a minimum of drama and found key information on the Paula Drakes case.

Brenda stopped by the office after leaving Debbie and Abby. She wanted to make sure Cubbie was holding her own and still sane. She gave her the key to close the office at five and headed home. To Malfour. It was going to take some time to get used to having her own office. Brenda had always dreamed of seeing her name on a door; she just didn't expect Private Investigator to be tacked on to the end of it.

After having a large Greek salad for dinner, Brenda started on the new Capricorn bear, Cappy. Since she made so many bears from one pattern, she'd invested in a rubber stamp of the pattern parts so she wouldn't have to trace so many. This way, she merely stamped the pattern parts onto the fabric.

She'd bought some of her favorite upholstery fabric at the teddy bear show in Orlando. Long pile was the preferred fabric among many miniature teddy bear makers. Brenda loved it because it looked like the mohair used for larger teddies. She also picked up some synthetic suede in assorted earth tones for foot and paw pads. One can never have enough synthetic suede, she told herself.

What she liked about this particular long pile was the crosshatch backing. When she first started making the miniatures, by using fabrics with the crosshatch she learned that the small squares helped with the alignment of the seams.

Brenda laid out the chocolate-brown fabric and carefully stamped the tiny body parts on the back. She ran her hands over the soft fabric, lost in its velvety nap.

She might have remained that way if not for the loud noise that jarred her out of the moment. Something had fallen and broken. It was outside. The backyard. Brenda ran swiftly from the studio to her bedroom and pulled the Walther PPK semiautomatic out of the drawer.

Not again, her heart said, still recovering from the last time she had pulled the gun. The image of a dead body in the library hadn't had time to fade. She stuck the gun in her pant waist and ran down the stairs.

She stopped at the foot of the stairs. "Carlotta?"

"There is no one in the house, Brenda."

"I know that. It came from out back."

"There is no one outside either," Angelique chimed in.

"I'm going to check it out."

At the back door that led into the garden porch, Brenda peered out the glass panes of the door and saw nothing. Pulling the gun out, she opened the door and stepped outside.

It was dark. The clouds that had threatened rain earlier lingered into the evening, swallowing the stars and any moonlight. She heard the palm trees swishing back and forth in the strong wind, looking like whips against the night sky.

She strained to listen beyond the racket of the crickets. Nothing. She looked around the porch and right away spotted what had made the noise. One of her small pots of begonias lay shattered on the ground.

Brenda was pretty sure the wind hadn't been the culprit. The pot was too heavy. Without warning, something small and furry darted in front of her, cut across the garden and disappeared behind the fountain. It was a kitten! She was sure of it.

She tiptoed toward it, careful not to frighten the kitten away. Brenda leaned over the fountain to see a small white kitten with darker patches, maybe orange or brown; she couldn't tell in the dark. The kitten was no bigger than a large Jersey rat.

It caught sight of her before she could reach for it, and it scampered away into the overgrown mangroves and trees beyond, lost in the darkness.

Brenda had no intention of going after the kitten, at least not in the dark, but she also knew that if it was a stray, she wasn't going to let it starve to death. Calling Animal Services wasn't an option. Deep down inside, her thumping heart already told her she was keeping it. She'd never had a pet as a child and Tina turned out to be allergic to the one cat they had almost adopted.

Brenda stayed on the back porch a few minutes longer, hoping the kitten would venture back out, but it was cold. She hadn't thought about grabbing a jacket when she rushed outside and now icy shivers were slicing through her. She wrapped her arms around herself and reluctantly headed back inside.

By the time she got back to her workroom, she'd already made up her mind. It was time for a new addition to her life. This tiny, frightened kitten had come to her doorstep seeking companionship—well, food, at the very least. It could have gone anywhere in the Tides. But it had picked Malfour House. Just as she had.

Chapter 9

The following morning, Brenda showered, threw on a sweater and corduroy pants and was headed downstairs for a quick breakfast when she paused. Something was different.

Was it the shadows cast by the rising sun, or was the floral wallpaper darker along the upper walls? She ran a hand over the entire length of wall. There were definite patches where the print appeared dirty, while other areas sparkled in the light.

Brenda proceeded slowly down the stairs, taking one last look behind her. Carlotta and Angelique's words crept into her mind and sat there. She shook off the ill feeling and decided to call the contractors who'd applied the wallpaper. They'd better have an answer why this was happening.

Brenda didn't want to waste time preparing a hot breakfast this morning, so she spooned down a bowl of corn flakes with her favorite soy milk and went in search of cat food. She couldn't shake the look of desperation in that kitten's eyes. She'd stayed up half the night planning the pampered life the cat would have with her. She went through female and male names, deciding on none.

She hadn't gotten to the stack of Steffi Vargas's mail, although that was her top priority this morning. She found flaked tuna cat food at the Quick Stop on the causeway, grabbed several cans, sped back to Malfour, popped open a can, dumped it onto a bright red bowl, grabbed the stack of letters and headed to the back porch.

It was a clean, brisk day, with the brightest blue sky she'd ever set eyes on. The wind had calmed down to barely a whisper. Brenda inhaled the cool air and marveled at the sheer beauty of it all.

She placed the cat dish on the very edge of the porch and sat down on the top step. She couldn't help but think of Cubbie. She pictured Cubbie arriving at Strange Investigations, plopping down at the desk and flipping through the channels until something caught her eye. Brenda smiled to herself. It felt surprisingly good to imagine the scenario. She was the boss of her own business. She could go in when or if she pleased.

The shrill ring of the cell phone spoiled the moment.

"Sugar, you've got the life. Slacking already while the hired help slaves away." It was Cubbie.

Brenda laughed hard, unable to make up a good excuse.

"Okay, boss lady, you can laugh, but I've got a real message for you." Cubbie turned serious. "Manda Jones called. She sounded surprised you actually had an office." Cubbie harrumphed into the phone. "I wonder why?"

"Cubbie, I don't pay your high salary to wonder." Brenda was still amused.

"Yeah, well, she wouldn't talk to me. Wants you to call her. Sounds like you're gonna be busy. I guess that means I'll be seeing you sometime soon?"

"I'll be in later, Cubbie, as soon as I feed a kitten and call Manda."

"I know I'm going to regret it, but you didn't say 'feed a kitten,' did you?"

Brenda laughed again. "It showed up on my back porch and broke one of my potted plants then took off into the bushes. I haven't seen it since. Probably a stray, but I've decided to keep it if I can get it to trust me."

This time, it was Cubbie whose laughter echoed over the phone. "Listen, sugar, you dragged me away from my fifteen-year job to come sit behind some fancy desk and watch soaps all day because I trusted you. That poor kitty doesn't stand a chance."

Brenda decided to call Manda. She rang off and clicked Manda's number at the association. Manda answered the phone.

"I got to thinking real hard about Paula after you left." Manda spoke softly. "You know, Brenda, we really did have a good friendship. Went through a lot together. This one incident popped into my head. I remember thinking it was bad when it happened. I thought you might want to know."

"Every little bit adds to the big puzzle. Thanks for offering to help." Brenda propped her notebook up on her lap, eyes still alert for her furry little stray.

"Yeah, well, I told you I was pushing Paula real hard to stay clear of Joan Davis. She never did, but there was this one night when Paula came over to my place in a foul mood. She looked real bad. I could tell she'd been drinking. She was talking all crazy, you know. Said Joan wanted to quit seeing her. Well, I jumped for joy, but Paula, she kept talking how she wasn't going to let Joan fuck her off like that. Swore up and down that she couldn't love any woman but Joan and there was only one way she could get Joan to see she belonged with her."

Manda paused and Brenda heard her sigh.

"Paula wanted Stewart out of the picture and told me, through slurred words, that she was going to spill the beans to Stewart about her relationship with Joan. She was hoping Stewart would divorce Joan. And to ensure that would happen, Paula said she had something else on Joan that would deliver the killing blow. According to Paula, Joan was also having an affair with Phil Brown, some gallery owner."

That came as no surprise. Brenda had already guessed that by seeing the chemistry between them at the gallery. It did, however, open up nasty little scenarios that added Phil Brown into the mix. He might be worth checking into.

"Thank you so much for calling with this, Manda. You've been a big help."

"It's tough when somebody you loved isn't around anymore. You just keep replaying these little snippets of your life together, like some movie trailer or something." She sighed into the phone again.

"Manda, I promise I'll let you know when we get something solid on the case. Thanks again."

Brenda pressed the "end call" button on the cell phone and took one last look around her backyard and beyond. It was becoming clear her stray wasn't going to take the bait. Obviously, it was too frightened for open confrontation. She'd have to keep her eye out for it later tonight.

For the moment, there were more pressing things knocking at her door. Brenda thought now would be a great time to go back and visit Joan Davis. It was a beautiful day. Why waste it?

Brenda grabbed her cell phone, laced up her sneakers and left on foot for the Davises' mansion.

The first thing she noticed was the big black Rolls-Royce sitting out front. Was it Stewart's? Joan's red BMW wasn't anywhere in sight, but that didn't mean it wasn't nestled safely in their multicar garage.

The same housekeeper stood at the door, her smile in place, her blue uniform clean and pressed.

"Hi. Is Joan in?"

The maid shook her head politely. "I'm sorry, no. But Mr. Davis expects her back this morning."

Okay, so Joan was absent, but this would be a good opportunity to catch Stewart. Brenda couldn't help but wonder why Stewart wasn't at work already.

"Well, perhaps I can speak with Stewart then. Thank you."

Brenda stepped into the familiar Davis foyer. Stewart Davis practically bounded up the steps from the sunken living room and greeted Brenda with a crooked smile. He wore dark brown corduroy pants and tan sweater. He definitely wasn't dressed for the office.

"Brenda, how good to see you again."

Brenda hardly believed that. "Stewart, it's an unexpected pleasure to catch you home on a weekday."

He eyed her with interest. "Listen, I didn't get a chance to thank you for coming to my rescue the other night. Allow me to do that now."

There was the same twinkle in his eyes Brenda had noticed the first night she met him right here on this spot. She allowed herself only a moment to savor the memory of her and Tina and a glamorous night.

"Anything for a neighbor in distress. And that's why I'm here, actually. I wanted to talk to Joan about her nightmares."

Stewart stuck his hands inside his pockets. "Ah, well, I'm sorry, she isn't here." He stepped back slightly, a quizzical look on his face. "You do know Joan's been going up to see Tina in Newark?" He left the taunting question dangling in the air.

It was as if a fire rushed through her entire body. The sounds of the room faded and Brenda felt the smile on her face droop. Stewart must have seen the flush on her face.

"You didn't know?"

Brenda couldn't answer.

"I'm sorry, I thought Tina would have said something to you." It was obvious to Brenda he was enjoying her discomfort. She disliked him for it. "Tina's been helping Joan put together a presentation for gallery proposals in New York," he continued. "Joan wants to expand her artistic exposure. Truth is, that Rolls outside is my gift for Joan. It's a surprise for our anniversary. That's why I took the morning off. Her flight is landing in twenty minutes. I expect her within the hour." He glanced quickly at his watch.

Brenda hadn't heard much of what he'd said. Her insides had somehow turned to solid stone. She felt sure she couldn't move. Her thoughts kept repeating images of Tina and Joan. Together.

She shook her head to get rid of the pictures. She'd come here to get answers. If Joan wasn't going to supply them, Stewart might.

"I'm sure Joan will love the Rolls. Happy anniversary. But since Joan isn't here, do you mind if I ask you a few questions?"

Stewart crossed his arms. "Questions? What kind of questions?"

"I'm sure Joan told you I'm investigating the Paula Drakes case."

The millisecond of surprise on Stewart's face was priceless. Seems neither Joan nor Tina played the communication game well.

Stewart recovered quickly, breaking into a quick smile. He started to shake his head. "I think I'd rather wait for Joan, if you don't mind. She'll be here shortly."

"I'll be shorter than that." Brenda stared and smiled politely. "I promise I won't keep you long."

He raised an eyebrow. "Tell me I'm not a suspect?"

"Not if you can tell me where and how you spent your Memorial Day this year."

"Oh no, not again, Brenda. Your desire to see me handcuffed and behind bars is really something you should see a therapist about, you know."

"Just make it easy, Stewart. Can you tell me where you were?" Brenda was having a very good time. "You know, I really do want you to have an airtight alibi."

"You're a PI, can't you find out?"

"Don't act like a suspect, Stewart."

"I was in Tallahassee," he said, exasperated. "The governor is an acquaintance of mine. I was planning a surprise birthday party for Joan and was there trying to convince him to make an appearance at the party." Stewart smiled sarcastically at Brenda. "He didn't make it."

"Neither did Paula Drakes. Did you know she and your wife were good friends?"

"They were the best of friends," he said evenly.

"So you didn't mind the boat Joan gave her as a gift?"

He laughed. "I thought it was a wonderful and generous gift."

"Did you fly or drive?"

Stewart looked confused. "What in heaven's name are you asking?" He unfolded his arms and glared at Brenda.

80

"To Tallahassee, Stewart." She gave him her sweetest smile. "Did you take a commercial flight or did you drive to see the governor?"

"Does it matter?"

Brenda looked at her wristwatch. "And I thought you wanted to get this over with quickly?"

Stewart moved toward the door, indicating that she was to follow. "I flew. My private jet comes in handy for such a situation."

They were standing at the front door. Stewart pulled out his wallet and handed Brenda a business card.

"I imagine you'll want to check it out. My hangar number is on the card. My pilot will verify the story." Stewart opened the door.

Brenda was halfway out but turned back, her hand on the door-knob. "By the way, any leaky footprint problems while Joan's been away?"

Stewart frowned. "Since Monday? Not a one. Thank you for asking." This time, he closed the door shut, barely missing her behind.

Brenda stuck her hands in her pockets and started on her way back home. It was a struggle to keep her thoughts on the case. At least now she knew why Tina wasn't calling. She was busy. With Joan. Granted, putting together a gallery presentation for an artist was hard work, but why hadn't Tina told her?

The temperature had warmed considerably. Brenda unzipped her jacket as she rounded the curve to Malfour. She stopped in her tracks. Parked in front of the house were a yellow cab and a brand-new, gleaming gold Jaguar. The cab's motor was still running.

Brenda picked up her pace. As she approached the cab, she noticed it was empty.

"Brenda, darling."

Her father practically ran down the stairs, arms open wide, with a tall, sturdy black man behind him struggling to keep up. The cab driver, Brenda surmised.

She wrapped her arms around her father and held on tight. He hugged her just as fiercely. Brenda finally pulled back and tried to study his face. He wouldn't keep still.

"Thank you, my man." He turned to the cab driver, unfurled a wad of cash in his hand, pulled out a one-hundred-dollar bill and tucked it into the man's shirt pocket.

The driver flashed a big smile. "Thank you, sir. Thank you." He kept smiling and nodding his thanks as he jumped in his cab and drove away.

Brenda slinked her arm through her father's, finally focusing on his light blue eyes. He was clean-shaven and his graying hair was perfectly in place, but the stress of his suffering was shockingly apparent in his face. There were dark, puffy circles under his eyes and the craggy lines Brenda found so handsome had deepened and spread, looking more like scars.

Brenda's heart ached.

"Dad, this is such a surprise. Where's Mother?"

"She's inside, honey."

Brenda didn't really want to know more about her mother. She dragged her gaze from her father's face and glanced at the Jag. "Now what is that all about?"

Her father walked her toward the car without replying.

"Dad, is this what I think it is?" Brenda ran her hand over the glossy, clean lines of the hood.

"The S type R. One of the first off the assembly line," her father said with pride. "This is the big horses model, baby. She's got the four-point-two-liter V-eight and six-speed transmission."

"Not your ordinary Jaguar." Brenda's blood was racing. She wanted very much to sit behind the wheel of this beauty.

"Zero to sixty in five-point-three seconds." Her father had that old glimmer in his blue eyes as he smiled at her.

"Dad, this Jag is beautiful, but who drove it down and why? I mean, you did fly in from Tarrytown, right? The cab?"

He took her arm and gently nudged her toward the steps. "We did fly, honey. The Jag was delivered here. It's yours." He turned to her and smiled. "Happy birthday, baby."

"Dad, no." Brenda was shocked and delighted at the same time. "My birthday isn't until February."

82

"Well, consider it an early birthday gift. Besides, since we're going to be here for the holidays, we expect you to drive us around in style." He tried to keep his smile but lost it. He took her hand and started into the house. "C'mon, your mother must be wondering what happened to us."

Her mother stood behind the wing chair in the living room, holding on for balance.

"Mother?"

Brenda approached as her mother made a feeble attempt to open her arms in welcome. The fur coat she wore drooped on her painfully thin frame. She looked like some rich kid's scarecrow. Brenda became aware that her father had remained at the doorway.

"I love Mommy."

The whispered words were like the flutter of a sparrow's wings in her ear. The baby-soft touch of tiny fingers on her hand made Brenda's heart thump. Timmy.

"You love Mommy."

The color of her mother's face was of dead wax. The makeup she over applied couldn't hide the pallor.

"I love Mommy."

The blonde designer wig she wore glowed unnaturally in the sun-drenched room, stray gray hairs snaking down her cheek.

"You love Mommy."

The skeletal face attempted a smile as the arms took hold of Brenda. She wanted to run from the embrace.

"You love Mommy. Please."

"Good heavens, Brenda, this house is gorgeous." Mercifully, her mother didn't hold on for long. She backed off, a low sigh escaping her thin lips. "Oh, I'm afraid I'm going to have to sit down."

Brenda's father was at her side in seconds, helping her into the plush velvet chair.

"Mother, can I get you anything? Water?" Brenda felt helpless. She wanted to avoid looking too long at her mother. The effects of the uterine cancer growing inside her mother chilled her blood.

Her father smiled up at her as he struggled to remove his wife's fur coat. "Your mother will be fine, sweetheart. She just needs her rest."

Brenda's mother barely managed to wave a painfully thin hand in the air. "Yes, darling, just go on about your business." She made a strange sound that could have been laughter. "I spend most of my time resting and your father spends most of his time attending to me, so we won't be in your way. But you will have to give us a tour of this lovely Malfour House."

"Of course, Mother. You just, uh, rest and when you're ready, we can do that."

Brenda watched her father as he did everything he could to make her mother comfortable. She had to get out.

"Dad, Mother, I really do have to get to the office. I've, uh, got a case I'm working on. The guest room is past the dining room and through the kitchen. Make yourselves comfortable."

"Of course, sweetheart. You get on to work," her father said. "Will we see you for supper?"

Brenda bit her bottom lip and raised her hand. She'd already made dinner plans with Eddy. "I'm sorry, Dad, I have plans tonight. But I have a great chef you can call." She pulled out Chef Standau's business card and handed it to her father. "Just tell him I sent you."

"Brenda, why don't you take the new car?" Her mother suddenly became more animated, although she struggled to catch her breath. "Now you can get rid of that dreadful SUV thing."

Brenda could never convince her mother that the Jeep was Tina's way of lugging her sculptures around. Once she had left, Brenda had paid the penalty for breaking the lease and turned it in. As usual, her mother spoke before having the facts.

Her dad dug into his pockets and flung a set of keys toward Brenda. "It's all legal and in your name. Go ahead, open her up."

Chapter 10

The new Jaguar was more powerful than Brenda imagined. It was smooth, the engine singing as she pumped up the speed over the Twenty-second Causeway Bridge. She'd gotten a late start, but the day wasn't lost yet.

Brenda hadn't forgotten the card Stewart had given her. She was more than willing to take him at his word. She took I-275 to the Tampa International Airport exit. Airport authorities directed Brenda to a group of hangars that housed private jets. She pulled her brand-new Jag in front of the hangar number on Stewart's card. There were several mechanics in blue jumpsuits working on a sleek new jet. Stewart had extravagant taste.

"Excuse me, where can I find the pilot?"

The man wiped his hands on his jumpsuit. Black grease left streaky stains. He eyed her with suspicion. "Who's looking?"

Brenda pulled out her PI license card. "Stewart Davis suggested I talk to his pilot."

The mechanic looked over her card and nodded toward a glass door inside the hangar. "Damon is inside."

Brenda went through the door and into a tight little office with a small desk littered with papers. Photographs of various 747s and commercial airliners hung on the light blue wall. A thin man with salt-and-pepper hair and a white shirt sat behind the desk, thumbing through a magazine. A small gold pin with wings was tacked on his shirt pocket.

He put the magazine down and stood up, smiling. "Hi, what can I do for you?" He was staring at her. Brenda could guess what was coming next. He shook his head. "I hope I'm not being rude, but has anyone ever told you—"

"No, you're not being rude." Brenda smiled as she handed him one of her cards.

He pulled out a small metal chair for Brenda.

"I checked with Stewart Davis before talking to you. I won't keep you long." She leaned back in the chair. "You are his pilot, I assume?" Brenda glanced at the name tag on his other shirt pocket. Damon Kingston.

"Sure. Stewart hired me about five years ago."

"Stewart and I were talking about his trip to Tallahassee this past Memorial Day weekend. Last weekend in May. You flew Stewart to Tallahassee that weekend?"

Damon Kingston hesitated. He just stared at her, smile still on his face.

"Don't worry, you're not going to get yourself in trouble. I need to confirm what Stewart already told me. You filed a flight plan, didn't you?"

He put both his hands on the desk. "And you're sure Stewart sent you here?" He shook his head. "That's not information we normally pass out."

Brenda pulled out her cell phone and held it out for him. "Go ahead. Call Stewart. He assured me you would cooperate."

Damon backed off. "Don't get me wrong, it's just that this is highly unusual."

"All you have to tell me is if you flew Stewart Davis to Tallahassee that weekend." She smiled back at him.

He started a slow nod, still hesitant. "Um, yes, I did fly Mr. Davis to Tallahassee."

"When did you fly back?"

"I flew the jet back that same night. Mr. Davis stayed the weekend."

"Stayed the weekend? Stewart didn't fly back with you?" It sounded odd to Brenda.

"Mr. Davis was staying the weekend with the governor and his family." Damon stopped. "That's about it."

"How did Stewart get back? Did you fly back for him?"

"No, I didn't fly back. I wanted to stay here with my family. We had plans for the holiday. Mr. Davis was okay with that. I assume he took a regular flight back." He stopped and looked suspiciously at her. "Excuse me, but I thought Mr. Davis discussed this with you?"

That was all Brenda was going to get. It wasn't much, but it was an alibi. It appeared Stewart had told her the truth, but she still wondered why he didn't just have Damon fly back to get him.

Brenda smiled and got up. She stretched out a hand toward Damon. "Thanks for your time, Damon. You've been helpful."

She left the hangar and found two of the mechanics circling her Jag. One of them whistled as she approached.

"She's a real beauty. This is one of those brand-new V-eights?"

"Are you a Jaguar enthusiast?" Brenda loved to share her enthusiasm for Jaguars with others who appreciated them.

He just nodded, not taking his eyes off the gleaming golden car.

"It's a birthday gift," Brenda said, feeling like a proud mom.

She drove off, somewhat disappointed that once again Stewart came off clean. He'd managed once before to slide through the scales of justice. He'd done nothing illegal in the eyes of the law. But it had almost cost Brenda her life and Malfour.

She sighed. Too bad Stewart wasn't her bad guy. She still had to find out who had killed Paula Drakes. Brenda had to get to Strange

Investigations before going back to Malfour to ready herself for supper with Eddy.

Brenda sat in her office, a cup of coffee in one hand and one of Steffi Vargas's deliquent student loan letters in the other, waiting for the information to come up on the laptop.

In seconds, she had her answer. She'd entered Steffi's Social Security number into a national database where anyone with the first three digits of a Social Security number could locate the state it was issued in.

"Alabama," Brenda said out loud.

Cubbie poked her head into the room. "You okay?" Today, she had on a red Chicago Bulls cap, red sweatshirt and black pants.

Distracted, Brenda barely glanced at her. "Know anything about Alabama?"

"Yeah, they still fly the Rebel flag, don't they?"

Brenda reached for the phone and dialed Lisa Chambliss. Cubbie headed back to her desk, shaking her head.

Brenda counted down the number of times Lisa's phone rang. She could locate Steffi Vargas in Alabama herself, but Lisa had the powerful resources of a police department behind her. She would find Vargas in half the time.

"Detective Chambliss."

"Lisa, Brenda Strange."

"Brenda, I'm going to start believing in your psychic powers." There was a smile in Lisa's voice. "I had my finger on the buttons to dial you." She went on, "Good news. We got an extension on the Paula Drakes case. Two weeks. No more, no less. If we can't bring anything new to the table, kiss it good-bye."

"Well, don't pucker up yet. Paula was murdered and I'm going to prove it." She paused. "With your help, of course."

"I have a feeling you're going to ask a big one from me." Lisa Chambliss laughed and Brenda liked the sound of it. "See, maybe I have psychic powers myself."

"If you can find Steffi Vargas in Alabama, you might convince me you have psychic powers."

"Aren't you supposed to be a private eye? It's the staple of your business to locate missing persons. Besides, who is Steffi Vargas and why are you looking for her?"

"She's Paula's jilted lover. She could have useful information. Besides, she skipped town before or about the same time your department pulled Paula out of the bay. I've got a Social Security number issued in Alabama and two friends who say Mobile might be where she was heading when she took off like a bat out of hell."

"Running scared?"

"She was running. I just need to know from what or who."

"I can run the SS number through our computers. I'll also check the airlines and travel agencies to see if she booked a flight through any of them."

"Thank you, Detective."

"Lisa, remember?"

"Sorry. Lisa. My family always taught me to respect the law. Habits are hard to break."

"Brenda, you were a lawyer. You spent half your life trying to find holes in the law. I ran your background. Hope you don't mind?"

"You ran a check on me?" Brenda felt ambivalent about a police detective digging into her life, friend or not. She wondered just how personal those checks went.

"Standard procedure, Brenda, don't get worked up about it." Lisa stopped abruptly.

Brenda got the distinct impression she wanted to say more. "Police procedures. Now that's a topic I have issues with. Too many to get into now but maybe over coffee sometime." The words tumbled out of Brenda's mouth before she realized it.

"We'll be seeing lots of each other. Remember, we've only got two weeks."

Brenda knew Lisa Chambliss was still smiling on the other end and oddly felt deprived of the real thing. Pushing those thoughts aside, Brenda looked at her watch. It was after four P.M. She was running late for supper with Eddy. She'd have to run home, shower, change, say a quick hello and good-bye to her parents and rush out the door.

Eddy's townhouse lacked nothing in luxuries. It was one of ten homes sitting high above the Gulf of Mexico waters near Gandy Bridge. Brenda stood in front of a large picture window in his living room looking out at the breathtaking sight of the sun setting behind the bridge.

"A little piece of heaven on earth," she said softly.

"I see Florida's already got her hooks in you," Eddy said as he came into the room with two martinis. "Cocktails are now served."

Brenda tore herself from the window and settled comfortably on the rich, red leather couch. She couldn't suppress the sigh that escaped her lips. Right here and now, her troubles seemed so very far away. Paula Drakes. Her mother. Tina. Good food and good company replaced the shadows gathering around her.

"I hope that sigh was pure contentment." Eddy came and sat next to her, holding his martini glass toward her in the air. "Cheers."

Brenda bumped her glass against his. "Here's to the zucchini Marquesa baking in the oven. I can't wait to try it."

She took a long sip of the vodka, allowing the cold liquid to travel slowly down her throat. "Eddy, your place is divine. You really captured the look of old Hollywood."

Eddy Vandermast was born sixty years too late. His entire home was an homage to the 1940s and the glitter of Hollywood's golden age. There were elaborately matted and framed portraits of Hollywood icons on every wall. Some were autographed.

Overstuffed leather chairs, ottomans and art deco combined to create the illusion of having stepped into some famous director's home, fresh off directing Bogey and Bacall.

Brenda put her martini down and picked up the expensive photo album on the table.

"I can understand why you wouldn't want to display your expensive pieces. The sun coming through those windows would make that old fountain pen ink fade like invisible ink."

"You're one of very few who can understand and appreciate my obsession with collecting autographs."

"I don't see it as an obsession at all," Brenda said.

"Well, dearie, having over fifteen thousand dollars invested in photographs pressed between plastic protective sleeves in leather binders isn't exactly Wall Street."

Brenda took another sip. "Yes, but your collection is so much more fun than reading numbers in a newspaper."

Eddy laughed, put down his martini and looked at Brenda. His eyes had the gleam of a scheme. "Say, listen, why don't you come to an autograph show with me?"

Brenda started to shake her head.

"No, seriously, Brenda. Think about it. I belong to the autograph collecting organizations. They hold autograph shows around the country. There's one next week in Fort Lauderdale."

"I don't know, Eddy. I'm working on a case."

Eddie reached out and touched Brenda's shoulder, barely able to control his excitement. "Oh, come on. Leave the Drakes case behind for a day. I can fly us down at the crack of dawn, have breakfast on the beach, hit the show and be back before supper."

"You fly, Eddy?" Brenda asked, surprised.

"I've had my pilot's license for five years. Own my own Piper Malibu Mirage. I'm a very safe pilot," he added, teasing her.

The possibilities were bouncing like bingo balls in Brenda's head. Suddenly Alabama didn't seem so far away.

"I can't give you a definite on the autograph show, but it does sound interesting."

"You know, I fly all over the country for autographs."

"Stewart must really pay you well." Brenda winked at him. The martini felt good.

Eddy shot back with a wicked grin, "Stewart and the five other multimillion-dollar companies in Tampa and St. Petersburg."

91

Brenda fingered the stem of the crystal martini glass. Now would be the time to sneak in some questions. Eddy was a friend to both Stewart and Joan.

"How long have you known Stewart and Joan?" she asked, her tone conversational.

"Oh, about ten years. Stewart had just married Joan and was on the way to the top."

"So they've been married some time, then?"

"Oh, yeah. Stewart's first marriage, Joan's second."

Brenda smiled as her heart skipped a beat. So Joan had a past marriage. She'd forgotten how she enjoyed the hunt.

"Sounds like Stewart almost made it to permanent bachelorhood. Joan must have really tickled his fancy."

"You could say that." Eddy frowned and shook his head slowly in thought. "But you know what they say. The honeymoon doesn't last forever. Things change."

"Sometimes you have to take extra steps to keep a relationship together." The words tumbled out of her mouth as the picture of Tina refused to form without Joan.

"Well, you could say Joan found herself with lots of time on her hands. Stewart's business keeps him away from home often." Eddy's tone was accusatory.

"That's why she took up painting?"

Eddy laughed. "Stewart indulges her."

"Come on, Eddy, you're painting Stewart as a good guy and Joan as the heavy. I don't necessarily buy it."

"Stewart's basically a straight-up man, Brenda. Really." Eddy leaned in closer toward her. "If you only knew about Joan . . ." He sat back and finished his drink in one gulp.

Brenda knew about Joan. Knew more than she wanted to.

"What happened to Joan's first marriage?"

"Stewart refuses to talk about it and Joan seems to have had it electronically removed from her memories. All I know is that he was a much older guy. There was a big rift between the old man's family and Joan."

"That's it? Was she married here in Florida?"

"Oh, yeah. Here in Tampa." Eddy stood up in a flurry of movement and tapped Brenda on the leg. "Okay, enough of Joan and Stewart. Dinner should be ready and then we'll get you all squared away with your papers."

The temperature had dropped considerably since she'd first arrived at Eddy's. Brenda wrapped the leather jacket tightly around her and pulled the belt snug. Eddy's zucchini Marquesa had been divine and he'd done a thorough job with the papers. They were safely tucked in her bag.

As she pulled out of the private garage, she could see the tiny parade of car headlights strung across the Gandy Bridge like a string of Christmas tree lights. It brought back the memory of fireflies and her youth.

She and Timmy would spend nights running after them, open jar in hand, trying to capture the elusive bugs. They managed to snag a couple of them once, proudly displaying the jar in their room, fascinated by the faint glow like a night-light of their very own. How Timmy cried when the fireflies died the next day.

Her dad would always hug them and in a calm, patient voice explain how all of nature's children shouldn't be trapped to live in captivity. He continued to tell them how all living things needed freedom to live. Air to breathe. She understood. They shouldn't capture any more fireflies in jars.

She and Timmy listened intently to their father each night, but nonetheless, the following evening, they were back out after supper, open jar in hand, running after little blinking fireflies.

As she worked her way down Gandy Boulevard, Brenda gunned the Jaguar. She felt the powerful engine purr and the rush of the car pushed her back into the seat. She knew she was going too fast and had had one too many martinis to be considered sober, but tonight, caution wasn't the little angel sitting on her shoulder. It was the devil with a very sharp pitchfork.

When she reached Bayshore and eased the car onto the smooth, open curves of the boulevard, the pungent scent of Tampa Bay at low tide seeped through the air vents and into the car. She inhaled deeply, oddly enjoying the comforting familiarity of the smell.

Brenda pressed down harder on the accelerator and watched the speedometer hit seventy-five. The hum of the car and the road unfolding before her was like what she'd imagine a dose of pure cocaine in her system would be. Maybe she was drunk on more than just vodka? Her mind was talking faster than she could listen. Paula Drakes was leading her into uncharted territory. She couldn't get the markings on Paula's body out of her head. Gills. It was on the autopsy report in black and white. The medical examiner said they were gills.

How did she end up with these crazy cases anyway? It seemed she was always turning to Mark Demby and his expertise. Brenda was sure he had something on this. Somebody had to help her out with the crazy ideas staking out space in her head. Maybe when Susan Christie arrived, she would have something to offer.

Brenda pulled up to the guardhouse, flipped her card to the attendant and continued on to Malfour. When she pulled the Jaguar to a stop in front of the house, all the exhilarating recklessness she had reveled in came to a screeching halt, replaced by the gruesome thought of her mother in her designer wig.

Brenda took one last look at her golden Jag gleaming in the moonlight, smiled and walked into a dark, quiet Malfour.

"Carlotta? Angelique?" she called out.

No answer, of course. That was the trouble with ghosts. Not very dependable. And Angelique and Carlotta had been moody and distressed lately. Did ghosts have mood swings?

"Mother? Dad?"

They didn't answer either. Obviously, they were already in bed. It was only 9:30. She wasn't anywhere near retiring for the night. A nightcap was what she needed. Well, maybe not needed, but she sure as hell wanted one. Brenda made sure to keep her bar stocked.

Pulling down her favorite snifter, she poured the golden cognac slowly, watching as it settled smoothly into the glass. The effects of food and drink at Eddy's were wearing off, and she wasn't ready to let go of the high the alcohol brought.

Walking quietly past the stairs, she glanced up, suddenly stricken by a morbid curiosity. How tight was her father wrapped beside her mother? Did she wear her wig to bed? Was the pain unbearable each time she fluttered her eyelids?

Brenda swirled the cognac in her glass and headed to the living room. Her father had left a fire burning in the fireplace. She sat down and settled back into the velvet of the couch. The crackling of the flames, the cognac in her system and exhaustion worked some kind of magic on her memory, because she was suddenly back with Timmy in their old backyard on that fateful day over twenty-five years ago.

"It wasn't your fault." Carlotta was beside her.

"I was angry with him." Brenda stopped a moment, looking up at the ceiling. "He disrupted my stupid little tea party." Her mouth formed a sad smile. "A bloody little tea party." She shook her head.

"You were just a child too."

Brenda looked sideways to the door and the steps that led upstairs to where her mother lay asleep.

"She should have been watching Timmy," Brenda said. "He would be alive today if she'd been there."

"And we could have had a full, rich life of love together, if we'd been able to escape Albert," Angelique whispered.

"But we didn't. You cannot blame your mother forever. Or yourself," Carlotta added.

"I don't know how to let go of the bitterness, the resentment." Brenda felt the tears pooling in her eyes.

"Brenda?"

She jumped up and saw her father at the doorway looking concerned. He was in his favorite pajamas and a black robe with red trim. She wiped her eyes with the back of her hands and smiled. "Hi, Dad."

"I thought I heard you talking with someone." He came and sat down beside her, gazing at her intently. He could get anything out of her with those eyes.

"Oh, no, I must have dozed off. Was I talking in my sleep?" She had to play it off.

"So now you're talking to yourself in your sleep? Brenda, are you okay here? I mean, you're all alone and this is such a big house." He scanned the room, then returned his focus to her.

"Dad, please, I'm fine. Malfour is my home, and I've never been more comfortable. I don't feel alone, really." If only he knew, she thought, not without a trace of amusement. She smiled and took his hand. "Don't worry about me. You're going to have to save all that energy for Mother. Promise you won't worry?"

Her father tried to smile, his eyes turning watery. "What's wrong? Can't I worry about the both of you at the same time?" He bowed his head. "Can you promise me you won't worry about me?"

She reached out and hugged her father hard. "I love you, Dad."

She wanted very much to ask him about his plans for his future. His life without her mother would be different. Did he intend to stay at their home, Montepoint? Would he be able to live with the memories?

"Dad, have you thought about . . ." She paused, choosing her words carefully, fighting the emotions. "Have you considered what you plan to do after . . . after Mother . . ."

He got up abruptly and ran his fingers through his gray hair. "I really don't want to think about that right now. My time belongs to your mother." He smiled at her and reached out for her hand. "Listen, sweetheart, she's going to need all our love and strength."

Brenda noticed the tiny tears at the edges of his eyes.

"I'm not going anywhere, Dad." She squeezed his hand.

He shook his head. "Sweetheart, you've been running from your mother since Timmy's death." He stopped and eyed her, not letting go of her hand. "It was an accident, Brenda. No one was to blame."

Brenda didn't see it that way. "She should have been watching, Dad. Timmy . . ." She stared at the ceiling, fighting back the tears. "Why wasn't she there?" She looked at her father, her cheeks wet with the tears she couldn't hold back. "She was never there for any of us."

He said nothing, just pulled her close and held on tight. "Your mother loves you very much." He brushed the stray hairs off Brenda's face.

"Why can't she tell me that?"

"For the same reason she never told me. For some people, it can be difficult to express themselves in a relationship. I learned to love your mother even though she never understood why. It was always enough for me to know she loved us."

Brenda wiped the tears from her face and looked hard at her father. "It wasn't enough for me, Dad."

"Brenda, your mother asked to come here so she could be with you. She made me promise not let you know that." He tried to smile. His lips quivered. "Maybe this is the chance for the only healing your mother can hope for."

Brenda knew what her father was trying to do, and his effort made her smile.

Her father sighed. "I'm going to check in on your mom and turn in for the night." He turned to go but paused. "Oh, by the way, your mother put some food out for this little stray kitten you've got out back. Were you planning on taking it in?"

"Mother fed the kitten?" Brenda asked, not sure she'd heard right.

"Yes. Came right up to her. She said you had cat food, so she assumed it was for the kitten."

Brenda jumped up and started out of the room. "Oh, Dad, he's beautiful. I think he's a stray, but I've decided I want a cat. I wonder if he's still out there?"

She could no longer control herself. Brenda left her father behind and went outside, where a slight breeze was sweeping the leaves up and about. The little red bowl was empty and no kitten in sight. Brenda peered into the darkness, straining to catch sight of the furry stray. There was nothing.

She went back inside and locked the back door, trying to make sense of why the kitten preferred the company of her mother over her.

Chapter 11

The intrusive sound of the cell phone ringing woke her up. The knocking on the door was even louder.

"Yeah?" Brenda called to the door as she wiped the sleep from her eyes and reached for the phone.

"Honey, Ed Banners is here to see you." It was her father. "Says you called about the wallpaper."

Lisa Chambliss was on the phone, her name and number showing up on the digital display.

"Dad, tell Ed I'll be right down. Thanks."

She answered the phone. "Lisa, awfully early to be on the case." Brenda couldn't help but visualize the slender detective.

"Top of the morning to you, Brenda. Hope I didn't wake you."

Brenda looked at the alarm clock. Eight in the morning. She sat up in bed and reached for her clothes. "What's up, Lisa?"

"Two things. I got a trace on Steffi Vargas. Your little runaway must have flaked out. She checked herself into a nut house."

The butterflies fluttered in Brenda's stomach. "Where? In Alabama? Do you have a name?"

"Denning Center for Mental Health in Mobile." Lisa rattled off the address. "I'd book you a plane, but I wasn't sure if you fly first class or economy."

Brenda couldn't help but smile. "What else do you have?"

"Nothing directly related to your case, but something you might want to know." She paused. Brenda never liked what came after such pauses. "Stewart Davis filed a missing persons report early this morning. Seems his wife, Joan, didn't come home."

Brenda sprang out of bed and maneuvered the phone between her ear and shoulder as she hopped around and slipped on her pants. "Got any details?"

"Sorry, I'm not working the case, but I'll keep you posted on what I get."

A certain uneasiness crept into Brenda's bones. The conversation with Stewart yesterday morning and the image of the sleek, black Rolls-Royce came up like food poisoning in her stomach.

"Thanks, Lisa. I'd appreciate it." Brenda clicked off and quickly threw on a sweatshirt. As she came down the stairs, she eyed the wallpaper. The stains were still there.

Ed Banners was waiting in the library, her father deep in conversation with him. Her mother was nowhere in sight.

"Good morning, Ed. Thanks for coming so quickly." Brenda shook his hand.

"Ed here was telling me about the restoration of Malfour." Her father looked rested, relaxed.

"It's a beautiful home, but I hear you're having problems with the wallpaper installation?" Banners looked at Brenda for the answer.

"Let me show you where it's gone bad."

Brenda led Ed, with her father in tow, into the hallway. When she pointed at the wall, she shuddered. If anything, the dark splotches were spreading.

"See the dark patches running the length of the wall? They go all the way up the stairs." Brenda pointed.

99

Both Ed Banners and her father followed her hand. Banners took two steps up the stairs and leaned closer to the wall. He ran his hand slowly over the wallpaper.

"You mind if I go upstairs?"

Brenda just nodded and encouraged him up. Banners continued up the stairs, examining the wall.

"Brenda, I don't see anything," her father whispered in her ear. "Am I looking at the wrong place?" He squinted at the wallpaper.

Brenda only smiled, suddenly overcome with a bad feeling that Banners wouldn't find anything either. Banners worked his way back down the stairs. He wasn't looking at the wallpaper anymore.

"It looks okay to me, Ms. Strange." He scratched his head and avoided looking at her. "Do you still see the dark spots?"

They're still there! The stains are still there. Brenda wanted to scream. The memory of the first time she walked into Malfour and smelled the acrid smoke of burning wood that no one else did was still fresh in her mind.

She ran a hand through her hair and looked up at the stains staring back at her. "Well, maybe it is the light coming through the library windows." Averting Banners's gaze, she turned away from the stairs. "I'm sorry I got you out here, Ed. I guess I should have figured it out."

All three walked to the front door.

"It's no problem, Ms. Strange. I want my customers to be happy with the work we provide." His smile was friendly as he opened the door. "Don't hesitate to call if you have any problems." He shook Raymond Strange's hand. "Good to meet you, Mr. Strange."

Ed Banners was barely out the door before Brenda walked quietly back to the stairs. She stood perfectly still, the sun-dappled hallway alive with light and dark playing tag. The spreading stain on the wall mocked her.

Her father came up unexpectedly from behind and wrapped his arms around her shoulders. "You know, honey, with the sun coming through like that, it's easy to see dark areas up on the walls." His eyes were kind, and Brenda understood that he was just trying to make her feel better.

She slid her hair behind her ears and stood a moment longer hugging her dad. No one could help her. How could they when they couldn't see?

"Dad, where's Mother? Is she up yet?"

"Oh, sure. She was up before sunrise. You know, I think coming down here has been good for her. She's out back with your kitten."

Brenda opened her mouth in surprise. She sprinted away toward the back porch, unable to control her excitement.

Brenda wasn't expecting the sight that greeted her. Her mother sat in one of the Adirondack chairs on the porch. She wasn't wearing a wig, but rather a black turban neatly wrapped around her head and a heavy robe the color of eggplant. At her feet sat the smallest, most beautiful kitten Brenda had ever seen. He was mostly white, with patches of a color she could best describe as butterscotch.

Brenda stopped abruptly, trying to make sense of the scene. Her mother put one bony finger to her lips, motioning for Brenda to be quiet, and pointed to the kitten. It was curled up at her mother's slippered feet. The red food bowl sat empty on the other side.

Brenda hunched down low and tiptoed to crouch beside the sleeping bundle of fur. She just had to touch it.

"How long has it been here, Mother?"

"Since both the sun and I got up." Her face struggled with a smile.

Again, Brenda wondered how painful it was for her mother to even smile. She shoved the dark thoughts away and put her hand out toward the soft kitten.

"Be careful, Brenda, or you'll scare him off."

It didn't run away at all. It didn't even wake up. Brenda ran her hand gently over the white fur. When she touched its tail, the kitten yawned, stretched and opened its eyes.

Brenda pulled her hand away, afraid it would bolt. Instead, the kitten extended all four legs, blinked at her in curiosity and, deciding she was not a threat, curled back up into a ball.

Brenda's mother leaned over and petted the kitten. She had never taken kindly to cats. Brenda looked up at this woman she no longer knew.

"Do you think it's a he, Mother?" She noticed the soft, faraway look in her mother's eyes.

"It's a he, dear."

"We've got to give it a name," Brenda said, the bond with her mother growing stronger through this lost, sad stray at their feet. Perhaps her father and Angelique and Carlotta were right. It was time to seal the gaping wound that had existed since Timmy's death.

Brenda watched as her mother, deep in concentration, continued stroking the kitten.

"Butterscotch," her mother suddenly blurted, clearly proud of the name.

The truth was that Brenda liked the name. She looked at the tiny feline face tucked away in the fur coat, the nose a perfect shade of butterscotch. She looked back at her mother.

"I like it, Mother. Butterscotch."

"Remember those scenarios we talked about?"

Brenda sat in her office at Strange Investigations, Cubbie fidgeting uncomfortably in the chair across from her.

Brenda shot her an amused smile. "Would you care to bring your chair in here? You've got a fight going on with my imitation Eames." Brenda looked at Cubbie and the chair.

"No, sugar. I mean, these chairs just weren't meant for women my size."

Brenda shook her head, still smiling. "Cubbie, Stewart Davis didn't murder Paula Drakes."

"Well, hell's bells, boss, you never told me it was Stewart you were after again." She held up the *Tampa Tribune* newspaper. "Did you see this? Joan Davis is missing. If I remember what we talked about, you gotta be thinking Joan Davis is your culprit. I mean, people don't just run away from such a lavish lifestyle unless they're running from something." Cubbie shook her head, her mop of curly red hair peeking out from under a red Chicago Bulls cap. "Probably got scared with all the questions you were hitting her with. She's guilty as sin, Brenda."

"The police don't know what's happened to Joan. Lisa Chambliss said she was missing. I haven't spoken to Stewart yet. In this business, those that run always have reasons and Joan's may very well be murder. But Stewart is definitely off the suspect list."

By the way Cubbie was looking at her, she knew the next question. How could she be so sure?

"He has an alibi," Brenda said.

She believed Stewart couldn't have killed Paula Drakes because Paula wasn't haunting him. It was only Joan who was losing sleep and waking up screaming at the slimy apparition of Paula.

Brenda was convinced that Paula was spooking only her murderer or murderers. It made sense. But just because crazy theories were second nature to her didn't mean people like Cubbie and Lisa Chambliss were going to follow her Pied Piper's tune. And just because she went through a near-death experience and came back with an extra awareness of the "other side" didn't make her an expert in the paranormal.

The saltwater puddles were very real. Brenda was convinced they were footprints. Not necessarily human, but footprints nonetheless. Cubbie would just shrug and argue that someone could be trying to frighten Joan Davis. But if so, why? Was there another person involved in the murder?

The natural explanations just didn't add up. Whatever made those footprints in Stewart and Joan's bedroom was not human. And not a ghost.

Brenda kept thinking back to her sixteenth birthday and the set of books her grandmother had given her. The shiny leather covers smelled new and exciting. It was a series on unexplained phenomena.

Brenda remembered devouring each volume. She went through severe withdrawal symptoms after finishing the last book. It was in that last book that she read about a city older than Atlantis, the lost city of Ithea, which had met the same fate as Atlantis, thousands of years before. Atlantis was swallowed by the raging waters of the Atlantic and settled deep below the ocean floor, toppling what little was left of the decaying city of Ithea.

But Ithea was not a dead city, according to the book. A new race had evolved within the watery tomb that was Ithea. A hybrid race of half fish and half men. A race born from the crossbreeding of the drowning Atlanteans and the Itheans.

Brenda had never forgotten that story. Her fascination led her to seek out one of the books from the list of "recommended reading." Ironically, she no longer had that leatherbound set her grandmother had given her, only that one volume by Quentin Trask.

Trask had written extensively in the field of lost underwater civilizations, but his work was never taken seriously. He published several volumes on Atlantis and Ithea, but they were considered fiction by many and, at worst, the ravings of a madman without factual evidence or scientific merit. Some even put him in the same category as H. P. Lovecraft, the eccentric author of science fiction and fantastic tales.

Nonetheless, in Trask's most compelling work, *From the Depths to Madness*, he persisted in presenting his theory that another race existed on this planet with us, hiding deeper than explorers could ever go below the ocean floor.

What if that was what happened to Paula Drakes? It was in black and white on the medical examiner's report. Paula had developed, in his professional opinion, gills. What if she wasn't dead at all, just living life under the waters of Tampa Bay as a mermaid or fish or whatever Quentin Trask wrote about? Her body was still missing.

"Well, you're the PI, you know." Cubbie's voice broke Brenda's far-fetched contemplation. Cubbie got up slowly, looking at Brenda with one eyebrow arched. "Listen, boss lady, I know when you get that look on your face it's time for me to button up, but I thought sure you'd want nothing to do with Stewart Davis after what you and Tina went through with him." She moved toward the door. "Enough of bad news. I've got fresh coffee and some leftover Danish I picked up on the way in this morning. Had breakfast yet?"

"As a matter of fact, I didn't have time for breakfast this morning." Brenda smiled halfheartedly, remembering Ed Banners's expression, the wall, her mother and Butterscotch. The coffee and Danish sounded good. "I'll take that coffee, and do I have a choice in Danish?" Her favorite was raspberry.

"Sorry, no raspberry, but there's a cream cheese and strawberry swirl still left."

"Still left?" Brenda smiled. "How many have you had already?"

Cubbie put up her hands in defense. "Hey, now, if you got in the office on time every morning, you wouldn't be getting the leftovers."

They both laughed as Brenda reached for her phone and watched Cubbie walk out. There was no doubt she had to get to Mobile to find Steffi Vargas. Eddy could get her there. She punched in his number.

"Oh, my God, Brenda. Did you hear about Joan? Are you on the case? Did Stewart hire you?"

"Hey, hold on, Eddy. I know about Joan, but I haven't spoken with Stewart, and no, I'm not on this case. The police are going to do everything they can to find her, I'm sure. Are you holding up okay?"

"I've been a little shaky this morning." Eddy exhaled into the phone. "I'm sorry, Brenda. Here I am acting like a big baby. I'm glad you called. Your papers are legal and I've got three charities you'll want to look at."

"Great. Thanks, Eddy, but I'm not calling about the papers. How'd you like to take your mind off things? Take a break for a day or so?"

There was a brief pause on his end. Brenda could sense his hesitation.

Cubbie came in holding a tray with a coffee mug and a Danish wrapped in a paper towel. Brenda motioned for her to set it on her desk.

"Eddy, I'm asking for your help," Brenda continued in soft tones. "Last night at your place, you mentioned you owned a Piper Malibu. Bottom line is, I need you to fly me to Mobile, Alabama."

"Alabama? Land of the KKK and the rebel yell?" He sounded interested.

105

"Can you do it, Eddy? I can pay you."

"Forget the pay. Should I ask if this is about the Paula Drakes case?"

"You can ask. I've got a hot lead on an ex-girlfriend of Paula's. She's in a mental institution in Mobile. Her hometown, as it turns out. So how flexible are you?"

"Hold on and I'll check my calendar."

Brenda waited and pictured him behind his big desk and wall of hunks.

"We can fly out tomorrow morning if you want. I don't have any appointments that my partner can't handle. All I'll need is to file a flight plan."

"Tomorrow is better than I hoped for. Thank you, Eddy."

Brenda hung up the phone and took a bite of the Danish. The blend of tart strawberry and creamy cheese filling tasted better than she imagined. Knowing that Cubbie liked to serve what she termed "piping hot coffee," Brenda took a cautious sip. It was black the way she preferred. Black, the color of the shadows swallowing the walls at Malfour.

Before she left the following morning, Brenda made her parents promise they'd watch over Butterscotch. She left strict instructions that the kitten was to be kept indoors.

Butterscotch had to get used to his new surroundings. Brenda didn't know how old he was, but one of the first things she needed to have done when she got back was to take Butterscotch to a vet.

She'd bought a litter box, a kitty transport and premium kitty litter. With assurances from her father that he would call in case of an emergency, Brenda and Eddy left Tampa en route for Mobile, the morning sky enfolding them in clouds of lavender and orange.

Chapter 12

Leaving Eddy to discover the charms that Mobile, had to offer, Brenda took a cab to the Denning Center for Mental Health. She'd already spoken to a Doctor Richard Smith, who'd agreed to meet her.

The Denning Center was a bland two-story building of white stone with small, rectangular windows dotting the length of it. The landscaping was sparse and the overall feeling Brenda got was one of cold detachment.

Dr. Smith greeted her in the lobby. He wore a white lab coat and was tall with thick, sandy-colored hair and attractive wire-frame glasses. Brenda pegged him at thirty-something, more or less her age. His eyes were gray, the color of the tiled floor.

"Ms. Strange, this is an unexpected request." He eyed her with interest as he extended his hand.

"Please, call me Brenda." She had her PI card ready. "I'm sorry the timing is so abrupt." She handed him the card. "Getting to see Steffi is of the utmost importance to this case. I hope you understand." She watched him study the card for a brief moment.

"Of course, Brenda, follow me to my office and we can discuss Steffi." Smith stuck the card in his coat pocket and pointed Brenda toward one of the corridors.

Brenda couldn't suppress a shiver as the overwhelming scent of disinfectant assaulted her. On the surface, the Denning Center was spotless, with off-white walls and colorful wall trim along the baseboards, but the unsavory odors reminded her where she was.

She followed the doctor down another hallway and past a nursing station until he finally stopped at a door with his name etched on a black nameplate.

"I'll be as helpful as I can." Dr. Smith motioned Brenda in and directed her toward a brown vinyl chair. He sat behind a small desk littered with folders and papers. "Without violating patient confidentiality."

"Client confidentiality is something I take very seriously, Doctor Smith. I'm not asking you to break that. I want Steffi Vargas to answer some questions, that's all." Brenda smiled in that innocent manner she'd found mostly got her what she wanted.

Smith eyed her steadily, an annoying hint of flirtation in his eyes. He finally sat back in his chair and formed a pyramid with his hands. He gave Brenda back her smile.

"Steffi Vargas came to us as a voluntary walk-in. She checked herself in with strict instructions that no one be contacted."

Brenda arched an eyebrow. "Sounds like someone trying to hide from something. When did she check in, Doctor?"

"She arrived in early June, just after Memorial Day. And that's all I can tell you, I'm afraid. It's up to Steffi if she wants to talk to you about it."

"Doctor Smith, I'd like to see Steffi."

He looked at Brenda for a moment, then reached for a small photo lab envelope on his desk. "I suppose this would be okay." He picked it up and handed it to Brenda. "These might be of interest to you. I don't know any of the people in the photos."

Brenda opened the envelope and pulled out a handful of color snapshots. Steffi had definitely been stalking Paula Drakes. The photos were shots of Paula playing tennis. Paula dining at an outdoor restaurant. Paula going to the gym. Some of them showed Paula and Joan Davis together.

Brenda held two of the photos side by side. These caught her attention. Wearing shorts and tank tops, Paula Drakes, Joan Davis and Phil Brown all stood on what looked like a pier of some sort under a bright blue sky. They were in the middle of a large crowd of people. Brenda looked closer. There were boats behind them and large banners. Brenda couldn't make out all the words because they were so small, but *Tampa Bay Boat and Oars Club* stood out boldly.

Brenda looked up at Smith. "Do you mind if I take these to Steffi?"

Smith shook his head. "Not at all. But if you want to take them with you, you'll have to ask her permission." He got up and Brenda followed him. He stopped at the door. "I know you'll use common sense, but if Steffi gets agitated in any way, I can't let you stay in the room. I'll warn you. She's taken to hiding the pills the nurse brings her. Skipping her medication makes her unstable at times."

"Does that mean you'll let me talk to her alone?"

"Don't give me a reason to be there. I'll go in and explain to her who you are. Just remember that to the best of my knowledge, she doesn't know that this Paula Drakes woman is dead, and I don't want her to find out from you."

Steffi Vargas was a beautiful young woman, a real stunner with jet-black hair, golden eyes and an ivory complexion. Brenda stood in the white-washed room that had a small window, bed, a table and two chairs. Steffi Vargas stood near the window, eyeing her with a mix of suspicion and curiosity.

"Hi, Steffi. I'm Brenda Strange." Brenda smiled, trying hard to comprehend how someone like Steffi Vargas could end up in a place like this. She gestured to one of the chairs. "Do you mind if I sit?"

"I'm not crazy," Steffi said quickly, not answering Brenda. "I'm here cause my brain is a little scrambled. Manic depression and borderline schizophrenia. I admitted myself, you know." She wrapped her arms around herself. "I can't let my parents know. Mom will scream and Dad will beat me." Steffi was suddenly focused somewhere else, beyond Brenda. "Paula did this to me."

Brenda took the chair and pulled it closer to Steffi. "Steffi, can we talk about Paula?" Brenda knew she needed to proceed slowly.

"Why should I? She doesn't give a shit about me." Her words were venom.

"Okay, do you mind then if you and I spend some time this morning looking at your pictures?" Brenda looked squarely into Steffi Vargas's eyes. "I could use your help." Brenda took one of the photographs and held it up. "Do you remember when this photo was taken?"

The pain in Steffi's face was heart-wrenching as she eyed the photograph. Brenda held it closer.

"Please, Steffi, I know it hurts to see these, but I need you to remember."

Steffi shook her head violently. "I don't know. I don't want to know."

"Try, please. May? June?" Brenda persisted. "Did you see Paula and the others get in the boat?"

Steffi stopped shaking her head and stared at Brenda, tears swelling in her eyes. "Paula doesn't care about me anymore. Why did she send you here?" Her lips quivered.

"Paula didn't send me, Steffi. I'm here because Paula needs your help." It wasn't exactly a lie.

Steffi wiped the tears with the back of her hand and looked at Brenda with renewed interest. "Paula needs my help? For real?"

Brenda smiled and nodded. "For real." Steffi seemed like a lost child.

Steffi snatched the photo from Brenda and looked intently at it.

"Memorial Day." Her gaze lingered on the photograph. Her entire body was motionless.

Brenda allowed Steffi several moments of quiet with her memories, then softly said, "Steffi?"

Startled, Steffi jumped. "How could I forget that day? Paula and I argued. She was going out on Joan's boat." She frowned in concentration and studied the photo again. "I told her not to go. She's deathly afraid of the water, you know. I was so worried about her." She stopped and looked at Brenda. "Is Paula okay?"

Brenda knew hesitation could cost her. "Helping me will help Paula, Steffi, so please stay focused. Did you actually see Paula get onto the boat? How many others went on the boat with her?"

"I didn't stay long enough to see much more than Paula, Joan and that guy get onto Joan's boat. It was some kind of boat race or rally. I was afraid Paula or Joan would see me, so I split as soon as I took the pictures."

"How long after that did you leave Tampa?"

"I left that week." Steffi struggled to remember. "Late that week, maybe Wednesday or Thursday." She looked directly at Brenda. "Why is that so important? You never answered if Paula was in trouble. Is she okay?"

Steffi Vargas may have stalked Paula Drakes, but that was all she was guilty of. Brenda was convinced she had nothing to do with the murder.

Brenda held up the two photos of Paula, Joan and Phil. "Steffi, I can't tell you too much in regard to the case I'm working on, but it would help me and Paula out a great deal if I could take these back with me?"

"Sure, but I don't want them back. I'm through with her." Her attitude had changed like lightning, her face twisted in anger. "I hope she's happy with that bitch."

❦

Brenda and Eddy had supper at a mom-and-pop restaurant called Minogue's near the Mobile airport. Dr. Smith had said the restaurant was a Mobile institution. Brenda couldn't find much in the menu for the vegetarian and opted for a bland-tasting chef's salad with mostly romaine lettuce, and soup.

Eddy took every free moment between bites of his patty melt to pump Brenda for information on her visit with Steffi Vargas. He was worse than the most curious of cats. When she skirted around his prying, he rattled on about his excursions to Mobile's antique shops.

The case had taken an unexpected turn. Could Paula have been murdered that day? Was Phil Brown on the boat with Joan and Paula? Phil Brown and Joan Davis were having an affair. Did Paula know it? Could she have been so jealous that she confronted Phil or Joan about it? It sounded like a sordid little situation to Brenda. One that could have led to murder. With Joan Davis missing and Phil Brown now apparently involved somehow with the activities of that day, Brenda had no choice but to question him.

Brenda paid for their meal in cash. Eddy filled up on black coffee, and they left Mobile. Brenda missed Malfour and wanted very much to be back in Tampa.

They were a good forty minutes from Tampa when Brenda's cell phone rang.

"Brenda, Lisa Chambliss. I hope you're sitting down."

"I'm sitting in the cockpit of a Piper Malibu halfway between Mobile, Alabama, and Tampa. Got news on Joan Davis?"

"Did you get to see Vargas?"

"I did more than that. I've got a very strong new lead. But I know you don't call PIs just to chitchat."

"Chitchat isn't exactly what I'd call this."

There was one of those long pauses that Brenda hated.

"They've found Joan Davis's body."

There was an unnatural silence. A silence that screamed. Brenda tried to keep her thoughts from scrambling in different directions at once.

Lisa said, "I don't know if you two were friends."

"No, not friends," Brenda replied quickly.

"They found her in a dumpster behind Le Galleria, a gallery on Seventh Avenue in Ybor."

"I know the place. Phil Brown owns it."

"Hey, Brenda, how much of a serious kink does this throw into your case?"

"My number-one suspect just got eliminated. I would say that leaves me back on square one. Any leads on who could have done it?"

There was another one of those pauses. "We've got the murderer in custody. He confessed."

Brenda swallowed the lump that traveled up her throat. Eddy was eyeing her with a hungry curiosity.

"He? Do I know him?"

"Brenda, I can't go into the details, but I will tell you that you might want to come down to TPD as soon as that plane sets down in Tampa."

Chapter 13

It was after eight by the time Brenda found her way to the tall blue glass building of the Tampa Police Department. Downtown Tampa was a wasteland at this hour.

Lisa Chambliss met her outside Homicide Division and escorted her to another room down the hall. She said nothing to Brenda, her face devoid of that enigmatic smile Brenda found attractive.

When Brenda entered the cramped, dark room that she followed Lisa into, her heart froze. Directly in front of her was a large window with a view into another room. A two-way mirror. Phil Brown sat on a chair, his hands folded on a long table. Two men, one standing, another sitting, were the only other people in the room with him.

"Now you see why I couldn't give you any details on the phone?" Lisa eyed Brenda steadily. "Phil Brown caved in after he was questioned."

"He admitted to killing Joan?" Brenda couldn't tear her gaze from the haggard Phil Brown and the two detectives who circled him like animals in for the kill.

"Well, not exactly." Lisa followed Brenda's gaze.

"Am I supposed to guess?" Brenda was tired, slightly agitated. She studied the profile of the woman standing next to her. A long, thin nose curved into thin lips that at this moment betrayed controlled anger.

Lisa turned to look back at Brenda. "He's pulling the multiple personality shit. He says his other personality killed Joan."

Brenda didn't think Phil Brown stood a chance. The detectives in that cage with him were barely under control, their faces hot with contempt. Brenda could hear the agitation in their voices.

"You had an affair with Joan Davis," the tall, wiry detective with dark hair stated rather than asked Phil Brown.

"Yes, I did." The Phil Brown who sat in that room looked liked he'd aged ten years.

"She was paying you to show her paintings in your gallery."

"That has nothing to do with this."

"Don't interrupt me, buster."

"I didn't do anything," Phil Brown insisted.

"You murdered Joan Davis in cold blood."

"I didn't kill her."

"Cut this Doctor Jekyll, Mr. Hyde shit." The other detective, a shorter man with muscles bulging through his white shirt, leaned down and got into Phil Brown's face.

"This guy is taking the nut route." Lisa leaned closer to Brenda. "It's his only defense. He was traced to the airport where he had picked Joan Davis up. Dear Mr. Brown started giving the detectives the details about how 'Jake' had killed Joan."

"Jake?" Brenda shot her a questioning look.

"Oh, it gets better." Lisa refocused her attention on the scene unfolding in the holding room.

Phil Brown looked shaky but unfazed. If he'd killed Joan Davis, he wasn't showing an iota of remorse or guilt.

115

"I've given you everything already in my statement. And where is my doctor? I asked that he be here."

The taller, thinner detective kept circling the room, his gaze firmly on Phil Brown. "Okay, Brown. Suppose I come with you on this wacko ride you want to take us on. Let's say 'Jake,' your other personality"—his voice dripped with sarcasm—"killed Joan. You couldn't have stopped him? You just hung around and let him kill a woman in cold blood?"

"That's a crime too, Mr. Jekyll." The other detective still stood like a bird of prey over Phil Brown. "Oh, yeah, it's called accomplice to a murder. Your life of hanging overpriced bad art is over, Jekyll. You'll be doing it in a prison cell." He stared hard at Phil.

Brenda could see that the questioning was eating away at Phil Brown. She looked at Lisa. "Did they find any evidence to link him to the murder?"

"Oh, yeah. His gun was loaded with fingerprints. His. Same gun used to plug two bullets into Joan Davis. Our CSI unit says he murdered Joan at the art gallery and then moved the body to the dumpster behind the building where they found her. Not a very clean murder at all."

"Where is his lawyer? I hope he has a good one."

Lisa shook her head. "He said he didn't want a lawyer. Refused twice. All he's asked for is his doctor, whom we've called. He's on his way."

"Maybe he's telling the truth." Brenda heard the words come out of her mouth. She believed Phil Brown.

Lisa Chambliss looked at her in surprise.

"If he does suffer from multiple-personality disorder," Brenda continued, "then it's quite possible this 'Jake' really did kill her and was inept at covering his tracks."

Lisa was shaking her head, a smile of disbelief forming on her lips. "Brenda, you know how many times we hear this copout plea?"

Brenda said nothing.

"Look, Brenda, when these guys come in here with this bull crap, it makes it real messy for us. We've got to pull in doctors and shrinks. It never pans out. But let's just say we go along with Phil here. If we go along with him, we have to go into the psychological mumbo jumbo of who was who when the murder actually occurred. Was it Phil or Jake who killed Joan? Did Phil premeditate the murder and Jake carry it out? Who lugged the body out to the dumpster after the fact, Phil or Jake? Who do we prosecute? Get the picture?"

Brenda waited a moment before replying. She wasn't going for a confrontation. She was certain Lisa had come across all kinds of scum with the same excuses. But if Phil Brown was right and he did have another personality that was capable of committing murder, then he might have murdered Paula Drakes back in May. The pictures proved he was there that day with Joan and Paula. Steffi Vargas said they'd boarded the boat before she'd left.

The possibility of Phil Brown's multiple-personality disorder had to be explored.

"Lisa, can I talk to him?"

Lisa looked at her for a second before shaking her head. "Can't let you do that." She paused for another second. "But I might be able to get you a quickie at the jailhouse in a couple of days after they book him. I'd have to accompany you."

As soon as Brenda walked in the door, Carlotta was beside her, eyes wild with agitation.

"Angelique is out of control. That woman is driving her to act irrationally."

Brenda stopped in her tracks. It was just approaching eleven in what she'd hoped was the end of the most exhausting day she'd had since moving to Tampa. Evidently, she was wrong. It wasn't over.

Brenda scanned the hallway. It was empty, except for two large tripods topped with video cameras. Was this something her father set up? He hadn't said anything to her about shooting video in the house. What in heaven's name would he want with two video cameras?

Malfour was quiet. The soft glow from the fireplace in the living room was the only glimmer of light in the darkness. Her parents must have gone to sleep. She wondered where Butterscotch was hiding.

"What woman, Carlotta? My mother? What's Angelique doing?"

"*No, not your mother. The ghost finder. She can see us and talks into a tiny device that she points at us. I've been trying to hide from her since she arrived, but Angelique has become confrontational.*"

"Damn," Brenda whispered. "Susan Christie. That's who the cameras belong to. I forgot all about her. I haven't even made sleeping arrangements for her. Where is she, Carlotta?"

"*They're in the dining room. Hurry.*"

Great, thought Brenda, the guest room was only a kitchen away from the dining room. All she needed was for her parents to hear the commotion and join in the mix.

"Carlotta, you both knew this woman was psychic. You and Angelique are the reasons why she's here." Brenda treaded cautiously toward the kitchen, the ghostly form of Carlotta beside her. "Remember, you both encouraged her visit, against my wishes, I might add."

When Brenda pushed the French doors to the dining room open, she found a large woman with short blonde hair and razor-straight bangs sitting calmly at the dining room table. She held something small and black that looked like a photographic light meter pointed at Angelique, who hovered beside her.

Brenda looked to Carlotta beside her, but she was gone.

"Hello, Brenda, I'm Susan Christie." The woman got up and extended a big hand to Brenda. "Your dad let me in."

"I'm sorry I'm so late. Truth is, I'd completely forgotten you were arriving today."

Angelique, a small, wicked smile on her face, dissolved into nothing behind Susan Christie's large frame.

"You've got quite an active house here," Susan said, her round cheeks flushed with excitement.

"Yes, I do." Brenda's gaze traveled to the small instrument in Susan's hand.

"Oh, I'm sorry," Susan said, noticing Brenda's curiosity. "This is an electromagnetic meter. It helps us locate manifestations. It started buzzing as soon as I turned it on."

"Why don't we go into the library where it's more comfortable."
Brenda escorted her to the library, closed the doors and motioned
Susan to the couch. Brenda sat next to her. She was glad her parents
were asleep. She intended to spend most of the night getting to
know Susan Christie.

"I'm sorry for the cameras in the hallway. I wanted to get started
as quickly as possible," Susan said, looking at Brenda with a sheepish
grin. "I do have two more still cameras with tape recorders strapped
to them that I usually set up in other rooms of a house I'm investigating . . ." She paused. "But I wanted to get your permission before
I went any further."

"I don't feel comfortable with that," Brenda said. "My parents are
staying with me, and I'm also working on a case." She looked at
Susan Christie, who was removing the batteries from the electromagnetic meter. "Mark did tell you I was a private investigator?"

"He did." Susan glanced up briefly and smiled. "Don't worry,
Brenda, I won't get in your way." She pulled two new batteries from
her jacket pocket and plugged them into the meter. "I'm only staying a week, but I know I won't even need that much time." Her blue
eyes twinkled in the low light of the library. "I have to tell you,
Brenda, that Malfour is one of the most powerful houses I've had the
pleasure to encounter."

Susan set the meter down, smoothed out her dress and sat back
comfortably on the couch.

"I understand your psychic abilities are recently acquired, but I'm
certain that you can feel the forces in this house are drawing themselves around you." She paused, her gaze penetrating deep into
Brenda. "And you are feeding them. It's a symbiotic relationship you
share with this house."

Brenda remembered that Carlotta and Angelique had said almost
the exact same thing. "Since the first day I set foot in Malfour
House, I knew it was special," Brenda said, her thoughts floating
back to that shimmering day in May.

"Well, you've obviously adjusted quite well to your two new
roommates."

119

It took Brenda several seconds to realize Susan meant Carlotta and Angelique. She smiled. "It's been unpredictable, to say the least." Brenda leaned back into the creamy leather couch, intent on Susan Christie. "I have to tell you, it's refreshing to be able to talk openly about my . . ." She paused. "Gifts, to someone who understands. Mark told me you'd have a story or two to share."

Susan's laughter was pleasant. It almost succeeded in chasing away the nasty memories and fears the day had deposited in Brenda's head.

"Mark is trying to get me to write a book about my investigations and experiences, especially my channeling. Just because he can listen to my stories for hours, he thinks everyone else will find them that interesting."

"Channeling?" Brenda sat up. "You can channel?"

Susan didn't answer right away, and her smile changed. "It isn't something I advertise. Many of us have that power."

The way she looked at her made Brenda uneasy.

Susan put her warm, fleshy hand over Brenda's. "You have that power too."

Brenda's mouth opened but nothing came out. How could she channel? And why would she want to? The words tumbled out awkwardly. "No, I, uh, don't think I can do that."

"Look around you, Brenda. You are already doing it. Malfour has become a mirror image of you. Your life is displaying itself within the walls of Malfour."

The walls! Brenda knew immediately that Susan had seen the stains. Relief flooded through her. She wasn't imagining things.

"You saw the dark stains on my wall?"

Susan nodded. "They're reflecting dark times in your life. Or those yet to come."

Again, the same thing Carlotta had told Brenda. It was getting frustrating hearing all these veiled threats of doom and gloom with nothing to back them up. And even though she struggled to admit it, it was starting to frighten her.

Brenda shook her head. "I don't understand what I'm supposed to do with these warnings. Angelique and Carlotta have said the same thing to me."

"Harness the power you have within this house. Use Malfour as an oracle. The answers may come to you in sleep, in visions, or there are some mediums who scribble words on paper while under a trance." Susan moved closer to Brenda. "Meditate and find your voice. Let Malfour guide you."

"Yes, but will I like what I see?"

Brenda stayed up long into the night with Susan Christie. She'd finally drifted into an uneasy sleep when a sensation of freezing cold snapped her awake.

The left side of her body was numb. She rubbed her arm hard and ran her hand down her buttocks. She couldn't feel a thing. She sat up quickly and touched her cheek. It was numb and icy too. As unlikely as it seemed, she feared a heart attack or stroke. Thirty-somethings weren't guaranteed to be stroke-free.

When she started out of bed, she noticed an impression on the pillow beside hers. There was a clear imprint of someone's head on the pillow. Brenda peeled the comforter slowly away from the bed, and there beside her was the outline of another body on the sheets!

Brenda jumped out of bed, grabbed her chenille robe and wrapped it tightly around her. The room was frigid. What was wrong with the heater? She continued rubbing her left arm, hoping to get the circulation going. Could Carlotta or Angelique be the cause of the cold in the room? The thought flitted through her head, but she dismissed it. They visited her bedroom often without this bone-chilling cold.

Brenda started to jog in place. She did that for a few minutes until she could feel the warmth returning to the left side of her body.

She looked at the clock radio and moaned. It was only five in the morning. Since she was already awake, and the chill was starting to ease out of her system and the room, she decided against crawling back into bed. A hot mug of coffee was what she needed.

When she opened her bedroom door, she nearly tripped over Susan Christie. The large woman was still in her clothes and sat cross-legged on the floor, the electromagnetic meter in one hand and a video camera in the other.

"I think I'm bound and determined to have a heart attack tonight," Brenda said, annoyed. "What are you still doing up at this hour? Have you slept at all?"

Susan Christie's eyes were red and puffy, but her face looked like the wolf that had just eaten Little Red Riding Hood.

"Damn glad I didn't go to bed. Were you able to sleep?" She looked at Brenda anxiously.

Brenda wrapped her arms around herself. "I had trouble getting to sleep, but I finally did, until just now."

"Did the cold wake you? Was anything unusual going on in your bedroom?" The look in Susan Christie's eyes was starting to frighten Brenda.

"It was cold." She stopped herself from rubbing her left side, which was almost back to normal. And the imprint of another body still marked her fancy Egyptian cotton sheet. Should she tell Susan Christie?

"Cold?" Susan Christie raised an eyebrow. "That's all?"

"What is going on here, Susan?"

A chuckle escaped Susan Christie's lips. "Brenda, I've been tracking one of your ghostly roommates most of the night. She followed you into that bedroom and never left until a few minutes ago. I've been monitoring the magnetic fields." She let the words linger in the air. "That is one helluva long visitation." She looked closely at Brenda. "You sure you're okay? Your room must be like an icebox." She tilted her head, concern in her bright blue eyes.

Brenda faked a smile. Who or what had been in bed with her?

Chapter 14

Brenda woke with a headache. She'd managed to doze off after the early-morning coffee. Not even Susan Christie's persistent chatter could have kept her from sleep. She glanced at the bed beside her, apprehensive of what might have reappeared there. After getting back into bed, she had smoothed the sheets flat and fluffed up the pillow, leaving no trace of the ghostly silhouette.

Only a slightly rumpled sheet greeted her now in the too-bright rays of the sun. Relieved yet still distracted, she dressed and headed downstairs. She stopped abruptly at the foot of the stairs and looked at the wallpaper. The stains were still there. Brenda peeked in the library. Susan Christie was sound asleep on the leather couch. Brenda could have kicked herself for not remembering to get a roll-away bed into Tina's studio for Susan. That would have to be No. 1 on her list of things to do today.

As Brenda made her way to the kitchen, she came across her parents' neat pile of luggage in the hallway.

She found her parents sitting at the dining room table, fully dressed, her mother draped in a mink coat. Brenda stopped in her tracks.

"Going somewhere in a hurry? It's barely nine in the morning."

Her father put down his coffee mug. "West Palm Beach, as a matter of fact."

Her mother smiled weakly. "We have close friends I'd like to visit before . . ." She paused and stared down at the table. "Well, before we go back home."

"Your mother and I thought it would be an excellent time for us to go. You and your friend can have some space."

It took Brenda a few seconds to realize whom he was talking about. "Did you and Susan talk much?" Brenda asked, surprised.

"Oh, yes. She arrived early last night. Fascinating woman." Her father was smiling.

"Darling, you never told us you had ghosts," her mother said, taking a sip of her coffee. "Funny, I haven't seen one yet."

Brenda wished Susan hadn't spoken to her parents about Carlotta and Angelique.

"It's nothing to be frightened about, Mother."

"Oh, I'm not frightened, dear. I don't believe in such things." With a wave of her bony hand, she dismissed the notion.

"Good, then there's nothing to discuss." Brenda decided she didn't need breakfast after all. She was about to leave the room when she heard a sound that made her heart jump. "Was that a meow?" Brenda stood frozen, looking from her father to her mother. "Butterscotch?"

Her father walked slowly toward the double doors to the kitchen, pushed them open gently, and Butterscotch waltzed out, tail swishing back and forth.

He came up to Brenda and rubbed his little face against her leg, then wrapped his scrawny body around her other leg, meowing again at her with big green eyes. He blinked.

Brenda hesitated, then ran her hand down Butterscotch's back, watching him arch in delight.

"Your mother's been feeding him. He slept with us in the room," her father said softly. "Go ahead, pick him up. He won't run away."

Brenda swooped him up and cradled him in her arms, holding him gently against her chest. The blaring of a car horn outside frightened Butterscotch. He leapt out of Brenda's arms and scurried off in a blur of fur into the hall.

"That would be our cab," her father said, reaching for his wife.

"Dad, I could have taken you to the airport if I'd known," Brenda said, losing track of Butterscotch.

She followed her parents into the hallway and picked up one of the suitcases.

Her father put out a hand to stop her. "No, no. You leave those for the driver, honey."

"Come on, Dad, let me at least help take some of these for you."

"Need help?" The cab driver, a short, round man with dark sunglasses and no chin, stood at the front door.

"Yes," her father said, nearly yanking the suitcase out of Brenda's hand. "You can take these." The cab driver grabbed all four suitcases from the floor and lugged them outside.

Brenda stood smiling at her father. "You still have those annoying habits, I see." She shook her head.

Her father kissed her quickly on the cheek. "It's their job to load suitcases, and I tip them well for it. I never said I was perfect."

Brenda's mother walked slowly up to her and gently squeezed her daughter's shoulders. Her eyes were bloodshot, the tiny red veins snaking through the whites.

"Take care of Butterscotch. Now is a good time to bond with the little thing." She winked. Her mother had never, ever winked.

Brenda stood in mild surprise as she watched her parents walk out the door. "When will you be back?"

"Couple of weeks. Maybe a week and half or until your mother gets too tired. Don't worry, we'll be back in time for Christmas." Her father smiled and waved at her.

The phone started ringing as Brenda watched her father guide her mother gingerly into the backseat of the cab. Brenda waved to them and waited until the yellow cab drove away before sprinting into the living room for the phone. Susan Christie was still zonked out in the library.

It was Tina.

"Hi, princess, did I wake you?"

"Tina?" Brenda fought the lump in her throat. Tina's voice didn't sound the same. "No. I mean, no, you didn't wake me."

Tina laughed, a clipped, distant sound.

"I got the letter you faxed me." Brenda suddenly felt more like some adolescent schoolgirl talking to her first boyfriend. "Congratulations on your new position."

"Thanks."

Silence. Brenda should have said how proud she was of Tina. But she didn't. Tina shattered the quiet.

"Princess, I'll be coming home early." She paused. "For Joan's funeral. Stewart called."

The cold blast struck Brenda inside like frigid lightning.

"He must be taking it pretty hard." Brenda's own words sounded like someone else's voice. She didn't know what else to say.

"You haven't spoken to him?"

"I haven't gotten the chance. I thought it might be best if I gave him some time with his family and friends. I can pick you up from the airport."

"No, listen, I'll grab a cab."

"Tina, I want to see you. I can pick you up."

Tina sighed deeply into the phone. "I miss you terribly too. This may sound selfish and insensitive, but I'm glad I'll have more time to spend with you."

Now that Joan is gone, Brenda thought. She'd better be honest with Tina now. "Listen, my parents just arrived for the holidays but they're visiting with some friends in West Palm Beach first, and Mark Demby flew one of his investigators to Malfour. She's here for a week."

Brenda knew that the time she and Tina spent together would be crucial to the future of their relationship. She shivered involuntarily.

"Listen, princess, there are things we need to talk about. I mean, the way I left . . ." Tina's voice was soft.

"We can talk when you get home." Brenda stopped short of ending the conversation as she normally did. "Honey" just wouldn't come out.

The hard fact was that Tina was coming back home. The day after tomorrow, Sunday, her lover would once again be in her life. Brenda hung up the phone, wondering how she could save what was left of their relationship. In her heart, it was worth whatever it took to keep them together. She still loved Tina.

From nowhere, Butterscotch sprang up on the table, purring at a low rev and rubbing his furry face on Brenda's hand.

"Well, hey, baby boy." She ran her hand over the length of the tiny kitten and leaned her face into Butterscotch's cool, wet nose for a "kitten kiss." "Where did you run off to? I'm sorry we scared you off like that."

"You know, people really scare me when they use voices like that to talk to their pets." Susan Christie stood in the doorway, arms folded.

Brenda scooped Butterscotch in her arms. "I bet you don't own any pets." She smiled at Susan.

"I don't have enough time for a pet." Susan sighed.

"There is always time for a cat." Brenda looked at Butterscotch, who was purring even louder.

"Brenda, do you mind if I fix some breakfast? I make a mean El Paso scrambled egg."

"El Paso eggs? Doesn't include meat, does it?"

Susan Christie made a face. "Oh, don't tell me you're a vegetarian?"

"It's something Tina and I decided to try. I don't think I'm as dedicated as she is." Brenda walked out of the living room, Butterscotch happy and content in her arms. "I'll tell you what, Susan, I'll make a breakfast you won't forget as an apology for not having sleep accommodations for you." She looked back briefly at Susan. "By the way, now that my mom and dad have left for two weeks, you can stay in the guest room."

"Your parents seem like a nice couple. I didn't chase them out, did I?"

"No, no. They have friends to visit in West Palm Beach."

They headed toward the kitchen. "You know, breakfast isn't entirely free. I get to pick your brain some more." Brenda grinned sheepishly.

"At this hour in the morning, I'm willing to pay or submit to anything for food in my stomach." Susan laughed.

"Just out of curiosity, are you familiar with Quentin Trask?"

Susan smiled like the Cheshire Cat. "C'mon, Brenda, you've got breakfast to cook. I'll tell you all you want to know about Quentin Trask over a big omelette."

An hour later, Susan Christie took the last bite of her omelette, making happy faces as she swallowed. There was a big mug of coffee beside her plate.

"Who did you say taught you how to make this omelette?" she asked.

"My secretary." Brenda sat across the dining room table from her, already finished with her smaller portion. "She spent ten years in a restaurant before I stole her away."

"Well, my compliments to her." Susan raised the fork and winked. "And to the chef as well." She wiped her mouth and hands on the napkin, sat back in a show of contentment and picked up the coffee mug, peeking at Brenda over the rim. "So, why the interest in Quentin Trask?" Susan put the mug down after one big swallow of coffee. "I know you're a PI. Is this related to your current case?"

"It might be."

Susan arched an eyebrow. "You're not going to tell me more, are you?"

Brenda shook her head slowly and smiled. "I can't go into the case, no, but I was hoping you might be familiar with Trask's writings and theories. It would be a big help."

Susan put both her large hands on the table. "Well, I'm not exactly an expert on Quentin Trask, but I did do some research into his more outlandish theories."

Brenda inched up in her chair. "I had a set of books once, on all kinds of unexplained phenomena, and one of them had a chapter on sunken civilizations. It mentioned Trask's claims that the Atlanteans didn't all perish. That they somehow evolved into an amphibious race that to this day lives under the ocean floor, hidden so deep we can never find them."

"Oh, yes, the mating breath scenario." Susan nodded.

"Mating breath?"

Susan inhaled before continuing. "You know, Trask was never taken very seriously by the scientific community. As a matter of fact, he was dismissed as positively wacko. And the New Agers barely know his work exists."

Brenda found the whole idea of a hidden undersea civilization far-fetched but fascinating. She couldn't stop trying to connect the dots between Paula Drakes' autopsy report and missing body and the possibility that it all fit in with Quentin Trask's outlandish concept.

Susan continued, "Trask wrote four other books, all on Atlantis, Lemu and other lost civilizations. But it was in *From the Depths to Madness* that he exposed his beliefs on what really happened to Atlantis after it sank into the Atlantic. Trask really believed that since the beginning of time, as we evolved and became advanced cousins to the ape, others evolved under the oceans. When the ill-fated people of Atlantis followed their doomed city into the ocean, supposedly this other amphibian race saved many of the Atlanteans by breathing life into them through what he called 'the mating breath.'"

Brenda waved a hand to stop her. "Now wait a minute, you mean he believed these fish people mated by breathing into one another's mouths?" She had to admit how ridiculous the words sounded. She looked disbelievingly at Susan.

"That was the basis for his book. The Itheans reproduced by passing eggs through their mouths. They did that to the Atlanteans. Once a human mated with one of these amphibians, he or she would begin to change until they became an aquatic life-form. Trask persisted in writing about how this amphibious race still exists and thrives under our oceans. I mean, he went as far as to suggest that the Bermuda Triangle was a door into their undersea kingdom. Trask argued that all those disappearances in the Bermuda Triangle were the result of this other race kidnapping unsuspecting humans for mating, thereby procreating in the ocean." Susan paused. "Still think this helps at all with your case?" She had the beginnings of smile on her lips.

Brenda cocked her head and smiled back, hoping she could keep the thunder in her chest from exploding. It went against rational thought, but what if Paula Drakes hadn't really died. What if she was "rescued" by one of these amphibians? Given the "mating breath"?

"Do you believe any of it?" Brenda asked.

"Let's just say he never considered his work to be fiction. I think he firmly believed what he wrote."

Brenda shook her head again. "How did he back up his beliefs? Has anything half-human ever washed up on a beach? Did he have any scientific evidence to support his theories?"

"Not a shred of it," Susan said, shaking her head. "That's why he's pretty obscure. You can sometimes find his books alongside H. P. Lovecraft in the horror section of used bookstores. Pretty sad, actually."

"Don't knock H. P. Lovecraft," Brenda said. "I had one of his paperbacks tucked in my bag everywhere I went when I was a teen. I was a science fiction freak." Brenda felt like she was in a high-speed chase, her thoughts racing. She hadn't told Susan Christie about the saltwater footsteps in Joan Davis's room or the *X-Files*-like police report on Paula Drakes' body. Or that that same body had mysteriously disappeared from its crypt in New Jersey. The excitement in her stomach was gnawing to jump out. Did Quentin Trask's amphibious race exist? And was Paula Drakes now one of them?

"You could check out the Internet if you want more on Trask." Susan shoved her empty plate aside and put both her elbows on the table, her face suddenly serious. "Brenda, I wish I could say that I'm here with you today as part of a pleasant visit, but that isn't the case. Malfour House is a job I've been assigned to do, and I want to thank you for allowing me full access to your home, but I may need your help in order to finish my study of Malfour." She shifted her bulky body in the chair and stared at Brenda. "Forgive me, but I don't think you've been honest with me on what happened inside your bedroom last night." She searched Brenda's face.

Her question brought the memory of the frightening cold that had paralyzed Brenda, not to mention the rumpled bedsheets.

Susan continued softly. "I'm going to need your complete co operation." One hand landed over Brenda's.

Brenda had to tell her. She shook her head slowly. "I'm sorry, Susan. You're right. I was confused at the time. I didn't know if I wanted to talk about it." She met Susan's gaze. "I woke up with my left side paralyzed. I was frozen. The cold in the room had seeped into my body. That's how it felt."

Susan raised an eyebrow. "Yes, go on. What else happened?"

Brenda had to smile. Susan Christie should be in the psychic hot-line business. "Beside me on the bed was the clear indentation of a body, as if someone had been lying there."

"Or was still lying there." It wasn't a question.

Brenda opened her mouth to speak, but Susan Christie slapped her hand on the table, a twinkle in her eyes. "It was Carlotta." She pointed knowingly at Brenda. "She won't talk to me. She's evasive and distrusting, but she adores you."

Brenda was uncomfortable with the implication in Susan's words.

131

"Don't be so shocked, Brenda. You must realize she is attached to you." Again, it wasn't a question. Susan rubbed her hands together. She was spilling over with enthusiasm. "Brenda, I need to do a trance séance. Just you and me. And Carlotta, Angelique and whatever force is gathering in this house."

Brenda shook her head. "Susan, I don't know."

"It won't be anything flashy or dramatic. I simply go into a trance and allow for a spirit guide to speak to me." There was a crooked frown on Susan's face. "Well, sometimes they speak through me, if you can understand." She winked.

Brenda felt like she was on a roller coaster with no stop button. "I don't know much about spiritualism or séances."

"Very well, you think about it. You may not get another chance to get this kind of experience." She began collecting the plates and mugs from the table. "I hate to break this up, but I've got work to do. Listen, Brenda, do you mind if I set up some equipment in the attic and spend the day there?" She headed into the kitchen.

"Sure, that's fine." Brenda got up quickly and followed behind her, feeling as if she'd just been run over by a speeding locomotive. "Why don't you let me take care of those." She tried to remove the plates from Susan, who stopped, still holding on to the dirty dishes.

"You do have a dishwasher, don't you?"

Brenda thought a moment. "Dishwasher, yes. What I don't have is dishwashing liquid."

They both laughed out loud as Butterscotch weaved in among their legs, purring.

Chapter 15

Brenda hadn't been too keen on leaving Butterscotch alone with the whole of Malfour as a playground. With Susan Christie up in the attic for most of the morning and no one to watch him, there was no telling what kind of trouble a kitten could get into.

But Brenda had to get to her office. Lisa Chambliss had still not called and she was itching to talk to Phil Brown before the harsh realities of jail broke him down completely. She was convinced he held one or more keys that could open doors to her case. She also needed to get to her computer and check into what information might be out there on Quentin Trask.

When Brenda got to Strange Investigations, she didn't expect to see another car parked next to Cubbie's VW bug. The plain silver Crown Vic looked suspiciously like an unmarked plain Jane police car.

Lisa Chambliss sat in one of the chairs, legs crossed, flipping through an issue of *People*. Cubbie, sporting a multicolored Chicago Blackhawks hockey team cap, put the phone down as soon as she saw Brenda come in.

"Well I'll be, boss, I'm beginning to think you really do have psychic powers. I was just dialing you." She rolled her eyes toward Lisa. "She just got here."

Brenda pulled off the leopard-print scarf from her neck and smiled. "Lisa, this is an unexpected visit. I was starting to wonder if I would hear from you regarding Phil Brown."

Lisa got up, the TPD badge dangling from her waist, and pointed to the walls. "This isn't exactly what I expected." She shook her head slowly, not able to keep the smile from her lips.

"Private dicks have come a long way."

"This isn't a social visit, I hope?" Brenda asked, tucking the scarf into her sweater pocket.

Lisa said, "I can take you down to where Phil Brown is incarcerated. He's in the psycho section of the Orient Road Jail. They're expecting us, but we've got to leave now."

Lisa Chambliss was halfway out the door, waiting for Brenda.

"Cubbie, take my calls this morning. Don't forward anything unless it's an emergency with my mother."

"I didn't kill Paula Drakes." Phil Brown wore an orange jumpsuit, his hands and feet wrapped in chains. He stared intently at Brenda, the smell of desperation on his breath.

They sat in what Lisa called the "consultation room." Prisoners were allowed to meet with attorneys or police in this solitary room. There was a table and chairs. Lisa stood away from them against the wall, quiet contempt on her face.

"I'm not the one you need to convince," Brenda said.

"I don't want to convince you or anyone else." Phil Brown cast a frown at Lisa, then focused back on Brenda. "I'm not worried. When I go in for my hearing, I plan to tell the judge the whole truth. I'm not hiding anything. What I want is for you to know the truth about what happened that day."

"I'm willing to listen, but why should I believe you?"

His smile was tired. "I don't care whether I live or die. Maybe a death sentence will rid me of Jake forever."

"Are you sure about this, Phil? Have you given any more thought to a lawyer? There are advances in medicine. There might be a cure for you in the future?"

"I've made my decision. I know the state will appoint a public defender for me, so I'm going to defend myself. I won't change my mind."

"Okay. Go ahead, Phil," Brenda said.

Lisa almost jumped toward them. "You're not going to listen to this scum, are you, Brenda?"

Brenda couldn't help but admire the fire and passion Detective Lisa Chambliss carried around. But she'd come looking for answers and she wasn't leaving without hearing what Phil Brown had to say.

"Lisa, I don't have anything to lose." She didn't know if Lisa found it amusing or insulting, but it didn't matter. Lisa threw up her hands in frustration and backed into the wall, her arms crossed.

Phil was eager to continue. "Look, Brenda, I'm going to tell you the truth. Every summer in May, the Tampa Bay Boat and Oars Club holds its annual boat rally. Joan and I always did it, but this year, I had no idea Michelle and Paula were coming along."

Brenda held up a hand. "Hold on. Michelle? Who's Michelle?"

"Michelle Corby, Joan's sister." Phil studied Brenda. "You don't know Michelle?"

Brenda shook her head. "I didn't know Joan had a sister." She offered a fake smile. "We weren't that close."

When Phil Brown frowned, he looked dark and dangerous. "You didn't miss much." He shook his head. "She's a piece of work. Good-for-nothing gold digger."

Brenda arched an eyebrow. "You don't like her?"

His laughter was bitter. "There's nothing to like. She's a vampire.

She sucked Joan out of millions. Breast implants. Sports cars. Europe."

"So Joan and Michelle got along?"

Phil Brown snorted. "Joan did everything for her little sister."

"Why did Joan hand over so much money to her sister?"

"You obviously didn't know Joan very well. The Corbys were what you'd call low on the social ladder, if you know what I mean." Phil leaned closer to Brenda across the table. "Some would even call them trailer trash. That was until Joan married Stewart Davis. Stewart was the Corbys' meal ticket. They had everything they wanted. All they had to do was ask Joan."

"Besides Michelle, how many other siblings?"

"Michelle is the only sister. There are two brothers, one in the Army and the other in insurance."

It was apparent to Brenda why Phil Brown despised Michelle Corby. She was competition for Joan's money. The more she forked over to Michelle, the less there was for him.

"She was paying you to keep her art hanging in your gallery, wasn't she?" Lisa's voice sounded hollow in the small room.

Phil didn't look at her. "I loved Joan," he said to Brenda. "The trouble with Joan—" He paused, and Brenda noticed wet tears form at the corner of his eyes. "Joan wanted more than one man could give her. I saved her ass more than once when situations got sticky with her affairs."

Lisa Chambliss grunted. "You loved her so much she had to pay you to showcase her work?"

Phil became defensive. When he looked at her, there was a nasty scowl on his face.

Brenda slammed her hands down on the table. "Listen, I'm not here to talk about your affair with Joan." She shot a warning glance at Lisa before turning back to Phil. "Let's go back to that weekend in May."

Brenda dug in her purse and pulled out the three photos she had taken from Steffi Vargas. She laid them out on the table.

"Is Michelle Corby in any of these shots?"

Phil Brown looked them over and pointed to one, his handcuffs rattling on the table. "Yeah, that's her with the blue shorts."

Lisa Chambliss was at Brenda's side in seconds. Brenda picked up the photo and held it up for Lisa. Michelle was the short brunette with the tan, muscular legs standing just behind Joan. Brenda hadn't connected her with Phil, Paula and Joan. Michelle Corby didn't appear to be part of the group. Physically, she was the opposite of her sister. Brenda couldn't push back the image of Joan in her head. Thin as a curtain rod with that drape of blonde hair. She shook the ghost of Joan from her thoughts.

"Was this the first time Michelle or Paula had come along with you and Joan?" Brenda asked.

Phil Brown nodded. "Yeah, Joan and I had been doing it for years. I didn't know Joan had invited Paula and Michelle."

"Did Michelle and Paula know each other before the rally?"

He smirked. "I doubt it. They didn't seem to get along very well."

Lisa interrupted. "Brenda, this guy's going to say anything to take the heat off himself." She came forward a few steps, staring him down. "How do we know you didn't kill Paula Drakes too, just like you did Joan?"

Phil lowered his eyes, then looked at Brenda, ignoring the detective. "I didn't kill Paula Drakes."

"Maybe Jake did it?" Lisa's voice was taunting.

Brenda knew she was trying to agitate him. This was obviously Lisa's style of interrogation. But this wasn't Lisa's interview. Brenda cast a disapproving look at Lisa and set her gaze back on Phil Brown.

"I was drunk out of my mind," he continued. "I passed out. I don't even remember how I got home that night."

Lisa crossed her arms. "How convenient."

Brenda ignored her. Lisa was jeopardizing the relationship she was trying to form with Phil. The last thing Brenda wanted was for Phil to shut down and shut up. She needed to play along with him. Make him believe she was with him all the way. "Phil, is it possible that when you passed out, your other personality took over—"

"You don't understand," Phil interrupted, shaking his head.

"Jake lives to torture me. To undo everything I build up. He loves to boast of things he did that I would disapprove of. No, he would have been laughing in delight over getting away with a murder if he had done it." He stopped. "Besides, Joan would have told me about it."

He looked from Brenda to Lisa, desperate for either of them to believe him. Brenda remained quiet, still trying to fit Michelle Corby into her puzzle.

Finally she said, "Phil, is there anything else you can remember? Any little detail that might help me out?"

He bit his bottom lip. "They were arguing."

Brenda raised an eyebrow.

"Yeah, Paula, Michelle and Joan were at each other's throats," he said.

Brenda sat up and leaned across the table. "Can you remember what they were arguing about?"

He shook his head slowly. "No, sorry, too drunk. All I wanted was to throw up and go to sleep."

"Brenda, he isn't going to give you any answers," Lisa said, glaring at Phil Brown. Brenda wished she'd stay out of it.

"One last question, Phil. It may sound strange but think about it real good before answering."

"Sure." He shrugged, fidgeting in his seat. "I've told you the truth and everything I know."

"Are you having nightmares, Phil?"

The blank look on his face told Brenda he was lost. She couldn't suppress a small smile.

"Have you dreamed about creatures from the black lagoon? Has Paula Drakes been in your dreams?" She sat back into her seat and crossed her arms, still holding his gaze. "Any leaky water spots in your house you can't explain?"

Phil Brown looked at her, his eyes perplexed. "No, nothing like that. The only nightmare that haunts me is my own face in the mirror looking back."

"Brenda, this guy isn't a credible source. He's a whack job. But I don't know who's nuttier, Phil Brown or you, asking about dreams and nightmares." Lisa Chambliss shot glances at Brenda as she drove.

"I think he's telling the truth about Paula. He didn't kill her."

"Are you so sure? What if Phil Brown killed Paula Drakes because she posed a threat to his relationship with Joan? I mean, what if he was jealous of Paula? Or what if he was so scared of Stewart finding out about Paula and Joan's affair that he would divorce her. His sugar mama would be dirt poor again. So he kills Paula Drakes. When Joan starts to panic, and he fears she might spill the beans, he bumps her off as well, using that old double-personality trick. Motive, means and opportunity."

She gave Brenda a triumphant look. Brenda liked her smile and enjoyed the open dialogue. She shook her head.

"I admit Phil Brown is a suspect, but why give up to the police so easily? On the other hand, what if Michelle Corby was just as frightened to lose out on her sister's money? Her lifestyle would have drastically changed as well. Motive, means and opportunity."

Brenda watched the smile on Lisa's face widen as she pulled into the Strange Investigations parking lot. Brenda wasn't done.

"Look, Phil isn't completely in the clear until you get his doctor to release his medical files. Until then, Michelle Corby is the only person who can tell me what really happened on that boat." She opened the door to get out. "But her dreams will tell me even more."

She winked as she slammed the door, aware of the surprise on Lisa Chambliss's face.

Brenda sat in her library at Malfour; Butterscotch was sound asleep and purring on her lap. She had the laptop propped perilously on the arm of the leather couch. She hadn't seen or heard Susan Christie since getting home from her office.

Brenda had been searching the Internet for Quentin Trask and found one Web site with a local connection. *Nolan Canova's Pop Culture Review* was a fan-based online magazine that prided itself in its fannishness. It reminded Brenda of the *Star Trek* fan groups she had belonged to in her younger days.

The *Pop Culture Review* was made up of columns covering anything from films to comic books and everything in between relating to pop culture. But there was one column that related directly to Quentin Trask and his works. Will Moriaty's "La Floridiana" column for the month featured newspaper articles and sightings on what reporters called "Ole Three-Toed."

Moriaty provided newspaper accounts from the *St. Petersburg Times* and the *Clearwater Sun*, as well as eyewitness sightings of a large, hairy sea monster. The sightings took place in the months of March 1948 through August of the same year.

Brenda's eyes were glued to the screen, Butterscotch purring happily. The sightings seemed to have ended abruptly after August, as if the sea monster ceased to exist.

Or maybe we scared the hell out of it.

"The more sightings, the more chances someone would go looking for it and find it." Brenda was talking to herself. She reread the description of the sea monster. "Big, hairy and three-toed." It didn't exactly sound like anything Quentin Trask had written about, but the human race was filled with people of different colors, facial features, sizes and shapes. Why not our hypothetical undersea cousins?

Did one of these creatures give Paula Drakes "the mating breath"? Had Quentin Trask, taking a solitary walk down a deserted beach one summer night, witnessed a terrifying creature emerge from the ocean depths?

"I thought I heard someone come in."

The sound of Susan Christie's voice made Brenda jump. Butterscotch, frightened off her lap, scurried under the desk, his sleepy eyes blinking irritably at Susan.

"You've got to stop coming into rooms so quietly and frightening Butterscotch."

"Just Butterscotch?" Susan laughed. "I'm sorry, Brenda. I'll pound on the walls next time."

Brenda shut down the laptop, stood up and stretched. Twilight had crept in, deep maroon fingers prying into the room. Brenda realized she was starving. That smoothie at lunch was a distant memory. Dinner just hadn't been at the top of her priority list.

She walked past Susan. "I'm going to fix something quick for dinner. Have you eaten yet?"

"Forget food," Susan said softly, pulling Brenda by the arm. "Come with me."

She led Brenda to the stairs and nodded toward the wall. Brenda didn't expect the sight that greeted her. She stared, her mouth open in shocked silence. The stains had spread and now threatened to darken the walls in the hallway. The splotches looked like inky fingers greedily gobbling up all of Malfour.

It frightened her.

Susan stood eyeing her. "I thought this would alarm you. Brenda, let me do a séance. Tomorrow night. I've only got a few more days here, and by then it will be too late."

Brenda looked from Susan's determined eyes to the stains taking over her house. Hesitation flew out the window.

"What do you need me to do?"

Chapter 16

Brenda woke to low purring sounds and tiny cat claws digging into her side. Butterscotch sat atop her, kneading away happily.

"Hey, baby, take it easy on your mistress there." She smiled and ran her hands over Butterscotch's head.

The sun streaming through the window was bright. Too bright. Brenda guessed it was late. She looked over at the alarm clock. She was right. It was nine-thirty. Last night had drained her. It had been a week full of unexpected surprises, both in regard to the case and in her personal life.

Tina was coming home tomorrow and that made Brenda smile, easily forgetting how stress threatened to strangle her. She turned over to place Butterscotch on the other side of the bed and found two pieces of chocolate sitting atop the extra pillows. One was a Santa and the other a snowman.

Alarmed, Brenda eyed the room, wondering who had been there.

Nothing seemed out of place. She picked up the Santa, sniffed it to make sure it was indeed chocolate, then bit off Santa's hat. The creamy peanut butter melted in her mouth. Gertrude Hawk! That was her favorite chocolate. But Gertrude Hawk's chocolate was only available in select northern states. New Jersey was one of them.

Brenda shot up straight in bed. Tina. Could it be? Did she get an early flight into Tampa? A day early? The excitement sent a flutter through Brenda's heart.

Butterscotch meowed his objection as Brenda flung him aside, jumped out of bed and began scooping up clothes like a vacuum cleaner. If Tina was here, why hadn't she wakened her? Brenda dressed in record time and headed down the stairs, Butterscotch following behind her, his tail swishing.

But she stopped abruptly as she heard noises coming from Tina's studio. It was the familiar sound of hands pounding fresh clay. She walked slowly toward the room, trying desperately to control the flip-flop of her heart.

It was Tina. Her back to the door, she stood in front of her worktable kneading the clay. She wore black pants and a white sweatshirt; her hair was tied back in a velvet ribbon. Brenda tiptoed up behind her, wanting to reach out and touch the long, black hair, but she pulled her hand back.

"Tina."

Tina turned around. She smiled, but it wasn't quite complete. She wiped her hands on the sweatshirt. "Hey. I didn't want to wake you. I changed into work clothes when I got in."

She looked awkward. The way two people acted when time had passed between passions. If Brenda ever doubted her love for Tina, those doubts melted as she studied her.

"Thank you for the Gertrude Hawks," Brenda said, stuffing her hands behind her back. She didn't know what to do with them. "You got in early? Why didn't you wake me?"

Tina shrugged. "I changed my mind and had my agent move my flight. You were very deep into sandman territory. You looked so peaceful." She didn't take her dark eyes off Brenda. "Oh, yeah, that reminds me, there's more where that came from."

Tina grabbed a box sitting at the far end of her table and handed it to Brenda. It was the familiar Gertrude Hawk Chocolates box of Christmas "Smidgens" in the shape of Santa Claus, snowmen, Christmas trees and toy soldiers. Smidgens were chocolate and peanut butter candies, a Gertrude Hawk specialty.

"Those are your favorites, right?"

Brenda smiled. "I don't think I ever let you forget that."

The memories came rushing through Brenda of their first years together and her obsessive eating bouts when she would ravage a box of Smidgens in two days.

"I still don't understand how you can eat tons of those things and not gain a pound." Tina laughed. It sounded good.

But behind Tina, the ghost of Joan still lingered, and despite Brenda's struggle to keep the thoughts of Joan and Tina away, they remained persistent and intruding.

Tina was staring hard at her. "I missed you, Brenda." It was painfully obvious Tina was uncomfortable. "I was such a child when I left here, princess." She moved closer. "Things have changed." She took Brenda's hand hesitantly.

Brenda didn't back off. Tina's touch sent hot fire through her. She squeezed her lover's hand gently.

"I've missed you too." She smiled. "Why didn't you call after Thanksgiving?" Brenda was half-sure of the answer to that question, but she was a glutton for punishment. She wanted to hear Tina's answer.

Tina shifted her weight. "I've been incredibly busy." She dropped her gaze and let go of Brenda's hand. "I've been preparing for my new position. It's more demanding than I imagined." She paused and looked back at Brenda. "And Joan's been up a couple of times. We were . . ." She paused again. "I, uh, was helping her get a portfolio together. She wanted to try and get into some of the New York gal-

144

leries, but it wasn't exactly the best of timing." She paused. "After September eleventh, no one wants to deal with art, you know."

Her voice broke. Brenda exhaled. This was more difficult than she imagined. Tina hadn't lied about Joan or why she'd been so scarce. The shadows in the room began to melt away replaced by warm promises. The healing of their relationship had to begin somewhere.

Brenda fell into Tina's arms, digging her hands into Tina's thick, dark hair. "I'm so happy you're home."

The rest of Saturday was shot for Brenda. There was no way she was going to get any work done on the case at home or at Strange Investigations. She wanted all her attention on Tina.

After showing off Strange Investigations to Tina, they both decided on lunch at the Gulfbreeze. Although it was still her favorite restaurant, Brenda found how much she missed Cubbie's smiling face and extraordinary service.

After shopping at the malls and lovemaking in the afternoon, Brenda did exactly what Susan Christie had asked. It was early evening. She turned out all the lights in the living room, cleared one of the small antique tables and lit one solitary candle in the center of the table. The only fly in the ointment was Tina. She had grudgingly agreed to be part of the séance, but not before some strong-arm coercion.

She and Brenda sat side by side, Susan across from them, their hands linked atop the table. The light from the candle barely countered the darkness waiting to swallow the room. Brenda couldn't help but notice Tina's discomfort. She squirmed in her seat.

"Brenda, have you noticed the absence of Carlotta and Angelique?" Susan's voice was a whisper. Her face looked ghoulish in the candlelight.

"They must be avoiding you," Brenda teased as she looked around the darkened room, for the first time aware that her ghostly companions had been scarce.

Susan shook her head slowly. "It isn't me that's spooked them." She cocked her head in thought, then smiled. "Well, not entirely."

"Well, Carlotta and Angelique have never been afraid to communicate with me," Brenda said.

"It's not you either, Brenda." Susan patted Brenda's hand, casting a slow look around the room. "It's the house."

Brenda wanted very much to ask her what she meant, but Susan was way ahead of her.

"I know you've got lots of questions. So do I, and I think your ghosts might be able to help out with some answers, but they aren't very communicative with me, so I'm going to try and flush them out with this séance." Susan's tone took on a more somber note. "I'm going to start now. At no point should either of you let go of my hands. If you do, I'll lose my contact with the spirit." She waited for the both of them to respond.

Brenda, trying hard to banish the scenes of bad horror movies from her mind, fought to remain focused. Tina couldn't wipe the smile off her face. They both nodded stoically.

Susan seemed satisfied. She sat straight up in her chair, closed her eyes and began to speak in a slow, soft voice. "Angelique and Carlotta, I'm seeking your help tonight. Don't be afraid to make your presence known. You do not need to be afraid. Brenda is here tonight, and so is Tina."

She stopped and moved her head back as if listening but didn't open her eyes. Brenda couldn't figure out why Susan thought she needed this elaborate setting to get Angelique or Carlotta to appear. Then she noticed the candle. For a few seconds, she saw two candles. One wavered and melted into the other. Brenda blinked and the illusion was gone. She looked around the room. If Carlotta or Angelique were there, they were hiding.

Susan's shoulders started to sag, and her head was slowly dropping to her chest. Was she falling asleep? Brenda wasn't ready to pull her hands free. Without warning, Susan jerked up and opened her eyes. Except they weren't her eyes. It wasn't her face. Something else was trying to take shape. She stared directly at Brenda. Brenda shook her head hard and shut her eyes tight, hoping all would be back to normal. But when she looked again, the eyes that were not Susan Christie's were still staring back at her. Then Susan smiled.

It was subtle at first, a slight chill in the touch of her hand. Then a jolt of ice shot through Brenda, and Susan's hand gripped hers like a vise. It frightened Brenda. She was about to yank her hand away and break the circle, but Susan's hand suddenly felt warm and soft again. Except it was slender and gray. Not Susan's.

When Brenda looked up at Susan's face, it wasn't Susan at all. The porcelain blue eyes of Carlotta were locked on her, sparkling and wet with tears.

Brenda's world stopped. Nothing existed except for Carlotta's hand on hers. Tina broke the circle on the other side. Startled, Brenda pulled her hands away, watching as Susan collapsed on the table.

"Brenda? You okay?" Tina looked worried.

Brenda was concerned about Susan. She got up swiftly and turned the light switch on. The sudden bright light blazed into the room.

Susan sat up, rubbing her face, looking for Brenda. "Brenda?"

Brenda ran over to her, looking Susan in the eyes. She breathed a sigh of relief. It was Susan looking out at her. Brenda sat down, dazed, and shook her head.

"You put a bit of a scare in me." She noticed how drained of color Susan's face was. "Something happened, Susan."

"Your ghost, Carlotta, no longer has a problem communicating," Susan said. She patted her chest with her big hands and inhaled as she composed herself. She stared deep into Brenda's eyes. "Brenda, what happened here is an extremely rare event in the realm of spiritualism." She stopped, letting the words settle. "Carlotta was my guide, Brenda. She wanted to take one step further into our world." She stopped again, staring intently at Brenda and ignoring Tina.

"What exactly does that mean, Susan? What did Carlotta do, and why hasn't she talked about this to me?"

"She just wanted to touch you, Brenda."

Brenda dropped back into the chair. Was that the reason Carlotta was in her bed? She didn't know how to react to the nervous excitement running through her blood. She wasn't so sure how she felt about Carlotta's wanting to snuggle in bed. But ghosts weren't solid. They had no substance.

"I don't understand," Brenda said, confused. "How can that happen?"

Susan Christie smiled cryptically. "I became her host. She saw and touched through me."

Brenda couldn't let the knot slowly tightening in her stomach overtake her curiosity and hunger for the unknown.

"For a minute, it seemed like you were lost, Susan. Carlotta was here."

Susan sat back and exhaled. She closed her eyes and talked slowly. "We became one, Brenda. Two souls in one body, for lack of a better description."

"Is that it, then? I mean, is that all Carlotta wanted? To touch me?"

Tina suddenly rolled the chair back hard and bounded out of the room. "That's it. I can't take any more of this." She looked back at Brenda. "I'm sorry, princess."

Brenda had almost forgotten about Tina. After making sure Susan was okay, she ran upstairs after her. She found her sitting on the edge of the bed, her head buried in her hands.

Brenda sat down gently beside her. "Honey, I'm sorry all that freaked you out downstairs."

Tina sat up and looked at Brenda. "I should be apologizing to you. I better start getting used to all this." Tears were spilling down her cheeks. "I mean, this is who you are," she continued, waving her hands around the room. "I mean, I've got to accept everything in this house if I'm going to make this my home with you." She wiped at the tears with her sleeve.

Brenda blinked at Tina's last words. "You're staying here? In Tampa with me?" She must have had a shocked look on her face because Tina started laughing at her.

"Princess, I love you, and I don't want to be where you're not." She leaned over and kissed Brenda, a light meeting of the lips.

Brenda felt the fire ignite in her blood. "Tina, I need you to be sure. You have so much to lose now with your new position at the institute."

Tina put another gentle kiss on Brenda's lips. "It's either the institute or you. No contest, princess. After September eleventh, I can't see New Jersey as part of my life. I can create a life here. With you." She smiled her slow, sexy smile.

Brenda wanted to smother her in her arms, but a little voice in her head started chittering. Joan. She had to put that to rest before she and Tina could move on. She searched Tina's face for the answer. Her hand traced Tina's cheek.

"Tina, we vowed to be completely open with each other when we got together."

Unexpectedly, Tina took a deep breath and fell back on the bed, one hand over her eyes. Brenda had a feeling she knew what was coming.

"I love you, princess. Don't ever doubt that." She reached up for Brenda, and Brenda lay back to snuggle beside Tina. It was dark in the room; only the dim light from the hall cast soft shadows. Tina held on to Brenda tightly. "I'm afraid, princess. I'm afraid I've ruined everything." Her voice was a whimper.

Brenda knew then that Tina and Joan had slept together. The question now was whether the hurt was bad enough to make her lover suffer for the sin. Bitterness had never been a part of her life, and Brenda wasn't interested in adding it now.

She pulled Tina closer. "I wish I could understand the why of Joan, but it doesn't matter," she whispered into Tina's ear.

Tina pulled back to look at her. "I never stopped loving you. I'm not sure I can explain Joan either. I know this sounds cliché, Brenda, but it just happened. I thought we had so much in common. It was a high. It passed." Tina shivered in Brenda's embrace, snuggling her face against Brenda's shoulder. "Please forgive me."

Brenda ran her hand through Tina's hair. "If something hadn't happened to Joan, would you be saying this to me?"

Tina nodded feebly. "It was over. I had told her I couldn't help her anymore. She was on her own. Now I feel so guilty." Tina sighed. "Why did she have to die like that?"

Brenda didn't know what to say. "Situations sometimes catch up with people. Joan played hard."

She kissed Tina, slow but passionate, running her hand down the length of Tina's shoulder. Their kiss became deeper as Brenda slipped her hand under Tina's sweatshirt.

"We have so much catching up to do."

Chapter 17

A cold snap had rumbled into Florida during the Monday morning hours, leaving a gray, chilly, misty rain and below-normal temperatures. It was a day that found most Floridians, if they weren't at work, scurrying to the comfort of their fireplaces.

Joan Davis didn't have much of a choice. They didn't cancel funerals because of rain. From the crowd that gathered at Heavenly Gardens Resting Place, Brenda could only figure that those huddled under dripping umbrellas either loved Joan fiercely or wanted to stand with Stewart in his time of grief. Many of Tampa's elite stood elbow to elbow, faces somber and wet. Many were people Brenda recognized from the Davises' party last summer.

As she stood next to Eddy and Tina, she couldn't help but wonder what was going through the mourners' minds. Joan's death was not your ordinary passing. There was a sensationalistic stink that surrounded it. Joan had not only been brutally murdered, a sordid enough exit, but her adulterous double life had been exposed and splashed in all the local papers. The funeral was news. Cameras in hand, several members of the press hovered at the edge of the cemetery grounds.

Brenda was conscious of Tina almost clinging to her. They both shared one large umbrella. When she looked at her lover, the blank look on her face didn't reveal the emotional turmoil that Tina must be struggling with.

The gaunt-faced minister, minus an umbrella, started the eulogy. Brenda tuned him out and scanned the crowd. Stewart stood beside the minister, looking like a lost, wet soul. Beside him was another man and a woman. Both looked enough like him to peg them as family. The woman clutched his arm tightly.

Directly across from Brenda was a small woman and large man, their faces wet not from the rain but with tears. She had mascara stains running down into her chin. He tried to blot her eyes with a handkerchief. Michelle Corby stood on the other side of the woman. Brenda's gaze rested on her. Michelle was fidgety, observing the crowd with interest. She offered little support to what Brenda now assumed to be Mr. and Mrs. Corby.

She caught Brenda's stare, and the corner of her mouth twitched downward in a sullen look. But it was her eyes that held Brenda.

Brenda averted her gaze and nudged Eddy. "Are those Joan's parents?" She motioned with her head.

Eddy whispered, "Mr. and Mrs. Gordon Corby. Valerie is devastated." A plume of fog escaped from his lips. "They'll never be able to celebrate Christmas again," he said in a sad tone. He rolled his eyes back at the Corbys. "That's John in the black coat. Terry is right behind him."

Brenda couldn't believe the contrast between the Corby brothers and Joan and Michelle. The two brothers were as blond as Joan. It was obvious now that Michelle took after her father. He was the dark side to Valerie Corby's light.

She had to try to talk to the Corbys. Maybe they could provide some tiny clue about Joan or Michelle that might help her. Brenda tuned back in to the minister as he continued his Bible quotes. She wondered how tacky it would be to speak with Michelle Corby after the funeral. Judging from her body language, Michelle had no interest in her sister's funeral. She was taking Joan's death well.

Brenda turned her attention to Tina. She stood as perfectly still as one of her clay sculptures. What was it like burying someone you'd had an affair with? Brenda couldn't stop the dirty little thought from flying into her brain and squatting there. Had it really ended between Joan and Tina? Brenda was only seven years old when they put her brother Timmy in the ground. She remembered what she felt that day. She couldn't stop crying. Not only because she was going to miss Timmy, but because she was afraid for him. What would happen to him down there? Where was Heaven? How would he get there? And she was angry. Angry at the man who ran his car into Timmy's tiny body. Angry at God for making her see it all before her eyes. The visions never went away. Of course, now she knew what a beautiful place Timmy was in. Now she was jealous.

Tina tugged at her sleeve and woke Brenda from the past. The minister had finished, and both Stewart and Gordon Corby placed roses atop Joan's gleaming casket. Many in the crowd had dispersed, walking quickly back to their cars.

Eddy and Tina worked their way toward Stewart and joined a small group of friends who were paying their respects with big hugs and pats on the shoulder. Brenda scanned what was left of the crowd for Michelle Corby. She couldn't find her. Gordon and Valerie Corby stood beside Stewart, but Michelle was not with them.

Brenda watched as first Eddy and then Tina wrapped their arms around Stewart. Brenda couldn't do it. She put out her hand and he took it, his eyes lost in sadness.

"I'm sorry, Stewart. If you need anything . . ."

"Thank you, Brenda." His focus shifted to the person behind her.

"Princess, we're ready." Tina stood with Eddy.

"Looks like it's going to get worse," Eddy said as he scanned the sky, turning up the collar of his coat.

"I wanted to talk to the Corbys or Michelle, Joan's sister," Brenda said. She saw Tina's eyes roll and chose to ignore it. "Eddy, do you think it would be disrespectful to ask the Corbys a couple of questions after the service?" Brenda asked.

"I can't believe you're thinking about the case at a time like this," Tina almost hissed at Brenda.

Eddy took hold of Tina's arm and pulled her away. "C'mon, Tina, we can wait in the car." He nodded at Brenda with a half-smile. "Just don't be too pushy, Brenda."

Stewart and his family had broken away from Valerie and Gordon Corby, leaving the distraught Corbys adrift in the thickening rain.

Brenda approached them slowly and extended her hand.

"Hi, I'm Brenda Strange. Joan and I were neighbors. You have my sympathies over the loss of your daughter."

Gordon Corby's face was as cold as the frigid air; the grim face and dark circles under gray eyes gave him a haunted look. Deep lines cut through his face. Brenda figured him to be in his sixties. He shook Brenda's hand and let it go quickly. "Thank you."

Valerie's curly blonde hair was so damp that it stuck to her forehead. She stared at Brenda curiously. "Aren't you a private detective? I think Joan mentioned you once or twice." She stopped abruptly, concentrating on Brenda's face.

Brenda didn't know what to say. "I am so sorry about Joan."

Valerie Corby smiled, the corners of her mouth curving down instead of up. She was younger than her husband. "Thank you, Brenda. It's kind of you."

Gordon took his wife's arm and moved her away. Brenda wondered if this was such a great idea after all. But she might not have a better chance.

"Excuse me, Mr. and Mrs. Corby." She walked beside them toward their car. "I was wondering if I might have a few words with you about Joan?"

The Corbys stopped and looked at her, as if not quite sure what to say.

"Please forgive me. I don't mean to be disrespectful, but the case I'm working on deals with a woman who was very close to Joan."

Gordon eyed her suspiciously. "What about Joan do you want to discuss? We just buried our daughter. Now isn't such a good time." He was shaking his head and tugging on his wife, but she resisted. She looked Brenda over with red, swollen eyes.

"I want to talk about my daughter." Tears pooled at the corner of her eyes. She gave her husband a defiant look. "You can come by anytime, Brenda."

Gordon Corby was impatient to get away. "Well, you heard my wife. Come and see us whenever. We're in the phone book." He finally took hold of his wife's shoulder, and together they walked off, two black-clad figures parting the curtain of gray rain.

Brenda and Tina invited Eddy to Malfour after the service. He had a way of brightening things up. He'd turned into a good friend. Eddy called the order in from his cell phone in the car and they stopped at the Chinese place on the way back to Malfour House.

As soon as they opened the door, Butterscotch came bounding down the hallway, his tail twitching high in the air. He was chewing on something bright.

"Butterscotch, what on earth do you have there, baby?" Brenda ran her hand through his fur as she pried the tiny plush reindeer cat toy from the kitten's mouth. Butterscotch looked up and meowed his disapproval. "Where did you get this, baby?" Brenda petted him.

"We're taking the food to the kitchen, princess." Tina kissed Brenda softly on the cheek and she and Eddy disappeared through the dining room door.

Brenda scooped Butterscotch up in her arms and pressed her nose to his face. Butterscotch rewarded her with a wet kitten kiss. Brenda laughed, then noticed the note on one of the small hall tables. It was from Susan.

Brenda,
Took a cab to the drugstore. Needed sinus medicine. Long story. Got distracted in the pet supply aisle. I couldn't resist an early Christmas kitty present for Butterscotch.
Susan

Both Tina and Eddy came from the dining room, plates in hand.

"You better come and get your food before Eddy takes it all," Tina said, taking a big bite out of an egg roll and licking her fingers.

"Sorry, dear Brenda, but I am ravenous." Eddy had half a dozen fried won tons on his plate.

"Susan was the one who bought Butterscotch the toy."

Eddy laughed and ran his fingers through the kitten's fur. "Tina told me about the new addition to the family."

"Tina told you?" Brenda leaned over and put an arm around Tina. "Does this mean you're okay with Butterscotch then? I mean your allergies and everything?"

Tina wrinkled her nose. "Hey, at least he's not a hairy beast like the one in Newark."

Brenda looked at Eddy. "She means the Persian we had for a while. Tina developed a nasty allergy to it." She kissed Tina on the cheek. "Poor baby couldn't breathe and sneezed till her nose was as red as this reindeer toy. It wasn't pretty." Brenda held Butterscotch up to Tina. "I'm glad you and Butterscotch are bonding."

Tina backed away and covered her nose and mouth. "Whoa, now, I didn't say we were that close in our relationship yet. We're taking it slow."

They all laughed and Brenda dropped Butterscotch gently to the floor as all three walked back into the dining room. There were open take-out containers dotting the table.

Tina slid the two boxes of veggies and steamed white rice toward Brenda as they took chairs and sat down. Brenda grabbed a plate and dug out some of the rice onto her plate.

"I'm starving," she said as Butterscotch circled around her feet, no doubt hoping for a scrap.

The Chinese food tasted heavenly. Eddy finished the last won ton, wiped his hands on a napkin and pushed his plate away. "Well, I'll take Chinese take-out any day over all that fancy, rich food that is probably piled high on Stewart's bar right now. Plus the company is much better." He winked.

"I hope you don't mind that Brenda and I didn't want to go. We just felt awkward, you know," Tina said.

You felt awkward, Brenda thought. But she didn't want to dwell on that. It was time to move on. "I'm glad you're here, Eddy," she added with a smile.

"Yes, thank you. And now that I am here and we've sated our stomachs, I'd like to propose a little getaway for the three of us. It'll be a chance to relax."

Brenda stopped eating and eyed him suspiciously.

Eddy leaned forward, shook his head and smiled. "Don't look at me like that. It's better than that last excursion you dragged me on."

"What excursion?" Tina asked, looking confused.

"I had to ask Eddy for help on the case, that's all. Nothing to worry about," Brenda said.

"Alabama is not a place I will want to visit again." Eddy rolled his eyes.

"Alabama? Well, I'm not as jealous as I was getting." Tina laughed.

"Brenda, remember that autograph show in Fort Lauderdale that I mentioned when you came for dinner?" Eddy asked.

Brenda remembered. She knew where he was going. "I can't go with you, Eddy. Not now."

"Oh, come on, Brenda. You'll love it. If you liked my collection, this autograph show will blow you away. Tables and tables of dealers with autographs of every kind." His face was beaming.

"I don't know, Eddy."

"Fort Lauderdale? I'd love to go to!" Tina's eyes were wide with excitement.

"There you go, Eddy. Tina will go with you."

"No, princess, let's all three of us go." Tina wrapped her hands around Brenda's arm.

Brenda dropped the chopsticks to look at Tina. "Honey, I'm deep into this case." She tried to say it with conviction, but it was going to be hard refusing her lover when she looked at her like that.

Brenda had to look away and stared down at the quickly cooling rice and vegetables on her plate. "I wanted to go and talk to Michelle Corby at the Tampa Bay Boat and Oars Club. I think she can be of help."

Eddy jumped up and slapped his hands on the table with a big grin. "Well, she can wait a day. We can have that breakfast I promised in Miami tomorrow morning and fly us back in the evening. Besides, it's a done deal. I've already filed the flight plan." He winked and stared at her with triumphant eyes.

Brenda knew she couldn't back out. There were no excuses. Well, there was one. "Hey, is there any takeout left for Susan? Where is she?"

"Don't change the subject, dear," Eddy said.

"I can't leave Susan." It was Brenda's last stand.

"She's a big girl." Eddy winked and burst into laughter.

"Be nice." Brenda stared at him seriously.

Eddy sighed and reached across the table toward Brenda. "Oh, c'mon, from what I've heard of her, she can take care of herself, unless of course you don't trust her here alone in Malfour."

Brenda thought about it. "I trust Susan."

"Then you'll come?"

"Princess, please?" Tina tugged at her arm.

Brenda was beaten. The walls of her castle had tumbled. "We'll be back the same day?" She locked her gaze on Eddy.

"Cross my heart." Eddy did. "I can pick you two up at eight, and we'll be back by suppertime."

Chapter 18

The Pelican's Nest was the in-house restaurant at the Regency Court Beachside, the four-star hotel where Eddy's autograph show was being held. Directly on a white, pristine stretch of Fort Lauderdale beach, the restaurant had a view that was breathtaking.

Eddy talked all through breakfast, giving Brenda and Tina a crash course on autograph collecting. The show was in one of the hotel ballrooms. Christmas decorations dripped from every inch of the darkly paneled hotel. It reminded Brenda how bare Malfour was of Christmas.

Eddy paid the five-dollar admission for each of them, and Brenda entered a huge room crammed with six-foot-long tables draped in white tablecloths with binders stacked atop one another. At each table, collectors sat or stood looking through the binders.

"Eddy, are all those binders full of autographed photos?" Brenda asked.

Eddy's eyes scanned the room. "Not all of them. Some dealers only handle things like historical documents. Civil War letters and stuff like that. Others sell sports collectibles like autographed bats, baseballs and photos. There's something for every autograph collector in shows like this."

He couldn't keep still. Eddy was eager to throw himself at the nearest dealer.

"Okay, Eddy, lead on." Brenda urged him ahead.

"This is amazing. I never knew this hobby was so popular," Tina said as she followed Brenda and Eddy to one of the tables.

The man behind the table smiled and thrust his hand out. "Eddy Vandermast, how nice to see you." His moustache and beard were sprinkled with gray, his small glasses halfway down his nose.

Eddy introduced him as Peter Stoner, one of his favorite dealers in vintage Hollywood autographs. Eddy sat down and tore into the first binder. With Tina by her side, Brenda had just opened the H-L binder when loud voices and a shifting of the crowd distracted her.

She didn't wait for Eddy as she made her way toward a table up against the back wall. People were huddled around a gray-haired man in a corduroy jacket and beret. His voice was angry as he pointed an accusatory finger at the woman behind the table. She was a handsome woman, somewhere near fifty or so, with dark hair swept back from a face with long, almond green eyes and tan skin. She looked embarrassed but cool.

"This isn't the place for this. I don't want to call security," she said in a strong voice.

"Don't think I won't do what I have to to get my money or my manuscript back. I have all the proof I need here." The man in the hat pounded a manila envelope on her table and held it up to her face.

The business of autograph collecting had come to a complete halt, judging by the near silence in the ballroom. Dozens of collectors were crowded around this one table.

Two security guards and another man in a double-breasted suit and tie approached the man with the hat. His agitation grew more intense when he saw them.

He addressed the man in the suit. "Arthur, I don't want to cause trouble, but you know all about this. You didn't do anything about it." He waved a scolding finger at the man.

"All we want you to do is calm down, Cliff. Let's settle this in a rational way. If not, we'll have to ask you to leave."

Cliff shook his head. "Damn it, Arthur, Hilda stole my manuscript. No one is helping me." His voice quivered. "Why are you trying to cover for her? I've got the proof right here." Once again, he held up the manila folder.

"Oh, my God, that's Cliff Satterly. I can't believe he showed up here like this." Eddy spoke in hushed tones into Brenda's ear. He stood behind her.

"You know him?"

"Sort of. We corresponded and met at a couple of the shows until he moved out of the country. We lost touch. He's very active in the organization, but he's caused problems with all the autograph organizations and some dealers over the Malenko manuscript that he tried to sell to Hilda."

"What's the Malenko manuscript?" Brenda asked.

"I don't really know. Some kind of rare, one-of-a-kind document, I think." Eddy nodded toward the man in coat and tie. "That's Arthur Clemens, the current president of Autographs International."

Brenda took note of Arthur Clemens, down to the impeccable fit of his suit and the air of superiority that oozed from his pores. Then she turned to the woman under siege and asked Eddy, "I take it she's Hilda?"

"Yes. She's a past officer of the club." Eddy tsked. "This doesn't look good."

"Eddy, maybe you can help out. You know, be a mediator or referee," Tina said.

"You better act quick, it looks like they're ready to take your correspondence buddy out the door," Brenda said.

161

The security guard had one hand on Clifford Satterly's arm.

"Excuse me." Eddy jumped between the guard and Satterly. He took hold of Clifford's hand. "Clifford, what a pleasant surprise to see you."

Clifford Satterly broke into a big smile. "Eddy Vandermast. This is wonderful." He kept pumping Eddy's hand.

Arthur Clemens waved off the security guards.

Eddy managed to distract Clifford and edge him away from Hilda's table and the crowd. Brenda followed with Tina close behind.

"Clifford, I'd like you to meet two good friends of mine, Brenda Strange and Tina Marchanti."

Brenda shook hands with him, noticing how closely he guarded the manila envelope.

"Good to meet you Brenda, Tina." His hand was cold. "I'm so sorry about that little scene back there."

"Well, Eddy, good to see you." Arthur Clemens had approached the group, a big smile on his face.

Brenda studied him as inconspicuously as possible.

He patted Eddy on the back and then turned to Clifford, the smile gone and his voice more restrained. "Clifford, I'd like for you to stay, but you must agree to handle this matter with Hilda privately. No more public spectacles." He paused. "If you don't, we will bar you from future shows. You understand?"

Brenda's stomach knotted. His eyes held dark menace and his words echoed a threat. It was obvious to her. She heard it just like everybody else.

Clifford Satterly suddenly lost all his bravado. His shoulders sagged and he lowered his head as he spoke to Clemens. "I'm going to settle this one way or another. I'll deal with Hilda privately. This won't happen again." He cast a quick glance back at Hilda, who had apparently washed her hands of it and was now engaged in conversation with a customer. Beads of sweat dotted Clifford's forehead beneath the beret. He was nervous. "I need some water. If you'll excuse me." He moved away without saying good-bye to Eddy or anyone.

Arthur Clemens shook his head. "I really do apologize, ladies." He turned his dark gaze briefly on Brenda, then back at Eddy. "Eddy, I've always known you to be a gentleman, and yet you haven't introduced us. Who are these lovely ladies with you?" He fixed his eyes on Tina this time.

"I had my hands full with Clifford, thank you." Eddy rolled his eyes, smiled and pointed at Brenda. "This is Brenda Strange and her friend, Tina Marchanti."

Arthur Clemens looked very much like the Grinch when he smiled. "Brenda and Tina. Delighted."

His hands are better manicured than mine, thought Brenda as he shook hands with her and Tina.

"I'm afraid that when the Malenko manuscript is the topic among autograph collectors, it often gets out of hand." The grin lingered on his face.

"You know about the Malenko manuscript?" Brenda's curiosity sparked regarding the mysterious manuscript.

"Anyone involved with historical documents knows about the Malenko manuscript outline," Arthur said.

"And you're involved with historical documents?"

"Well, not exactly. Rare autographed paper antiquities are my specialty. But what is the Malenko manuscript if not the rarest of antiquities?"

He looked Brenda up and down. "Are you interested in the manuscript as well? How long have you been collecting?"

Brenda smiled and shook her head. "No, no, nothing so controversial, I'm afraid, just Bette Davis."

Eddy laughed. "She's not really a collector," he said. "I had to drag her here. She's a private investigator."

"Who loves Bette Davis," Brenda corrected him.

Arthur Clemens arched one eyebrow. "A private investigator? How interesting."

A garbled voice from his walkie-talkie interrupted him. He spoke into it and told the person on the other end that he would be right over. Arthur Clemens smiled and put out his hand toward Brenda.

"A pleasure to meet you." He did the same to Tina. "I hope Eddy can sell you on the joys of autograph collecting. Enjoy the show." He turned and left, catching up with the security guard at the front door.

"Well, that was not the kind of excitement I wanted to introduce you to." Eddy waved one hand in the air and grabbed Brenda's arm. "Now follow me and I'll introduce you to the major dealers in vintage Hollywood autographed photos."

Tina hesitated. "Listen, princess, Eddy, I don't think I'm going to find anything of interest here. The truth is I am bored out of my skull. Do you mind if I hit the gift shops around the hotel and meet you back here in a couple of hours? I was thinking of doing some Christmas shopping."

Brenda laughed. "You better take longer than two hours. I have a feeling we'll be in this room till closing."

Chapter 19

The day at the autograph show had been a welcomed distraction for Brenda. She hadn't realized autograph collecting was such serious business. For many, it was far more than a hobby; they made a good living going from show to show. Others considered autographs as investments.

Eddy found a 5x7 signed photo of Clifton Webb. To Brenda's untrained eye, the photo appeared to be in mint condition, with a matte sepia tone finish and a bold signature inscribed to someone named Joey in dark green fountain pen. According to Eddy, since the ballpoint or Sharpie hadn't been invented, a Golden Era Hollywood autograph was a sure fake if signed with anything other than a fountain pen. Tina came away with nothing, complaining about the lack of really unique gifts in supposedly unique gift shops.

True to his word, Eddy got them back by suppertime. It was only 7:00, but Tina was exhausted. She fell asleep. Susan was in her room going through some of her notes, which left Brenda lots of time with her thoughts. She couldn't get the Corbys out of her mind.

With Tina fast asleep, Brenda decided to visit the Corbys. They had issued an open invitation, but she called first out of respect. Valerie Corby sounded pleased to hear from her and gave her their address. Brenda left Tina a note telling her where she was going.

Judging from her map, they lived in a section of Tampa called Seminole Heights. Brenda wasn't familiar with it, but she hadn't gotten lost yet with her trusty map. She'd decided that while she was at it, she would try to get as much information as she could on Michelle Corby. Maybe she still lived with her mom and dad. Now that would be luck. But with everything she'd heard about her, Michelle probably had some condo on the beach.

Seminole Heights was an older area of Tampa now referred to as "historic." Many of the wood-frame houses had been lovingly restored, the neighborhood a tight group of small and larger bunga-lows, some in colorful paint schemes, with large trees draping over the narrow streets.

The Corby house was pink with white trim and had big planters on the large wooden porch. The Corbys had strung Christmas lights along the front of the house. A three-foot inflatable snowman stood slightly tilting on the front lawn and plastic candy canes lined the walk to the house. Obviously, this was all done before Joan's murder. Instead of cheering Brenda, the chasing lights saddened her.

Valerie Corby peered through the screen door and opened it, ushering Brenda in with a tired smile.

"C'mon in, Brenda, I have hot tea brewing." She pointed to an old wing-back chair. "Have a seat."

Brenda sat down in the floral wing chair, amazed at the room full of photographs that surrounded her. All framed, they sat crowded on tables, fireplace mantel and piano. There were family group shots, single portraits and high school cap-and-gowns. Valerie and Gordon Corby lived surrounded by their children. Maybe it was their way of coping with empty-nest syndrome. The photographs took attention away from the six-foot Christmas tree in the living room, only a few presents lost on the tree skirt beneath.

Brenda heard a door slam somewhere in the house and, seconds later, Gordon Corby walked into the living room. He seemed surprised. And not in a good way.

"Ms. Strange. I had no idea we'd be seeing you so soon." He tucked his hands in his pants pockets and sat down on the couch across from her.

"I had free time. I promise I won't take up too much of your or Mrs. Corby's evening." Brenda didn't want to get off on the wrong foot with Gordon.

"Oh, no problem. I just don't know how we can be of any help." His smile wasn't reassuring.

Valerie came back in the room, holding a tray with a ceramic teapot and mugs. "Brenda, you've picked a good time to visit." She placed the tray on the coffee table, poured tea into the mugs and seated herself on the edge of the chair next to Brenda. "Are you investigating Joan's murder? I thought the police were doing that?" She seemed distracted.

"No, I'm not working on Joan's case. I'm working for Paula Drakes' sister." Brenda took the cup of tea Valerie Corby handed her. It was steaming and smelled of cinnamon.

Paula Drakes' name sparked recognition in Valerie's eyes. She cocked her head to one side, deep in thought, then said, "I seem to recall that name. One of Joan's friends, isn't it, dear?" She looked at her husband as she passed him a cup of tea.

He shook his head. "I don't know. She always talked about so many people."

"Your daughter and Paula were very close friends," Brenda said. "That's why I'm here. I was wondering if I could take up a few minutes of your time to talk about Joan."

"I'd rather not," Gordon said, clattering his teacup and saucer on the table. He got up with some difficulty and looked at Brenda. "My wife will be more than happy to help you out, Brenda. I've got to finish cleaning up the garage." He walked out, leaving Valerie and Brenda alone.

Valerie tried to smile away her husband's abrupt exit. "He isn't taking this too well. None of us are." She shook her head. "I'm not sure there is much I can help you with either. Joan was a very independent woman. She left home at seventeen to live with a boy from school. We couldn't stop her. She was willful. We never saw enough of her after she moved out."

Valerie sighed, lost in the ghosts of the past. Brenda sipped her tea and waited.

"They didn't last long, of course, but she just kept moving until she met Frank, her first husband." Valerie stopped again, her face sagging with the weight of her pain. "We were so happy when she married Stewart. She never came around much, you understand. She and Stewart belonged to a different circle. They had their friends, you know. But she helped us get this house, and she helped her sister Michelle too." Tears were spilling out of her eyes. Valerie's lips quivered. "She was a good daughter." She stopped, unable to continue.

"I am sorry, Mrs. Corby."

Brenda watched as Valerie Corby dabbed her eyes with a tissue she plucked from the pocket of her sweater. She had opened the door for Brenda to ask about Michelle.

"Were Joan and Michelle close?"

"Well, other than the usual sibling rivalries." Valerie smiled weakly. "Especially with boys, you know."

Brenda nodded. She had almost forgotten about John and Terry, Joan's brothers.

"Mrs. Corby, did Michelle and Joan spend much time together? Do you know if they shared friends?"

"Oh, no." Valerie almost laughed. "They didn't share anything. Definitely not friends." She took another sip of the tea. "But Joan and Michelle loved each other despite their sibling quarrels." She shook her head as she put the teacup down. "Michelle is taking her sister's death very badly. Gordon and I are very concerned about her."

Brenda's heart thumped harder. "I can understand, Mrs. Corby. I lost my little brother when I was seven." She needed Valerie Corby to open up. Sometimes, sharing a personal tragedy created instant bonds.

"Oh, I'm so sorry, dear. I hope you didn't suffer like Michelle is. Her nightmares are getting worse."

Brenda's ears burned and the insides of her stomach flip-flopped. "Nightmares?"

"Oh, yes, dreadful dreams. She's been to the doctor for sleeping pills. They seem to help sometimes."

"The circumstances surrounding Joan's death could give anyone nightmares."

Valerie Corby shook her head slowly. "Well, they started before . . ." She trailed off and Brenda didn't think she could go on. Her eyes were wet again, and her voice trembled. "Michelle had been having bad dreams before Joan's death." She wiped her eyes dry again. "They've just gotten worse."

"Did she ever tell you what the nightmares were about?"

"Something about the water. Monsters coming from the water or something like that. I mean, she's been seeing a psychologist, but nothing seems to help her."

Brenda mentally added Michelle Corby to the number of grow-ing suspects on her list. Paula Drakes was haunting her. Brenda was convinced the dreams were Paula Drakes' accusatory fingers. She got up and set her teacup on the tray.

"Mrs. Corby, thank you so much for your time. I appreciate your cooperation."

"I hope I was some help. Is this friend of Joan's in trouble?"

"I wish that were the case. She was murdered."

A surprise greeted Brenda as she drove into the Malfour drive-way. A big police-issue Crown Vic was parked in the front. Although it was dark, Brenda recognized Detective Lisa Chambliss sitting in the front seat under the dim glare of the dome light. And Tina stood on the porch.

Lisa got out of her car and walked up to meet Brenda and Tina, a manila folder in her hand.

"Been waiting long?" Brenda asked, happy to see her.

Lisa offered a short smile. "Not long." She pointed to Malfour. "Your friend inside is just short of weird. When she answered the door with some ghost-finder gadget or whatever she called it, I decided to wait out here in familiar territory."

"That would be Susan Christie." Brenda smiled. "She is a ghost hunter but harmless. She's doing an investigation of Malfour House for the San Diego Central Register of Paranormal Studies."

"You have ghosts?" Lisa shook her head. Her gaze breezed over Tina, then she held up the folder for Brenda. "I think you wanted to see this."

Brenda felt Tina's hand on her arm and realized she hadn't introduced them. She reached for Tina. "I'm being rude. Detective Chambliss, this is my partner, Tina Marchanti."

Lisa took Tina's hand. "Good to meet you, Tina." She smiled and looked at Brenda. "A professional partnership?"

"Not professional," Tina added quickly, grabbing Brenda's hand. "Brenda and I have been together for over five years."

Lisa only nodded, her Buddha-like smile fixed on Brenda.

"Lisa, come on in. I'll get us some coffee or hot chocolate," she said as she opened the door to Malfour. Tina was the last one in. "Why don't you go into the library while I start up the coffee," Brenda said. "Do you take sugar and cream?"

"Black. I'm on a late shift. I could use the caffeine." Lisa worked her way toward the library, leaving Tina following on Brenda's heels to the kitchen.

"When did you start working with the police?"

Brenda reached for the coffee. "Tina, are you having any?"

"She's pretty. Reminds me of some of the elves from the *Lord of the Rings* movie. How long have you been working with her?"

"Do you want to work on the case too?" Brenda shot her an arched-eyebrow look. "And the last time I looked, Lisa Chambliss doesn't have pointy ears."

"Don't be smart, princess. I'm just trying to take an interest in your work."

Brenda knew exactly what she was up to. She turned the coffee maker on and then faced her lover. "Tina, honey, don't be jealous. I need an inside connection at the Tampa Police Department. It's a good PI business practice." She kissed Tina softly on the lips. "Besides, you gorgeous Italian, you're the only woman I work full-time with."

Tina gave her the best puppy dog face Brenda had seen yet. "I'm leaving now. I've started on a new project upstairs, so I'll leave you and Detective Chambliss to your business, but I won't wait too long for you in bed, so hurry up."

She slapped Brenda on the rear end. Brenda rushed at her, but Tina was out of the room too quickly. She would make Tina pay later.

As she headed back to the library, Brenda wondered how comfortable or uncomfortable the detective felt about meeting Tina. Tina liked to live her life openly. Brenda, while out of the closet, just never felt the need to expose much of her personal life to anyone other than her closest friends and family.

Lisa sat on the far end of the vanilla-cream leather couch. The exact same spot she'd sat when she was here last.

"I'm sorry to keep you waiting, Lisa. The coffee should be ready soon. What do you have?" Brenda sat down next to her.

Lisa handed her the folder. "Take a look. The medical files for Phil Brown."

"Don't sound so excited," Brenda said as she opened the folder.

"You've got good instincts, Brenda. Your boy Phil is a bona fide whack job."

Brenda tuned Lisa out as soon as her hand touched the first report. Two doctors' signatures graced each page in the file, which was thick with page after page of medical reports, psychological profiles and patient studies, held in and out of office. Phil Brown had clearly suffered long and hard. The earliest report was dated 1985. This would require a week's reading.

"Our department shrink has gone over the file. The short of it is that Phil Brown, in the opinion of those in the medical profession, does suffer from a multiple-personality disorder."

"To the medical profession?" Brenda put the folder down. "But not to you?" She eyed Lisa for the answer.

Lisa didn't appear to be at all sympathetic to anything the papers in the thick folder had to say. She shook her head. "Brenda, I'm not into medical witnesses or psychiatric evaluations. Phil Brown brutally beat and then, in cold blood, took a gun and shot a woman because she hadn't died from the beating. I'm looking for the answers to murder, Brenda, not excuses from doctors."

"Those answers may take you down roads less traveled, Lisa. Are you willing to shine your flashlight down those roads? I'm looking for a murderer too, remember?" Brenda watched for any signs of a chink in the detective's armor, a tiny flicker of a willingness to open new doors, but Lisa wasn't playing.

"Those medical reports do nothing for our case against Phil Brown. Whatever *X-Files*-induced dark road you take in your investigations is entirely your decision. It doesn't concern me or the TPD unless that little less-traveled road has a detour to Joan Davis's murderer. Then I might be willing to meet you halfway."

"I can't believe how pigheaded and arrogant you can be, Detective Chambliss." Brenda looked at her in amazement as she held up some of the medical sheets. "Are you willing to completely ignore medical records because it might complicate your case? It's right here, Lisa. Phil Brown suffers from the worst kind of MPD. These records indicate that not only does his other personality exist, but Phil is aware of every action Jake takes yet remains unable to stop him, or himself. However you want to look at it"—Brenda

172

tapped the folder—"it's a medical fact. He's been diagnosed and is undergoing treatment. How can you turn your face to that?"

"I think your coffee is ready."

"My coffee?"

"Yes," Lisa said with a nod. "You might want to check on it."

Brenda couldn't believe how she changed the subject. She got to the kitchen in time to hear the coffee maker percolating loudly. Lisa had good ears, or maybe just a knack for knowing how long it takes for coffee to brew.

She poured two large mugs of coffee, cream and lots of sugar for herself, black for Lisa, and headed back to the library. Lisa was standing and had just put her cell phone away.

"Sorry, Brenda, I won't be able to stay for coffee." She pointed to the folder. "You can keep those. They're all photocopies. I'm sorry we couldn't finish our debate on criminal justice, but duty calls." She had that smug smile on her face. "Let's keep in touch."

She was out the door, leaving Brenda holding her silver tray with two steaming cups of coffee. She suddenly had wickedly dirty thoughts of her and Tina in bed. She smiled all the way up the stairs.

Chapter 20

Even though the lovemaking had been great with Tina, the Paula Drakes case insisted on being number one in Brenda's thoughts. Michelle Corby wouldn't leave her alone. And Phil Brown kept poking his nasty head in her thoughts as well.

Butterscotch had woken her up early and she'd tiptoed down to the kitchen so she wouldn't wake Tina. She'd decided to make a light breakfast for everyone, even though she hadn't seen or heard Susan last night. She figured Susan would be hungry no matter what part of Malfour she was hiding in. Brenda was beginning to wonder about Angelique and Carlotta. Since the séance, they had been conspicuously absent.

By the time Tina made her way downstairs, Brenda had set the table with whole-wheat English muffins, natural jams, Smart Balance butter substitute, Special K cereal, a basket of fruit, and fresh orange juice and coffee with soy milk.

Both of them were enjoying breakfast when Susan wandered into the dining room, rubbing her hand over her eyes, where the dark circles were more pronounced than ever.

"Damn, you look like shit," Tina said.

Susan Christie cast her the evil eye, pulled out a chair and fumbled for the food.

"Are the girls keeping you up late?" Brenda asked.

"Yes and no." Susan reached for a muffin and stopped at the Smart Balance. "Tell me this isn't the only thing you've got? There has to be some real butter around here?"

Brenda shook her head. "This is just as good, and the taste isn't much different. Your heart will thank you for it."

Susan Christie sighed as she proceeded to spread the butter substitute on her English muffin. "Remind me to have Mark check the eating habits of the hosts I'll be staying with on future field trips." She took a hungry bite of the muffin and reached for the fruit basket.

Brenda took a spoonful of her cereal. "Susan, what have you been up to? I haven't seen or heard Carlotta or Angelique since the séance."

Susan stopped eating. "I'll be leaving today, you know. I'm done. We need to talk before then. There is much to discuss."

"It sounds serious." Brenda didn't know what to think of Susan's dramatic response.

"Maybe your ghosts are gone, princess." Tina finished her orange juice and looked at Brenda.

Susan grinned in between bites of a banana. "Oh, they're still here. Brenda knows."

Brenda said nothing. She always thought she would know if Carlotta and/or Angelique had passed on to the other side, but she couldn't be sure. Her psychic bond with the spirit world was such a new experience. Untested. Deep down inside her, Angelique and Carlotta still felt alive.

Tina was looking at her funny, as if expecting her to respond, but Brenda didn't have the answer her lover wanted. She knew Tina wasn't comfortable with this side of her. Maybe she never would be. She didn't understand it.

Brenda patted Tina's hand and looked at Susan. "We can talk this afternoon." She got up from the table. "I've got work to do this morning." Brenda leaned down and kissed Tina's head. "Love you, honey."

She left Susan finishing whatever was left on the table and Tina checking into a company that promised job placement for professionals.

Brenda contemplated stopping by the office but decided instead to head directly to Michelle Corby. She didn't have to refer to her Tampa map to find Tampa Bay Boat and Oars Club. Davis Islands was a piece of Tampa she'd come to know and love. Estella's Mexican Restaurant was her favorite place to satisfy her Mexican cravings, and Pipo's Authentic Spanish restaurant was like going to Spain, complete with live Spanish music and Flamenco dancers on weekends.

The club was nestled at the tip of Davis Islands. Brenda drove past Peter O. Knight airport, a small airport for private planes, and the beach residents called Harbour Point. She followed the narrow curving road until she came to an open gate with big bold Tampa Boat and Oars Club letters in gold.

"Not pretentious, are they?" Brenda murmured to herself.

The road continued, leading into a parking lot bordered by bright green landscaping and a big building that looked like an old Southern home. Brenda pulled her new Jag into one of the front parking places that were marked Guest and got out. A strong, cold wind whipped around her, chilling her despite her sweater and leather jacket and flinging her scarf into her face.

Though the sun was shining without a cloud in the sky, it was fighting a losing battle for warmth to the battering wind. To her right, stretching far into Tampa Bay, lay a dock with what to Brenda seemed to be dozens of yachts, sailboats and speedboats bobbing roughly up and down in their slips.

With the sound of the slapping surf and rude wind whistling in her ears, she went up the white steps and through the dark wooden doors. Crossed oars adorned the lintel of the doorway. Inside, a deep green carpet with splashes of light blue, and brown and tan chairs and varying sizes of palm trees greeted Brenda. The room made a soothing impression. There were several men and an older couple sitting and chatting together. It reminded Brenda of a hotel lobby.

"Hi, can I help you?"

Startled, Brenda turned. A tall, slim woman with short salt-and-pepper hair, in white turtleneck sweater and blue pants, was smiling at her.

"I hope you can. I'd like to speak with Michelle Corby."

"Is Michelle expecting you?"

"No, she isn't."

"She is very busy."

"I'm the Davises' neighbor. Michelle's sister, Joan, was a friend of mine."

Okay, so that was stretching the truth like a piece of taffy, but at least the woman's face registered the connection. She nodded. "We were all so shocked and saddened by Joan's death. Stewart and Joan have their boats here and were very active members." The woman had a faraway look on her face. She looked at Brenda and touched her arm briefly. "Let me get her for you. I'm sure she'd love to see one of Joan's friends."

She left, disappearing down an arched hallway. As Brenda scanned the obvious luxuries in the clubhouse, she wondered what exactly the Tampa Bay Boat and Oars Club was. If you went on appearances, it was an exclusive hideaway for the rich and their boats, but in the research she'd done, the club was also a heavy hitter in the charity arena, responsible for donating thousands to local nonprofit organizations.

Brenda heard a door shut and watched Michelle Corby emerge from the same hallway the hostess had disappeared into. Michelle looked good. She wore a deep red blazer with an animal print blouse peeking out, black pants and a less-than-welcoming look on her face.

"Michelle, I'm Brenda Strange." Brenda put out her hand and Michelle shook it in one swift move. "Your sister was a neighbor. I hope you don't mind, but your parents told me where you worked."

"What can I do for you?" Michelle was annoyed. It was obvious in the fake smile.

"If you have a few moments, I'd like to talk to you about Paula Drakes."

"Paula Drakes? I don't know any Paula Drakes."

"You may not remember, but you did know her. She died this summer. I'm investigating her murder." Brenda handed her one of her PI cards.

Michelle nodded slowly as she scanned the card. "Murdered? Yes, I do remember now. She was a friend of Joan's." She fixed her deep emerald eyes on Brenda. "I only met her once or twice. I don't see how I can be of any help to you."

"I won't take too much of your time. Perhaps we can talk in your office?" Brenda persisted.

Michelle looked around the room at the few people and hesitantly pointed toward the hallway. "I suppose so, but I do have a meeting in thirty minutes." She started toward the hall. "That's all I can give you."

"That's all I'll need." Brenda followed her into a smallish office that made up for lack of space with luxurious accessories. Michelle had definitely made a place for herself in the Tampa Bay Boat and Oars Club. Brenda wondered what Michelle's job was. "This is a beautiful yacht club. What do you do here?"

"I'm the event coordinator." Michelle's answer was unfriendly. She circled around to sit behind her black lacquered desk and pointed Brenda toward a pastel chair opposite the desk. Michelle Corby had already started out with a lie by saying she didn't know Paula Drakes. Brenda wanted to balance her questions to get answers and to scare Michelle into pushing the panic button. If she knew anything at all about Paula Drakes' murder, Brenda wasn't about to put on the kid gloves. She was going to punch hard.

She dug in her bag and pulled out the photos Steffi Vargas had taken in May of Paula, Phil, Joan and Michelle. She laid them on the desk and slid them toward Michelle.

"You said your memory of Paula Drakes was vague. Maybe this will refresh your memory." Brenda watched Michelle handle the photos as if they were coated with anthrax or some deadly disease. She looked at each one carefully, finally flinging them back on the desk.

"Joan knew a lot of people. I had never met Paula Drakes before that day." She avoided Brenda's eyes. "Look, I don't know what you want. This woman was Joan's friend."

Brenda smiled. "What I want is simple. Can you tell me what happened that day on the boat?"

"I was drunk. We were all drunk."

"Did you get along with Paula?"

"I don't remember much."

"Phil Brown remembers you didn't like Paula. He says you three argued."

"Phil Brown?" Michelle Corby laughed. It was an unpleasant sound. "He's a slime ball in fancy clothes."

"He killed your sister. I understand your feelings of hostility."

"Stewart and I both insisted Joan stop supporting his little poor excuse for an art gallery." She shook her head. "But no, Joan didn't listen to anyone. Look where she is now."

The hostility made her face ugly; her words were venom. She certainly wasn't using up her box of tissues drying tears for her murdered sister.

"You sound angry with Joan."

"My sister is dead."

"Did you two get along?" Brenda asked.

Michelle narrowed her eyes as she stared at Brenda. "What do all these questions have to do with this case you're working on? My relationship with my sister is none of your business."

Brenda met her stare and held it. "Paula Drakes was murdered, possibly the same day these photos were taken. Someone went to a lot of trouble making it look like a diving accident. I can't ask Joan." Brenda settled back in the chair. "I will find out who murdered her."

"I can tell you what happened if it will make you go away and leave me alone." Michelle's attitude was suddenly conciliatory.

"Anything you can remember will help."

Michelle Corby leaned back and formed a pyramid with her hands. "We were drinking. Joan wasn't really interested in the race. She paid the entry fee for the charity and just wanted to party. Phil drank till he passed out, and I wasn't too far behind. I don't remember much. Joan and I were pretty drunk." Michelle paused, staring into space for a moment. "To be honest, I don't know how any of us could have driven that boat back to the marina. Driving a boat that drunk I'm sure is illegal." She smiled.

"So you're saying that day was a complete blackout? You don't remember how you got home either, I suppose." Brenda sat back. "How convenient."

"You wanted me to tell you what happened." Michelle scowled impatiently at Brenda. "I told you how drunk we were. We didn't do anything wrong. Are you accusing me of something?"

Brenda didn't take her eyes off her. "I'm trying to get to the bottom of a murder, that's all."

Michelle Corby snapped, "Look, you've had your thirty minutes. You should have talked to my sister while she was still alive. Maybe she could have helped you, assuming she wasn't drunk."

Brenda didn't think Michelle missed Joan much. She clearly harbored more resentment and hostility than grief. This set off red flags for Brenda. It was obvious that Joan and Michelle hadn't been close, and in Brenda's experience, that kind of sibling relationship always proved to hide deep resentments. Brenda wanted to find out what those were.

"Did you know your sister and Paula Drakes were having an affair?"

Michelle Corby's face froze. Her green eyes looked away from

Brenda's stare as she rose from her chair and pointed toward the door. "You're not the police. I don't even have to speak with you. I think you know the way out." She stood in a defiant stance with her arms crossed.

Brenda got up slowly but didn't leave. "You're right, Michelle, you don't have to talk to me, but you might have some explaining to do to the police. They're going to reopen Paula's case." She turned toward the door but stopped, giving Michelle one of her most unassuming smiles. "By the way, did you know Paula was from Jersey City, New Jersey?"

Michelle looked at her, exasperated and angry. "Are you nuts or something? Why should I care where Paula Drakes was from?"

"Just thought you'd like to know that Paula's grave was broken into and her body is missing. The Tampa Police are working with the Jersey people."

Michelle inched toward Brenda, but it wasn't to kick her out of the office. Michelle fluttered her eyes and asked, unbelieving, "The woman drowned, so what would the police want with her body?"

Brenda intended to spook Michelle. She'd missed her opportunity with Joan but was hoping Michelle's brushes with the same nightmare would cause her to panic.

"Well, there are all sorts of crazy scenarios being thrown about. Some think Paula isn't dead at all. Maybe her body wasn't really stolen? Maybe she's risen from the dead to come back and seek revenge on her murderer or murderers."

Brenda let the words sink in. She hoped they dug in deep under Michelle Corby's skin. Give her more nightmares to add to the one she was already a slave to.

Brenda reached for the door and turned one more time to the speechless Michelle. She looked her over carefully.

"By the way, you really should get more sleep. Those dark circles under your eyes do nothing for your complexion."

Chapter 21

Brenda left the Tampa Boat and Oars Club with more questions than answers. Michelle Corby didn't have a heart and was clearly hiding something. She'd lost Joan, her source of money, and seemed deeply resentful. Desperation sometimes made people do careless things. Brenda hoped Michelle Corby would get just desperate enough to get careless. Maybe then she would be ready to tell her what really happened on the boat that day in May.

It was obvious she was lying. But why? Brenda wondered. Was Michelle Corby protecting someone? Or was she the murderer?

Brenda stopped by Strange Investigations and invited Cubbie to a pre-Christmas dinner that evening at Malfour. She also called Chef Standau, her favorite traveling chef. She couldn't wait to see what kind of amazing holiday magic he would come up with. She sorted through her mail, mostly junk, and headed back to Malfour. She still had that conversation with Susan Christie to get through and Felice had popped in asking about the Cappy bears, so Brenda had to somehow find time to make more bears, unless she could convince Tina to learn how to make them. That would help her out immensely.

When she got home, Brenda found a note from Tina. And a Christmas tree. The big seven-foot Douglas fir stood in the room, bare and waiting for decorating. There were no ornaments in the house. She hadn't bought any. Christmas had never been much of a holiday for Brenda once she grew up. She just never found the time and energy to decorate and, frankly, found the commercialism connected with the holiday season offensive.

Brenda read the note. Tina had gone on an interview. She had also bought the tree. It was always Tina who bought the trees. She'd had a hard time understanding Brenda's aversion to Christmas. Tina ended the note with: *You old Scrooge.*

Susan Christie's large trunks and suitcase stood in a neat cluster near the staircase. It was there that Brenda stood perfectly still, her eyes locked on the wall. The stains were reaching out like the tentacles of an octopus, stretching and grabbing for the surrounding walls. As Brenda's eyes followed the shadowing walls, she saw Susan Christie, standing with her arms crossed, watching her.

"Just what I wanted to discuss with you," Susan said.

"You have quite a knack for popping up on people." Brenda laughed.

"This isn't the worst of it." Susan pointed to the wall. "Follow me upstairs."

No, not upstairs. Those are our rooms. You can't have them, Brenda thought. She shivered. Up until now, the spreading shadows had eaten up only the downstairs walls, but the knot in Brenda's stomach was uncomfortably tight as Susan headed toward Tina's workroom.

There were no shadows along the upstairs hallway, but when Susan pushed the door open, Brenda was immediately struck by the darkness. It was mid-afternoon yet the room was deep in shadows. The two windows bathed in sunlight could only offer a light glow against the blackness on the walls.

Brenda focused on one area just above Tina's large worktable. Her heart almost stopped. She put a hand to her chest, reassuring herself she was still breathing. A distinct shape was taking form on the wall. It looked like a head with mushrooming hair, like a blurring, smudging outline of a drawing.

"Yeah, I thought you'd see it." Susan's voice was somber. "Listen, Brenda, I know we've talked about this, but I'm not sure you understand the sheer magnitude of what you have here."

Brenda only half listened to Susan. She couldn't believe the shape on the wall. What was it and what had caused it? Something was happening to Malfour. To her. She could feel it and see it. She just couldn't touch it. Not yet.

"Brenda, you've formed a psychic bond with this house. It's a very rare occurrence in paranormal history. In my professional opinion, Malfour has become an oracle of sorts, feeding off your energies and reacting to your life force in revealing ways. This may take different forms, and it may not happen often, but these shapes on the walls are trying to show you something that is either happening now or may happen to you or those around you."

Brenda understood what she was trying to tell her but she couldn't accept it. She'd been a lawyer, for Pete's sake. She dealt with facts and reality. She had never been into any of that psychic, New Age paranormal stuff. She wasn't even much of a religious person. Visions, ghosts, seeking the meaning of life had always been just some kooky movement equally kooky people indulged in.

Almost dying and taking a trip through the tunnel of light had brought her crashing through the doors of a world she had always insisted did not exist. Brenda was willing to explore and even accept paranormal activities. Malfour, Angelique and Carlotta were constant reminders that the supernatural did indeed coexist with the natural, but there was no way she was going to believe her "life force" was staining the walls of her home.

"You're telling me that my house is a fortune teller?" She cast an unbelieving look at Susan.

Susan held up one finger to stop her. "You're smarter than that. You know what I'm saying." Her eyes bored into Brenda. "Your problem is that you're frightened of this. First Carlotta and Angelique, and now this. I know it's a lot to be responsible for, but don't close the door on this, Brenda. Your ghostly friends can't help you. They're earthbound here with you. Exploring this could be something that might lead to astounding revelations and psychic growth."

There was nothing Brenda could say. Susan was right. The shadows on the wall did frighten her. But the thought of communicating with Malfour through her mind paralyzed her.

A car horn blared outside, interrupting her thoughts.

"That would be my cab," Susan said. "Please promise me you'll at least think about everything I've told you and that you'll call me soon?" She pulled out a business card from her jacket and handed it to Brenda. "Don't waste this opportunity. My new address and two numbers to reach me at are on the card."

Brenda suspected Susan Christie wanted very much to be invited back to Malfour.

Susan put out her hand. "Have a great holiday season. All my luck to you and Tina."

Brenda looked deep into the other woman's eyes and saw genuine concern. She couldn't help but smile. "I'm glad Mark sent you."

Brenda followed Susan downstairs and helped her lug her equipment out to the waiting cab. She waved good-bye and watched the cab meander out Malfour's driveway and disappear down the road.

As soon as she closed the front door behind her, a rush of cold brushed her cheek as a familiar voice whispered in her ear.

I'm glad she's gone.

Brenda jerked her head around. "Angelique?"

Don't mind her. She's jealous, that's all. Carlotta brushed Brenda's arm.

"I'm glad we've got our house back too," Brenda said, unable to suppress a smile. Her ghosts were so temperamental. She found herself thinking of the séance and what happened with Carlotta. Much had been left unsettled. But there wasn't time to delve into it. Brenda had things to get ready before Cubbie arrived for dinner. She hoped Tina would be back in time.

Tina showed up shortly after Susan left, pumped up about her interview at South Tampa University and bags of Christmas ornaments in her arms. She decorated half the tree before Cubbie showed up at five-thirty. Brenda opened a bottle of Australian Shiraz red wine and Cubbie proceeded to join Tina in finishing the tree.

Decorating a Christmas tree was not something that had been part of Brenda's life. Her family always paid to have their giant Christmas tree gloriously decorated. She didn't miss any part of those yearly rituals. She was more than happy to let Tina and Cubbie decorate the tree.

Chef Standau, who'd been responsible for that magical evening when she and Tina spent their first night at Malfour, never disappointed. He prepared roasted duck in marmalade sauce, stuffing and a plethora of raw and cooked vegetables, including one of Brenda's favorites, baked squash soufflé.

Dinner was served at seven, and by eight-thirty, Tina was halfway up the ladder at the Christmas tree, Cubbie handing her ornaments from below. Brenda was contemplating a glass of cognac when the phone rang. She answered it by default. It was Michelle Corby.

"You said you wanted to talk." It wasn't a question.

Brenda's stomach curled into a knot. "Let me switch phones. I've got company. Will you hold on?"

"No. I won't wait. Meet me here at the club. Now."

Brenda looked back at the happy pair trying to make a Christmas tree come alive. Chef Standau had cleaned up in the kitchen and left. The fireplace was roaring, the house warm and cozy. It would be difficult to get away, not to mention being rude to Cubbie. But she knew she would go. "I'll be there in under ten minutes, but will I be able to get in the gates?" It was late. She wondered why Michelle was working such long hours during the holiday season.

There was a click, and the dial tone droned in her ear. Brenda would have to take her chances.

"Everything okay, princess? Was it your parents?" It was Tina, standing beside her, concern etched on her face.

From the beginning of their relationship, Brenda had never been able to hide much from her lover. Tina had some kind of radar that seemed to pick up whatever little vibe Brenda might manage to put out.

Brenda ran her hand down Tina's arm. "No, not my parents, honey. Michelle Corby. She wants to meet me at the Tampa Bay Boat and Oars Club."

Tina stared at her. "Not now?"

Brenda didn't answer. She knew what the reaction would be.

Tina shook her head, a look of disbelief on her face.

"Princess, you can't go now. It's late." Tina glanced at Cubbie, who was oblivious to their conversation as she continued decorating the tree. "Cubbie is our dinner guest. You can't just leave. It's so late." She inched closer to Brenda. "Honey, this is a special night. C'mon, we're decorating the Christmas tree . . ."

It was more difficult than Brenda anticipated. Tina was making a monumental effort to please her and make a home here at Malfour, willing to sacrifice her new position in Newark. But Brenda knew that if the relationship was going to work, it would take even more from Tina. Tina hadn't necessarily liked it when Brenda did the odd PI jobs for Kevin. But they'd been fluff cases. She was now making a living as a private investigator. Rough and sometimes dangerous scenarios came with the job. It was what sparked her to make the decision to become a full-time investigator in the first place. Brenda liked the thrill of the unknown. The scent of danger and the satisfaction of justice were like an aphrodisiac for her system.

She took hold of Tina's hand. "Honey, I've got to go. I'm this close to solving the case, and Michelle Corby could hold the one final clue to help me piece it together."

Tina pulled away, refusing to hear. "I'll come with you."

"Don't be silly. Cubbie—"

"Cubbie can come too," Tina interrupted her.

This time it was Brenda who walked away, making for the hallway and the closet. Tina followed her.

"Tina, you know I can't let you or Cubbie come." Brenda reached into the hall closet for her long wool coat.

"Too dangerous for us but not for you, Miss Superwoman?" Tina's tone was turning ugly.

Brenda turned to face her as she buttoned up the coat. "Tina, please, not now. I won't be long, I'm just going to talk to Michelle. I'll probably be back before you and Cubbie are done decorating that tree."

Tina stood at the door watching Brenda get into the gold Jaguar. "If you're not back within the hour, I'll be tracking you down."

Brenda drove off, the cold night chill seeping through her coat and settling in her bones.

Chapter 22

The drive down Bayshore was breathtaking. The sickle moon was high and bright in the December sky, stars dotting the blackness like tiny sequins.

The situation Brenda left behind was sticky. She had been naïve to think Tina's feelings about her doing this kind of work could change so quickly. Brenda knew that allowing distractions—even holidays—to affect her case was committing professional suicide. Somehow, she had to bring both Tina and her love of PI work to the altar in a holy union.

Brenda pushed aside those concerns and concentrated on her meeting with Michelle Corby. As she wound her way past the dark road toward Harbour Point Beach, she couldn't help but wonder why Michelle Corby was keeping such late hours. Brenda tried to come up with logical explanations. It was possible that with Joan now gone, Michelle would have to put in longer hours in order to make enough money to support her lavish lifestyle, a lifestyle her dead sister helped support. But how many events would be planned over the holidays?

The gate to the Tampa Bay Boat and Oars Club was open. No security guard. Pushing aside her nagging apprehension, Brenda drove toward the clubhouse. As she pulled into the empty parking lot, she noticed that the clubhouse was dark. It appeared to be closed. Was Michelle working inside her office?

Fighting off the fear that Michelle might have led her out on a wild goose chase, Brenda had to get out and at least try the door. The distant sound of a buoy and the rippling waters of the bay were the only sounds disturbing the night. Brenda took in a whiff of the strong and pungent scent of Tampa Bay. Rotten eggs. It reeked.

She pulled and twisted on the clubhouse door. It was shut tight. Brenda still hadn't seen any sign of after-hours security at the Tampa Bay Boat and Oars Club. Perhaps there were hidden security cameras peppered about? Hoping that Michelle might be in her office locked in for safety purposes, Brenda decided to circle around to the side of the building where her office was.

Her boots crunched on the dry grass. There wasn't a single light on in the building. Michelle Corby's office was dark. Brenda was disappointed and definitely angry that she'd been led here maliciously. What purpose could Michelle have for bringing her out here in the dark?

Brenda was turning toward her car when a bright light flickered from one of the boats. It was coming off a boat way down the dock, far into the bay. Abruptly, the light blinked off. Then back on again.

Could it be a signal? Brenda wondered. Was someone trying to catch her attention? Maybe it was Michelle Corby? Although she was clear she expected Brenda to meet her at the clubhouse, plans might have changed.

Brenda had left a warm and satisfying evening with her lover and good friend to come out here. She was here now. Out in the cold damp night. She could turn back around and head home or go out on that dock and check it out. Her case wasn't going to miraculously come together with her sitting in the comfort of home, and besides, it was only a short walk to the edge of the dock.

Brenda crossed the parking lot and approached the dock cautiously. She hesitated a moment as she set foot on the wooden pier. The dock stretched far out in the Tampa Bay waters. Both the night sky and deep water below were black. Should she listen to the little voice inside her head? It was beginning to sound an awful lot like Tina.

She decided to put duct tape on the warning voice and continued walking down the dock, her eye on the bright light ahead. When she was here during the day, she hadn't paid much attention to how large the Tampa Bay Boat and Oars marina was and how far into the water it stretched.

She took another step forward when the light from the boat beyond went out again. Brenda froze. She swore she could hear the blood rushing to her head. Should she continue? It was difficult to tell in the dark how much farther out the boat was docked. The light popped back on.

It wasn't much farther. She had to keep going. Brenda looked behind her, the nippy wind whipping strands of hair into her eyes. The shoreline seemed small. She passed more boats as she walked slowly ahead. There were sailboats, speedboats and yachts, the smaller ones bobbing up and down in their slips.

She approached the boat with the large floodlights. Brenda assumed they were more like searchlights, for when someone went overboard. It was a medium-sized yacht, maybe a 23-footer, and the lights were mounted at the very top. They illuminated everything inside and around the yacht. There was a short ramp with rope handrails leading from the dock to the boat.

Brenda couldn't help but smile when she saw the name painted in bold, colorful strokes on the side. *Davross One*. Stewart's luxury yacht. Was Stewart onboard?

"Stewart?" Brenda called out, her voice almost drowned out by a circling seagull.

There was no answer. She had to go aboard. She hadn't come this far to come back empty-handed. The yacht appeared to be properly moored and the bright lights would allow her to see.

Once again stifling the voice of caution, she put one foot on the ramp and proceeded. "Stewart? Michelle?"

As she reached the top, she noticed a large object covered in dark clothes slumped on the yacht floor. Was it a body? Brenda jumped on board and approached carefully. There didn't appear to be anyone above deck.

Brenda whirled around as the sound of the yacht's engines fired and engaged. She looked up and around and could find no one. She stepped back and accidentally kicked at what she thought had been a body. Orange life vests scattered out on the floor. Why had someone carefully covered up life vests with clothes?

Her instincts told her to get the hell off, but before she could react, Brenda was rushed from behind and pushed forward so hard that she had no time to catch her balance or find anything to grab. She went sideways into Tampa Bay.

The cold water attacked her body immediately, clogging her nose and pulling her under. She gulped deeply of salt water before closing her mouth, her father's harsh words screaming through her head. He had been a ruthless swim instructor but once he was done, Brenda could at least swim as well as most people. She never thought she'd be deep in dark, cold water in the middle of a Florida winter night.

She kicked hard, her legs feeling the strain of water pushing against her. As she fought to stay above water, she looked back toward the shore. It was her only hope. No way was she going back on board *Davross One*. Someone didn't want her there.

Before Brenda had a chance to act, *Davross One* began to move away from the slip. Someone had undone the ropes. The yacht was veering sideways, straight into her. She could feel the powerful propellers as they churned the water around her.

Brenda's chest heaved with fear and her legs struggled against the water trying to drag her down. She struggled to remove her heavy coat. It would be easier to swim without it. The bow of *Davross One* loomed above her. She turned and swam as hard as she could. Maybe if she swam underneath the hull of the boat, she could jump back up on the dock. She didn't think she could outswim the big yacht. Her legs cramped and the pain stopped her dead in the water.

She heard the crack of gunfire before the bullet skimmed the water beside her. Someone was shooting at her from *Davross One*! She pushed back the panic that seized her. Then something bumped against her legs. Something big. Brenda didn't know what was more frightening, bullets whizzing by your head in the dark or a shark taking her for its next meal. Brenda kicked hard beneath the dark waters, hoping to break free, but whatever was down there grabbed hold of her legs and wouldn't let go.

A bullet screeched past her shoulder. Brenda had forsaken religion early in her childhood, but she was very willing to faithfully attend Sunday services if God could give her some sort of guiding light right now. Instead of big teeth taking a bite of her legs, whatever had her under the water suddenly began pulling her along toward the shoreline, away from *Davross One*. Her legs were held firm in what Brenda could only describe as an embrace.

Brenda was almost gliding atop the water, her arms stretched out, the cold wind sending freezing droplets of salty water that stuck to her face and hair. They were moving so fast that she couldn't dive below to see what was saving her from sure death. She glanced behind her at the yacht that seemed far away now. Whoever was firing at her had stopped. As the rocky tip of Harbour Beach came up fast, the thing holding her below let go, and Brenda sank slowly down into the water. Her feet hit rocky bottom as she struggled to gain her balance.

Dripping wet, cold and unsure of what had saved her life, she stumbled up onto dry land. The Tampa Bay Boat and Oars Club stood like a silent sentinel to her frightening ordeal in the bay. She looked out toward the water, hoping to catch a glimpse of something, but there was nothing. The water was still in the pale moonlight. Brenda scanned the marina and the bay beyond, looking for Stewart's yacht. She caught *Davross One* in the distance, speeding out toward the gulf.

Brenda wrapped her arms around herself, hoping for some warmth from the chill seeping through her body. Her clothes and hair soaking wet, she got into her Jag, wondering if the stink of rotting seaweed would ever come off her skin.

The sound of the crackling fire was better than any drug. Brenda sat on the velvet Victorian sofa in the living room, a warm blanket wrapped around her, watching the tiny embers float and dance around the logs. Tina was snuggled beside her, already asleep. In the corner of the darkened room, the Christmas tree lights blinked and chased each other around the ornaments at random speeds. Tina and Cubbie had done a beautiful job of decorating the seven-foot tree.

It was impossible keeping what had happened to her from Tina or Cubbie. They were both waiting for her when she got back. Cubbie reprimanded her in her own inimitable fashion, rushing to fix Brenda a bowl of hot soup. Tina made a valiant effort of restraint. Brenda waited for her lover to instigate the old argument over her reckless ways of investigating. But instead, Tina had gritted her teeth and listened to Brenda tell the story of what happened. Tina then rushed upstairs, got Brenda a fresh change of clothes and the blanket.

As they both sat before the fire, Brenda wondered about the apparent changes Tina had made. Last summer, she had been confrontational, unaccepting of Brenda's new psychic gifts and unwilling to make sacrifices for their relationship.

Brenda looked down at Tina sleeping beside her and marveled at how beautiful she was. The pouty, full lips took center stage on a thin, angular face topped with an abundance of black hair. Brenda leaned over and kissed Tina's head lightly so not to wake her, then got up as quietly as she could off the couch. She couldn't wait any longer to telephone Detective Lisa Chambliss.

Brenda tiptoed out of the living room, leaving Tina sleeping soundly. She headed to the library, shut the double doors and reached for the phone. It was almost midnight. Would the detective be on duty? Brenda dialed the Tampa PD first.

Lisa Chambliss's voice mail answered on the first ring. Brenda left a message with minimal information. All Lisa needed to know was that Brenda had an important new lead.

She went back to Tina, who was still sleeping and snoring lightly. Brenda put a couple more logs on the fire and snuggled back into Tina's arms. Tina mumbled a few incomprehensible words in sleep and held on tighter to Brenda.

It wasn't long before the quiet crackle of the fire made Brenda forget the unquiet spirits of her mind and embrace the sleep that beckoned.

Chapter 23

The following morning was a Thursday, and it started with surprises. Tina received a call for a second interview from one of her initial job inquiries. South Tampa University seemed very interested in her to direct their evening college arts program.

It was hard for Brenda to gauge Tina's true feelings on the offer. The previous night's happenings cast a strained air at the breakfast table and Tina wasn't saying much. It was an all-too-familiar scene. Disputes over the same issues had scarred their first summer at Malfour. Brenda wanted this time to be different.

"Will you be able to do actual classroom work yourself at the school or is it mostly a desk job?" Brenda asked, wanting to share in Tina's new professional life.

Tina didn't seem that interested. She took one spoonful of cereal before answering. "This sounds like small talk, princess." She put the fork down and looked at Brenda. "I'd rather talk about last night. It's much more interesting." She grinned, waiting for Brenda's response.

"I told you everything, but if you want to know more, I can repeat it."

"Take me with you on your investigations," Tina said.

Brenda shook her head. "I thought you wanted to talk."

There was no way Tina was coming with her on any part of her investigations. She'd made that clear several times. Last night only reinforced the dangers of the job. Granted, hopping into Stewart's boat hadn't been the smartest thing to do, but it had been her decision and hers alone.

Brenda got up and, ignoring her lover's puppy dog look, wrapped her arms tight around Tina. "Honey, we've got a real chance to make things work here. I love you and I know you understand that it's because I love you that we can't discuss this."

Tina didn't look convinced or ready to give up so easily.

"And it's because I love you so much that I worry, princess." Tina's eyes watered, a slight quiver in her voice. "I can't go through what happened back in Jersey . . ."

"Shush." Brenda put a finger over Tina's lips and hugged her even harder. "I'm never going to leave you."

With Tina off on her interview, Brenda decided now would be a perfect opportunity to pay Stewart Davis a visit. She needed answers on his whereabouts last night. If he wasn't aboard his yacht, she thought, he'd better have a list of people with access to it.

She called his office and was told he had taken a short leave. Stewart was still mourning his wife's death. Brenda wasn't fully convinced that Stewart Davis was so consumed with grief over Joan's death. It didn't matter where she talked to him. The Davis manor was just as good a place to grill him.

She'd just put on a brown corduroy jacket for the walk to Stewart's house, when there was a light knock on her door. Outside her window, she saw Lisa Chambliss's unmarked car.

Brenda was surprised at the early visit. She opened the door with a certain excitement.

"Detective Chambliss."

Brenda smiled, anticipating the conversation. Explaining what had happened to her wasn't going to be easy.

"Good morning, Brenda. I got your message. I'm on the way to TPD and wanted to stop in before."

They stood in the foyer. Brenda cleared her throat. "I will be as to the point as I can, but you've got to promise that you will listen with an open mind."

Lisa crossed her arms and raised an eyebrow. She said nothing.

"I gather that's a yes?" Brenda asked.

"It's early, Brenda, I had a late night entering reports, I haven't had my coffee, and my mind is still in first gear."

"I'll keep it short then. Michelle Corby set me up last night for murder. I was saved by Paula Drakes, or what was once Paula Drakes."

Lisa didn't answer. She just stared. Brenda laughed.

"I'm not going there with you, Brenda."

"Lisa, you wanted me to be quick."

"You need a shrink, Brenda."

They both locked eyes. Lisa started shaking her head in frustration.

Brenda sighed, her own frustration mounting. "Michelle Corby was in on Paula Drakes' murder or knows who did it."

"I have a bet on who did it. Phil Brown, better known as 'Jake' to you." Lisa's voice was curt.

"Butting heads will get us nowhere. You wanted me to share information with you on this. That's what I'm doing. I'm going to break this case soon, with or without your help."

Brenda had expected Lisa's disbelief but not the attitude. She was sorry their relationship had not strengthened.

Lisa sighed. "Tell me what happened. Be specific with the facts, Brenda. No monsters from the ocean or anything like that."

If Lisa wanted the facts, that was exactly what Brenda was going to give her. "Suppose we talk over that cup of coffee you obviously need?" Brenda smiled and pointed toward the kitchen.

Lisa's eyes twinkled as she bowed in gratitude. "Ahh, coffee, the magic word. You've got me for as long as it takes me to finish off a mug."

Over two extra-large coffee mugs, Brenda explained everything to the smallest detail, including her belief that it was Paula Drakes, or what she believed Paula Drakes had turned into, who led her safely back to shore.

"You wanted the facts." Brenda finished.

"Let me put this out on the table for you, Brenda. Give you a better picture of what I've got at stake on my end. Chief Hull granted me two weeks to get something new on this case. Something or anything that could remove that tacky little *X* Detective Cannello had jokingly scribbled on the folder. We were freaked out, Brenda. When your medical examiner tells you that without a doubt he believes the dead body you pulled out of the bay was morphing and sprouting gills over the human lungs, your rational head wants to throw all that crap out the window. You've got to understand why Chief Hull wants the men in black, or whatever they really call themselves at the FBI, to take this case off our hands." Lisa paused and exhaled. "Brenda, unless you give us something real, don't even bother. I had to do some hard convincing to even get the chief to trust a new PI with this particular case. You might as well even forget about us reopening it."

It was clear to Brenda that Lisa hadn't been listening. Working with her presented more of a challenge than Brenda had anticipated. But she wasn't ready to give up.

"Suppose we forget the mumbo jumbo stuff, as you like to call it, and stick with the cold hard facts you're so fond of. It's very simple. I was set up, pushed into Tampa Bay and shot at until I managed to swim away. I believe it was Michelle Corby."

This time, Lisa crossed her arms and cocked her head to one side, eyebrows furrowed. "First off, you trespassed, and second, you never even saw your attacker. You've given me nothing."

Brenda had to smile at the sudden enthusiasm in Lisa's voice. She had her attention now.

"It's about coincidences, Lisa. Michelle Corby calls and asks to meet with me at the Tampa Bay Boat and Oars club late in the evening. When I get there, the place is dark and empty. No Michelle. Just as I'm ready to leave, a bright light from one of the boats distracts me. The light leads me to *Davross One*, Stewart and Joan's yacht. As soon as I'm on board, I get shoved into the cold water and not only do I try to get rammed by the boat, but someone on deck starts shooting at me, hoping to finish the job." Brenda paused for dramatic effect. "What would you call that?"

"A bad night?" Lisa chuckled.

Brenda had done what she set out to do, which was to inform Lisa Chambliss about the attempt on her life and her suspicions about Michelle Corby. It was up to Lisa to do what she wanted with the mix.

"Listen to me, Brenda. What I'm going to tell you is an official statement. I do not want to hear any of your crazy monster stories. Do not call me unless you have solid, real facts or leads to offer." She stood up and headed for the door.

Brenda followed close behind. "I'm going to find who murdered Paula Drakes," she said.

Lisa stopped abruptly. Brenda almost ran into her.

"Brenda Strange, I am this close to scratching you from my list of reliable working contacts. Please don't make me do that."

She was out the door and gone before Brenda could say another word. Brenda was stunned, barely able to comprehend the hostility in Lisa's words.

The morning was cool, but not a cold freeze. Brenda took her time walking to Stewart's home. There were several cars parked out front. One of the men she recognized from the funeral opened the door. She introduced herself and asked to see Stewart.

The man extended his hand. "Come in, Brenda, I'm Lamar Davis, Stewart's brother." He ushered her inside. "We're having a heated discussion about the Buccaneers this morning."

He flashed her a bright smile. It had to be the Davis trademark. As a matter of fact, he looked very much like Stewart, Brenda thought, give or take ten pounds and a few gray hairs.

They stepped down into the sunken living room, passed the wall of sliding glass doors and went into a screened outdoor pool area. It was a bit excessive for Brenda's taste. Way too big for two people. Lamar kept walking until they reached another door that led out into another room surrounded by glass. In the middle of the room was a huge water fountain as a centerpiece and three wrought-iron patio tables and chairs surrounding it.

Stewart, and a woman who Brenda assumed was his sister, sat at one of the tables. She had been at the funeral as well. Empty plates and coffee cups littered the table.

"We've got company, Stewart."

Stewart, coffee cup in hand, stood up. "Brenda, this is a surprise."

He introduced her to his other sibling, Lenore. They were staying another week to be with Stewart. The woman was not friendly. She sized Brenda up with cold, steely eyes.

"Can we offer you some coffee?" Stewart asked. "We also have scones." He pulled out a chair for her.

Brenda smiled and shook her head. "I'm sorry, Stewart, I can't stay, thank you. I was wondering if I could speak with you privately?"

Stewart, more relaxed than the last time she'd seen him, hesitated, exchanging glances with his sister and brother. He finally put down his cup on the table.

"Well, of course, Brenda. Let's go upstairs to the study." He pointed toward the door.

Brenda turned to Lamar and Lenore, meeting their curious gazes. "It was a pleasure meeting you both."

The study was almost the size of the massive living room. It was spacious with clean, angular lines and dotted with blond Scandinavian furniture and rows of tall bookcases filled with books, magazines and bronze sculptures. On one side, there was a shelf that covered the entire wall filled with colorful glass objects.

Stewart closed the door behind them and wasted little time in

201

showing his old colors. "Going by your previous visits, I can only guess this is an interrogation of sorts. I will not discuss anything to do with your case or about my wife. In my mind, that doesn't leave much to talk about."

His hospitality had gone out the window. Brenda couldn't help but smile as she shook her head. "Nice to see some people don't change. Do you miss Joan?"

He crossed his arms and gave Brenda the once-over. "Joan and I had a great relationship, Brenda, but I am not going to fall prey to your little mind games. If there is something I can really help you with, I will gladly subject myself to your silly questioning."

Brenda moved toward the shelf unit with the glassware, eyeing one piece in particular. It was a vase, the glass blending from crystal clear into a flaming burst of orange at the bottom.

"I have questions, Stewart. Nothing more, nothing less."

Stewart laughed. "Oh, there's always something more hiding in your questions."

"I had an unpleasant experience last night," Brenda continued. "Someone tried to kill me."

"Obviously, they didn't." Stewart thought he was funny. When Brenda didn't respond, he stuffed his hands in his pockets and shook his head. "You're not blaming me, are you?"

His smile irritated Brenda.

"Because if you are," he continued, "I hate to disappoint you. I spent the night here with my family. At nine we watched a DVD of old football games. Packers and Colts. Both my brother and sister are die-hard Packer fans." He waved a hand down at the floor. "If you'd like, go ahead and ask them. Satisfy your sick little mind. Honestly, Brenda, I first thought of you as a nice, decent human being. It hasn't been two weeks since my wife was brutally murdered and here you are harassing me. Don't you have a heart?"

Brenda found it difficult to feel sympathy for this man. Did that make her an insensitive monster herself? Right now, the answer to that question couldn't stand in the way. There was a murder to uncover. She had to do what she needed to do.

"Stewart, I'm sorry if I picked a bad time, but I almost lost my life last night, and it was someone on your yacht who almost took it. They shot at me."

His face dropped like a sack of cement. "*Davross One*?"

"Who has access to your yacht?"

Stewart turned his back on her and walked slowly toward one of the windows, running a hand through his blond hair. He stopped and looked back at Brenda. "I pay to have a twenty-four-hour crew on board." He shook his head in dismay. "I can't imagine why any of them would want to shoot you."

"Stewart, does anyone in your family, or maybe one of your friends, have access to the yacht? Someone who can run and maneuver it?"

"No, no one in my family. No friends, certainly. Just the crew."

Brenda hesitated. "How about Joan's family?"

Stewart gave her a blank expression, then put one hand in the air and snapped his finger. "Yes, of course. Michelle has keys and full access to the yacht. She and Joan often took cruises." He scratched his head. "But you can't mean Michelle . . ."

"I'm not accusing anyone, Stewart, just trying to make sense of what happened."

Stewart returned from the window and stood facing Brenda. "I don't know if this means anything, but Michelle has gotten friendly with my shift captain, Mario. He's a nice young man. She's been dating him. I've given them permission to have dinner dates on the yacht."

"So it's possible Michelle and your captain could have been on a date on *Davross One* last night?"

"Of course, it's possible, Brenda, but that doesn't mean Michelle or Mario were the ones who tried to shoot at you. I mean, why?" Stewart cast Brenda a perplexed look.

"That's what I have to find out."

Stewart inched toward the door. "Well, Brenda, I'll contact the firm who hired my crew and have them run background checks on each of them, and I'll speak to my night crew personally. If they know anything about what happened last night, I'll call you. I'll get to the bottom of it."

Brenda wasn't going to wait for Stewart Davis to check into anything. Background checks were something he should have done before he hired Mario or anyone else. Stewart had been helpful, more willing to tolerate her than usual. Was he doped up on some kind of tranquilizer? Brenda doubted it. Hopefully, after this case was done, she wouldn't have to spare any of her thoughts on Stewart Davis anymore.

Brenda knew she was getting close to Paula's killer and it wasn't just the tight knot of excitement in her chest. When attempts at your life start to get serious, somebody was feeling the heat. Brenda was now sure that Michelle Corby was a key player in the game that landed Paula Drakes in Tampa Bay last summer. She had to find her.

Brenda decided to head out to the Tampa Bay Boat and Oars Club today and see what kind of alibi Michelle Corby could come up with and what good reason she had for pulling the stunt she had. And while she was there, Brenda intended to do her own questioning of the *Davross One* crew.

Tina wasn't back from her interview, so Brenda made sure Butterscotch had food and water and headed to Strange Investigations.

Cubbie was caught up in a very loud game show when Brenda walked in. She greeted Brenda with a welcoming grin.

"Well, I'm glad to see you up and about, boss lady. You had me scared last night. Sugar, you looked like some drowned rat a cat brought in."

"Cubbie, did I ever tell you how grateful I am to be the beneficiary of your particular outlook in life?" Brenda slapped Cubbie on the back as she proceeded into her office.

Cubbie followed her. "Hey, I grabbed your favorite continental breakfast this morning on the off chance you'd be here. Raspberry cream cheese Danish." Her smile was as big as her face. The way she leaned on the door reminded Brenda of the Cheshire Cat.

"Yum. Thank you, Cubbie. Can you throw in some coffee too?"

"This is starting to remind me of my waitress days."

"Anything to keep you happy." Brenda smiled.

Cubbie started out the door but stopped. "Oh, yeah, that Detective Lisa Chambliss called. Three times. Said all good private investigators have their cell phones on at all times. It sounded urgent. She left her cell number. Said you should call her there."

Damn. The cell phone. It had gone into the water with her and was so water-logged, nothing worked. As Cubbie disappeared to fetch breakfast, Brenda reached for the phone and dialed Lisa's number. She was mildly surprised. Just a few hours ago, Lisa had basically told her to shove off. Something big must have gone down. Something to do with Joan's case or Paula Drakes. Or maybe both.

Lisa Chambliss answered before the end of the first ring.

"Brenda. You need to be here now. 'Jake' is asking for you. Says he won't talk to anyone but the Princess Diana clone." She paused and Brenda could swear she was smiling. "I could only think he meant you."

"I'm glad you still consider me of some use." Brenda couldn't help herself. Lisa's cutting words this morning had stung. "I'll be right there."

Chapter 24

Brenda didn't know what to expect. Her apprehension was so intense, it felt like baby *Alien* monsters were chomping through her stomach to get out.

When she arrived at Orient Road jail, Lisa wasn't waiting. A young police officer allowed her access and told her Detective Chambliss was waiting in the visiting room and that she was to go right in. Brenda remembered her last visit here.

Lisa stood outside the door to the visitation room. She grabbed Brenda by the arm. "Thanks for coming. Things are happening fast. 'Jake' has been with us for about an hour. All he's saying is that he can blow the lid off both the Paula Drakes case and Joan Davis's murder but he won't talk to any of us." She paused and shook her head. "He insists on you and only you."

Brenda moved away from Lisa's touch. "Don't look so troubled. I have that effect on people."

That brought the old smile back to Lisa's face. The smile Brenda found inexplicably attractive. "Listen, Brenda, I was out of line at your place this morning. Since we need your help right now, I hope you'll accept my apologies."

"I think this is the beginning of a beautiful friendship." Brenda smiled and moved toward the door. "Let's go talk to Jake."

Brenda didn't expect what waited in that room. Phil Brown was gone. Not in the physical sense, of course, because nothing physical had changed, but it was a different man who sat in the chair before her. She leaned toward Lisa. "What happened with the arraignment? No bail, I'm guessing?"

"The bastard keeps refusing a lawyer. Says he's tired of all the medicine and leading a double life. The judge refused bail."

"Do both Jake and Phil Brown plead guilty?"

Lisa shook her head. "Who the hell knows, Brenda. We're hoping you can get to the bottom of this freak show." She motioned for Brenda to proceed inside.

Jake, Phil Brown's alter ego, leaned back in a casual, almost defiant manner, a subtle grin pasted on his face. Where Phil Brown had looked like a wounded animal, Jake sat like a king among jokers, confident that he controlled the universe around him. The transformation was startling.

When he saw Brenda and Lisa enter the room, he got up in an angry rage. He couldn't get very far, though. Jake was chained to the table. He pointed a finger at Lisa.

"I said the Princess Diana dame and no one else." His voice was guttural and coarse, with a Bronx accent Brenda knew Phil Brown didn't have.

"I think you should do as he says, Lisa." Brenda didn't take her eyes off Jake.

"You'll be okay?" Lisa asked.

"Are you guaranteeing the life of those restraints?"

"We'll be right behind the mirror if we need to get you out."

Lisa cast a look at Jake that could have frozen the Hillsborough

River. He only smiled and shot her a bird as she closed the door behind her. There was a nasty smell in the room. Unclean clothes and dead skin.

"Goddamn pigs. They want a piece of everything." He spat a clump of phlegm at the floor. When he turned to look at Brenda, his face was twisted in an angry snarl. Brenda had seen that mask of hate before. Danny Crane wore the same look when he burst into her law office and massacred twelve people. She couldn't let those images into her thoughts, not if she wanted to deal with Jake.

She slowly sat down in the chair opposite him. He grudgingly sat back down, looking her over.

"If I'm gonna spill the beans on Mr. Big and Mighty, I want you to hear it first." The smile on his face made Brenda squirm in her chair. "Besides, Phil likes lookin' at you better. And so do I."

"Who is Mr. Big?" Brenda forced the words out of her mouth, making sure they sounded stronger than she felt. She glanced at the giant locks on the chains at his feet.

"Mr. Big. Stewart Davis. My girl Joan's good-for-nothin' creep husband."

The tiny knots clustered in Brenda's stomach suddenly formed into one giant one. She wanted to remain calm.

"You want to spill the beans on Stewart Davis? I'm listening. What do you have?"

He smiled even wider. "Well, Brenda babe, you're gonna wanna know that it was him who bonked Paula Drakes in the head and dumped her to the fishies. And it was the same who paid me big bucks to get rid of his wife for him."

Brenda could just imagine Lisa Chambliss's jaw drop on the other side of the mirror. She had to keep him talking. Brenda edged up in her seat, trying hard to stifle the excitement in her voice. She wanted to know about Paula Drakes.

"Wait a minute. Stewart was there on the boat?" Stewart wasn't in the pictures Steffi Vargas took that day, and his alibi checked out. He was in Tallahassee that weekend. Who was lying? What reason did Jake have to fabricate such a lie? Then again, was she crazy to even contemplate taking anything that someone with an MPD said seriously?

"Of course he was."

"Were you there when he murdered Paula Drakes?"

"Hey, baby, I'm here ninety percent of the time. Yeah, I was there. I saw it all."

"But Phil says he was drunk and passed out. He didn't see a thing. He didn't tell me Stewart was on the boat that day."

"What would you say if Stewart Davis was paying you big bucks to keep your pie hole shut?"

"Stewart Davis paid you to keep quiet?"

"Not me. Phil."

"Tell me how it happened."

"I'm gonna tell you once and only once. I am not going to repeat it. That boat rally was nothing out of the ordinary for Stewart, Joan and Michelle. They did the stupid thing for charity every year and I went along with them. Well, this time, they dragged along your Paula Drakes for the ride."

Brenda remained quiet. She wanted him to talk as long as he wanted.

Jake shook his head. "I gotta tell ya, she looked like a frightened rabbit. Man, she didn't want to be there. Like my stupid counterpart told ya, the dames were arguing. Michelle and her sister were like two female cats with claws extended. It was always about money. But what Joan didn't know was that for Michelle, it was also about Stewart. She wanted him. He was already dickin' her, but his dick didn't give her the name of Davis. Michelle wanted to be Mrs. Stewart Davis. Her sister stood in the way. Of course, Joan screwed her marriage up anyway, sleeping with every Tom, Dick and Paula—" He stopped, put two hands up in a stop signal and leaned back in his chair. "Hey, sorry about that joke, but it's the truth. I was Joan's lackey for many a night when she couldn't handle whoever the guy or dame she'd gone out with. She'd call me and I had to come and rescue her. Not Phil, but me, good old Jake."

"So Joan was playing the field behind Stewart's back."

Jake laughed out loud. "Hell no, not behind his back. He knew every little dirty night she spent with someone else."

"Why didn't he just divorce her?"

Jake leered at her, shaking his head. "Because he has secrets, Brenda. Secrets that Joan was privy to."

"Where does Paula fit into this? Why did Stewart murder her?"

The look on Jake's face froze Brenda's blood. His lips were moving but he said nothing. His eyes were spacey, unfocused. Without warning, he slammed his handcuffed hands on the table. This time Brenda pulled herself back.

"This is big, lady, big." He jerked his head up and screamed at no one. "Do you hear me? I'm gonna tell her everything!" He sat back down in one swift move, eyes staring straight at Brenda. "He doesn't want me to tell you. Phil is sweating bullets."

He stopped and watched Brenda's reaction. She needed him to keep talking. She said nothing, just met his gaze.

He grinned. "I like you. Yeah, I do. I'm gonna quit pussyfootin' around with you. Stewart and my boy Phil were involved in a fake art ring operating in Europe and America. They had people forging famous paintings. It was a big smuggling operation. There are hundreds on Stewart's payroll. Check out some of his overseas accounts. Paula found out about it, probably because Joan opened her mouth and told her. Well, your Paula threatened to expose Stewart to the police."

Jake sat back in his chair and shook his head. "Love is such a sad, pitiful thing. This poor lesbo thought she really had a shot at Joan with Stewart out of the picture. It didn't take much for Stewart to bash her brains out with the diving tank. He just fitted her out with Joan's wet suit and dumped her over. Paid that bastard Phil to keep his mouth shut and then threatened Joan that he could easily find an accidental death worthy of her if she whispered a word to anyone about it. Michelle was the only one he didn't have to worry about. She was in on the whole thing. When Joan started cracking and you started sniffin' too close to home, he came to me and said to take care of her. So I did." He smirked. "Too bad, 'cause the dame was really wild in the sack, you know."

Brenda let out breath she hadn't realized she'd been holding. It was an unbelievable premeditated murder plot Jake revealed. It changed her entire picture of the case. She thought she had the puzzle nearly complete. Brenda was convinced Michelle was the missing piece. Stewart had always been on her top ten list of people she distrusted, but she'd scratched him after his alibi appeared tight.

"Well, do you believe me?" Jake's eyes searched her face.

"Why should I believe you?"

"Well, Miss Private Dick, the way I see it, both you and me got nothin' to lose. Phil the pussy pissed his pants when the cops came calling and sent me down the river." He leaned in closer over the table. The smell grew worse. "If I'm going down, baby, Mr. Big Shot Stewart is comin' with me."

Brenda wanted to keep Jake talking but wondered how much more time Lisa would allow her.

"You realize there is nothing I can do for you. I'm not the law."

"You're a smart lady." He kept his grin. "While you're out there taking care of Mr. Big, get Phil the pussy to tell you about the fake art ring." He leaned back as comfortably as he could with chains on his feet and hands. "There is nothin' worse than fake art dealers."

He'd barely finished the last sentence when the door opened and Lisa Chambliss and two uniformed police officers walked in.

"The show's over, Brown," Lisa said. "Time to get back to the real world."

The two police officers grabbed Jake and lifted him up from the chair. He went without a word, smiling at Brenda all the way out. When the door shut behind them, Brenda got up and stood beside Lisa, who waited patiently with arms folded.

It was already obvious to Brenda by her body language what she thought.

"Isn't it at least worth looking into, Lisa?"

"The ramblings of a murderer who thinks he's some gangster from a bad B-grade movie and talks to himself doesn't constitute valid testimony."

Brenda couldn't handle Lisa's roadblocks anymore. She slammed a hand hard on the table. The sound echoed in the small room. The foul smell lingered in the air. She wanted out.

"I'm sorry, Lisa. We aren't going to see eye to eye on anything regarding this case." She turned her back on Lisa and started for the door.

Lisa grabbed her arm. "Hey, Brenda, don't be so hard on yourself." She smiled. "Or me. I'm gonna check a couple of things out, okay?" She released Brenda's arm. "I know we both want to find justice. We're going to get the bad guys, one way or another." There was a hint of a smile on her face.

Brenda couldn't agree more. "For once, you're right." She left the stink in the room and Lisa Chambliss, letting the cold, bracing air outside cool down the volcano that was building inside her.

Brenda drove off, her mind painting a new picture over the old one of Stewart Davis and his part in Paula Drakes' and Joan's murder. Was he the fiend that masterminded cold-blooded murder? Could he be involved in international art fraud?

In her mind, Brenda knew only one way to prove Stewart's guilt. Paula Drakes was pointing the way.

When she drove up to Stewart's house, all the cars that had been parked in the driveway this morning were gone. There wasn't a single vehicle at the Davis home.

She rang the doorbell, expecting the same maid in blue to answer. Brenda was surprised when an older man she didn't recognize opened the door and smiled.

"Hi, I'm Brenda Strange, a neighbor of Stewart's. Is he in?"

"I'm sorry, ma'am, Mr. Davis is running errands. Would you like to leave a message?"

Brenda didn't want to leave a message. She was going to walk away but stopped. She remembered Stewart mentioning someone named Wilson, his staff manager who had helped him clean up the water leaks in the bedroom. Could this be Wilson?

Brenda gave him her best smile. "You wouldn't be Wilson, would you?"

The look on his face told her she'd struck gold. He cocked his head in surprise.

"Why, yes, ma'am. My name is Wilson." He gave her an apologetic smile. "I'm afraid I don't recall your visiting."

"No, we haven't met, Wilson. Mr. Davis mentioned you."

"I am quite surprised Mr. Davis spoke of me. I'm afraid I don't do as much as I used to around here." He appeared flustered, arching one gray eyebrow. "I do hope it was in good terms?"

"Stewart is very happy with your service. As a matter of fact, Stewart and I were discussing the water damage and roof problems. He was very thankful he could call on you at all hours to help with the cleanup. I'm sure you're glad Stewart fixed the problem."

Wilson's smile faded. "Well, I'm afraid the problem isn't fixed at all." He scrunched his eyebrows. "He didn't tell you?"

Brenda tried hard to control the flip-flops in her stomach.

She attempted her most serious face. "With this horrible thing that happened to Joan, we haven't had a chance to do much chitchatting. Don't tell me Stewart still has water leakage?" She held her breath as she waited for Wilson's answer.

He shook his head. "I'm afraid it's quite a dilemma. Mr. Davis doesn't know what to do. It's gotten so bad in the Davis bedroom that Mr. Davis has taken to sleeping in other bedrooms."

"Other bedrooms?" Brenda silently wondered how many bedrooms the palatial home actually had. "Stewart still has water puddles?"

"Yes, ma'am. Except that water just keeps leaking from everywhere. I'm almost embarrassed to say, but I haven't been able to find

213

where the water is leaking from. Poor Mr. Davis has called every roofing company he has done business with, to no avail."

Brenda tried to remain calm. "Is it the same water with the seaweed smell?"

Wilson nodded. "Yes, ma'am. It started this past summer, even after Mr. Davis had a new roof put in." He stopped, thought hard about what he'd just confided and leaned closer outside the door toward Brenda. "Miss Strange, you won't tell Mr. Davis what I said?"

Brenda smiled. She had good reason to. "Wilson, we never had this conversation." She shook Wilson's hand, despite his reluctance. She guessed the staff was not in the habit of any such contact with visitors.

"Would you like me to tell Mr. Davis to return your visit?" Wilson asked.

"No, thank you, Wilson. I'll be seeing Stewart again soon."

Brenda got back in her car and cursed the lack of a cell phone. She had to get a replacement. She had no doubt who killed Paula Drakes. Jake was telling the truth. It wasn't just Joan who was tormented by Paula Drakes. Paula was pointing her webbed finger at both Stewart and Joan. Whether Lisa Chambliss bought the truth or not, Paula Drakes was still alive, except her new home was at the bottom of the ocean floor among a race of beings only few have been privileged to glimpse. Stewart could have lied about everything. A man with his money could buy anything, even alibis. Both he and Michelle could have been on *Davross One* that night.

Brenda thought about calling Lisa and filling her in but changed her mind. She would confront Michelle Corby on her own. First, she had to stop at home. This time, she wasn't going without protection.

Her new Jag was in the drive when she drove up to Malfour. Tina was home. This complicated matters. If Tina knew where she was headed there would be another confrontation. She didn't want to deal with that now. She was so close to breaking the case she could smell the adrenaline pumping through her system. Any delay could cost her the element of surprise. There had to be some way around Tina.

Tina was waiting for her as soon as she walked in the door. She grabbed Brenda from behind and kissed her hard. The big grin on her face told Brenda the job interview had gone well. She still wore the double-breasted pantsuit she'd selected for the interview. Tina must have just gotten back.

"You are looking at who could be the next Director of the Arts for the South Tampa University night curriculum." Her smiling eyes searched Brenda's face.

This was the news Brenda had hungered for. Her body and life had gone into a cold withdrawal when Tina left in August. It was she who insisted and argued for Tina to give up her position in Newark and stay in Tampa. Brenda remembered suggesting to Tina that she find a job and make a home of Malfour with her. That dream was now a reality and all Brenda could think of was Stewart Davis and Michelle Corby.

"I am so proud of you, honey." Brenda kissed Tina and held on to her tight.

Tina backed off. "Well, I know it isn't a sure thing, princess, but it's pretty damn close to being my job." She eyed Brenda intently. "I thought you'd be happy."

Brenda never could hide her feelings well from Tina. "Honey, I am very happy for you. For us."

"But?" Tina arched an eyebrow.

Brenda rubbed her lover's arm. "Why don't we celebrate tonight? Go out somewhere special for dinner."

Tina laughed. "Hey, I don't have the job yet." She kissed Brenda's neck and nuzzled her face into her hair. "I know another way we can celebrate, though. Upstairs." She moved her eyebrows up and down, making funny faces, and winked.

Brenda's insides turned to jelly. Tina wanted to make love. How could Brenda refuse without appearing selfish and insensitive?

Tina caught the hesitation. Her funny faces turned dead serious. "What is going on, Brenda? Please tell me, 'cause I'm not psychic like you."

This was exactly what Brenda wanted to avoid. Getting into a nasty situation with Tina wasn't in her daily planner. She wanted desperately to catch Michelle Corby at the Tampa Bay Boat and Oars Club but not necessarily more than she wanted an afternoon in bed with Tina. The trouble was that today she couldn't have both.

"You're working on the case, aren't you?" Tina was still eyeing her with suspicion. "I wondered where'd you'd gone to when I got home. Now I know." She walked away from Brenda and leaned against the wall. She slid her hands into the pockets of her pants, the expression on her face gone suddenly sad. "I'm not going to keep you, princess, but you'd better clear your calendar tonight. We'll have some making up to do."

Brenda wasn't sure what to make of this new, improved Tina. The Tina who had left her in August had chosen to close doors instead of opening new ones. They had butted heads and gotten nowhere.

"Baby, I promise we'll have a delicious night with nothing getting in the way." Brenda leaned across and kissed Tina in a slow, deliberate way, then broke off and headed upstairs.

"Hey, I thought you were in a hurry to get back to your case?" Tina asked.

Brenda had been caught off guard once already. She was going to be prepared this time. She dug out the Walther PPK 9MM, stuck it in the waist holster and then slipped on a jacket. It was better if the gun was out of sight. She didn't need to give Tina any more reasons to worry.

She bounded back downstairs, where Tina still waited next to the door, arms crossed. Brenda kissed her again softly on the mouth. "Just had to get my jacket. It's getting colder when the sun goes down."

"Princess, you're not going swimming in your clothes or anything like that again, are you? Remember, I expect you back for dinner."

"Don't worry, okay?"

Tina stood at the door as Brenda headed for her new Jag. She had all intentions of getting back to Tina and her offer.

Chapter 25

It was four-thirty. The day had slipped by like a lazy sailboat on the smooth waters of the bay. Brenda figured she had maybe thirty minutes to catch Michelle Corby at the club. The palm trees lining Bayshore Boulevard swayed in deepening shades of dusk as they stood in silhouettes against the sky of evening purple, fiery reds and lavenders. It would be dark soon.

Brenda sped through Harbour Beach and through the gates of the Tampa Bay Boat and Oars Club. As she pulled into the parking lot, she noticed how few cars remained.

She parked her Jag out front and hurried through the door. There was no one in the lobby. She was headed toward Michelle's office when the same woman who had greeted her before stopped her in mid stride.

"Excuse me, I'm sorry, you can't go in there."

Brenda stopped, whirled to face her and thrust a finger in the woman's stunned face. "You can call the police if you want to stop me. I'll be in Michelle Corby's office. I won't be long." She smiled and continued walking, leaving the woman frozen, mouth open, clearly unable to decide what to do.

Brenda wasn't about to let Michelle Corby go out the back door while she was detained. Of course, she realized she was taking a gamble on Michelle's being there at all, but it was a chance worth taking.

She opened the door without knocking and found an empty office. Brenda checked the one closet in the office on the off chance Michelle might have heard the commotion in the lobby and tried to hide. Nothing. Michelle wasn't there.

Brenda proceeded back out into the hallway and the lobby, where the hostess, wild-eyed, watched her, apparently unsure whether to approach Brenda again or not. Brenda walked up to her. She tried to speak in a calm voice. She didn't want to frighten the woman into silence. She needed to know where Michelle Corby was.

"Do you know where Michelle is?"

The woman cowered under Brenda's intense glare. She started to shake her head but then nodded. When she spoke, her voice was almost a whisper. "What do you want with her?" She gulped. "I mean, you aren't going to harm her or . . ."

Brenda dug out one of her PI cards and handed it to her. "I need to speak with Michelle. Can you tell me where she is?"

The woman scanned the card slowly, finally lifting her gaze back to Brenda. "She's on the *Davross One*, the Davis yacht. I can get you a dock map."

"Never mind. I know where it is."

Brenda left without another word. Michelle Corby could have been the one firing at her that night. There was little light left in the sky as she approached the dock. The waters surrounding her began to take on a dark and ominous look. She walked without hesitation past the boats. It was desolate. There wasn't any activity on any of the boats near the *Davross One*.

As she neared the *Davross One* she noticed the glow of lights belowdecks in the living quarters. Michelle Corby was home. But was she alone? Before stepping aboard, Brenda searched the deck. There was no one about. Trying to stifle the thumping of her heart in her ears, she stepped softly over the railing and onto the yacht.

Surrounding her were only the sounds of the rippling water and seagulls that circled overhead. To her right were two doors. One of them must lead down to the cabins; it was just a question of which one to choose.

Brenda was about to move toward one of the doors when the one to her right popped open and Michelle stood frozen in the doorway.

"Hello, Michelle. Surprised?"

Michelle inched onto the deck cautiously, looking like a trapped mouse. "What are you doing here?"

Brenda shook her head with a mocking smile. "Why is it that everyone who is caught red-handed asks that question?"

"You shouldn't have come looking for me," Michelle said, her voice taking a more defiant tone.

"Well, you see, Michelle, I don't take kindly to getting shot at. You tried to kill me."

Michelle shook her head furiously. "No, you're wrong. It wasn't me. I don't own a gun."

"You have some explaining to do. Care to start? Why did you drag me out here that night? Were you on board waiting for me?"

Michelle grinned. "I know my rights. I don't have to talk to you." She circled around closer to Brenda.

Like a shark going in for the kill, thought Brenda. The weight of her gun behind her back was comforting.

"You can't run away from murder, Michelle. Why don't you tell me what happened that Memorial Day? Did you kill Paula Drakes? Do you know who did? If you tell me the truth now, it may take years off your prison time."

Brenda didn't really know that, but she hoped the bluff might convince Michelle.

But Michelle merely laughed at her. "I think you've been watching too many *Law and Order* episodes. It's too big of a mess now." She stopped and eyed the doorway nervously. "I'm in way too deep."

"Stop while you're ahead, darling." It was a man's voice that interrupted her. A voice Brenda recognized.

Stewart Davis stepped out from the shadows of the doorway. Brenda caught the glint of the 9mm Glock he pointed her way. He looked at her with a smirk on his face.

"What a lovely scenario we have here." He shifted his gaze to Michelle. "The smart-aleck PI and my bitch." His smirk widened. "I couldn't have planned it better if I'd tried."

"Stewart, what the hell are you talking about?" Michelle's voice was a panicked squeak.

"Michelle, dear, let me spell it out for you. We have Brenda Strange, private investigator, who tracks down Paula Drakes' real murderer, except that in this case"—he pointed the gun at Michelle—"it's a murderess. Murderess shoots the private investigator, but not before the private investigator shoots her in self-defense." He shifted the gun toward Brenda. "You do have a gun, don't you?" His voice was harsh. "Hand it over now."

Reluctantly, Brenda reached behind her, slid the PPK from her belt and held it up to Stewart.

"Stop. Put it on the deck and slide it over here," Stewart said.

Brenda had no choice. In a slow, deliberate move, she sent her gun down the floor to Stewart. He picked it up in one swift move, never taking his eyes or gun off Brenda.

"A real tragedy, you see, Michelle," he continued, "because you both die in the shootout, leaving one eyewitness. Me." He smiled as he aimed one gun at Michelle and the other at Brenda.

"You murdered Paula Drakes and had your wife killed. You can't get away. Phil's confessed to everything," Brenda said.

"You fucking bastard. You won't kill me," Michelle hissed. She turned to Brenda. "I'll tell you everything. He did kill Paula Drakes and he had Phil Brown kill my sister." Her eyes were frantic.

"Tsk tsk," Stewart said. "By now, Brenda here probably knows all that. She knows you were with me all the way on those murders. Don't you, Brenda?" His eyes were menacing. "It was very easy with Paula. The stupid dyke threatened me then proceeded to get seasick. I just bashed her head in. It was easy to take her boat and let it float." He flashed Brenda a wicked grin. "And Joan. She just couldn't keep sober enough to stay quiet."

"Did you pay your pilot for that alibi, Stewart? You weren't really in Tallahassee, were you?"

Stewart chuckled. "I was in Tallahassee, Brenda. I merely booked a flight back to Tampa that same day. Too bad you didn't have that figured out. Too late now, I'm afraid."

"Paula will never let you go. You know what I mean. She'll follow you."

His face twitched. "Shut up."

Brenda tried a bluff. "I just came from the police department, Stewart. They're on their way here. You're not getting away."

In one swift move, Stewart aimed Brenda's PPK at Michelle and fired. The thrust of the bullet sent Michelle back like a stuffed doll. She lay lifeless. Brenda made a move toward her.

"Stop right there," Stewart hollered. "You're next." He had the Glock pointed at her head.

"Police. Drop the gun now!"

Lisa Chambliss's command broke the silence of the twilight. It came from behind Brenda somewhere. Panic clouded Stewart's eyes. He hesitated, then pointed the gun away from Brenda.

"Get down, Brenda," Lisa yelled.

The crack of two 9mm guns split the air as Brenda saw the spark from the Glock in Stewart's hand. Red-hot pain shot through her hand. She bent down low to the floor.

Stewart's body hit the deck hard, his Glock making a loud thud and sliding away. Even in the twilight, she could see the hole through his chest, blood already pooling on the deck.

Brenda's left hand was numb and it was covered in blood. She got up slowly, took her jacket off and wrapped it around her bleeding hand, squeezing hard to try and stop the blood flow.

Lisa checked out both Stewart and Michelle, who hadn't moved since getting shot, then moved swiftly to Brenda's side.

Brenda managed a smile. "I know it wasn't the mumbo jumbo, so what got you here?"

"Phil Brown managed to wrestle his way back to us. He fleshed out the rest of the story that 'Jake' had given you. I checked out the contacts that he gave us on the fake art ring. He was right. It was a big scheme. We've got arrests going in Europe as we speak. It seems like your guy Stewart was one of the ringleaders." She shrugged. "I just played a hunch and came looking for Michelle Corby, since I couldn't find Stewart at home." She smiled. "Glad to see me, huh?"

The pain in Brenda's hand was like a knife twisting into her. She winced. Lisa looked at the jacket wrapped around it. Blood was seeping through.

"You were shot." Lisa pulled out her cell and called for backup at the scene as well as paramedics. "I've got to get you to the hospital. TPD will be here any minute. Hang in there."

Brenda wanted to say no. Her head was confused; she couldn't focus. But she'd be damned if she passed out because her hand got shot. She tried to focus on something else. Get her mind off the pain. She looked at Stewart and then at Michelle.

"Is she going to make it?" she asked.

"She's still breathing, but it looks bad," Lisa said.

"Stewart?"

Lisa shook her head. "He's one less we'll have to prosecute."

Brenda heard the sound of an ambulance and police cars in the distance. She felt her feet buckle beneath her. The jacket on her hand was soaked in blood.

"Hey, stay with me, Brenda." Lisa grabbed her.

Brenda saw Lisa's mouth moving but heard nothing. The world went silent and black.

Chapter 26

Eddy and Cubbie had made quick work of the Christmas turkey Cubbie cooked. She'd also prepared extras of the green bean casserole, squash soufflé and fresh cranberries for Brenda and Tina, and several freshly baked breads from the Gulfbreeze for everyone.

Neither Eddy nor Cubbie was staying in Tampa for Christmas. Eddy had a new love in Boston and wanted to spend it with him, and Cubbie was heading out to Chicago to stay with one of her daughters. Brenda decided on an early Christmas dinner for the four of them. And that worked out perfectly, because her parents were due back the twenty-third to spend Christmas with her.

Malfour was alight with candles and Christmas decorations. But the Christmas tree was the center of attention. It stood as guardian to a small pile of brightly wrapped gifts huddled beneath it. Brenda and Tina sat on the couch before the roaring fireplace with Eddy and Cubbie settled in the two wing-back chairs. Butterscotch lay curled into a ball between Brenda and Tina, purring loudly.

Cubbie had a toothpick in her mouth, Eddy a glass of Dewars in hand.

He waved his drink in the air. "This is going to be a great Christmas, I can feel it."

Tina snuggled close to Brenda and squeezed. She looked at her, the fire reflecting in her eyes. "I'm just happy my princess is safe and sound."

Brenda leaned into her lover. "I'm always going to be safe and sound." She pointed to the ceiling. "Remember, I've got the other side protecting me."

They all laughed.

"Yeah, sugar, but it was one Detective Lisa Chambliss that got you out of this mess," Cubbie blurted out.

"It wasn't a mess, Cubbie. It was a situation." Brenda laughed. She was happy that she'd survived to joke about it and sit wrapped in her lover's arms. She could have been shot dead. She had Lisa Chambliss to thank for her life.

Eddy was looking intently at Brenda. "I'm glad you're safe too, Brenda. The whole Stewart thing seems so surreal to me."

"Yeah, well, he had us all duped," Tina said.

"No, not all of you," Cubbie added. They all looked at Brenda.

"Come on, everyone, this is our Christmas party. Let's not talk about that," Brenda said, uncomfortable with the conversation. She leaned over and picked up one of the Christmas gifts. "Let's exchange the presents."

She picked up the small box with the Christmas tag decorated in teddy bears. It was her gift to Cubbie. Brenda handed it to her. Cubbie's eyes lit up.

"Let's wait till we each have our gifts before opening, okay?" Brenda reached for another one. It was a small envelope made of red and green foil. Tina's name was boldly handwritten. Brenda handed it to her. "Merry Christmas, honey. I hope you can use this." Brenda had taken a gamble on Tina's gift.

She passed out the rest of the gifts. She had a gift each from

Cubbie and Eddy in her lap. There was nothing from Tina, who sat there with a permanent smile on her face.

Eddy and Cubbie were overjoyed with their gifts, Cubbie donning the Michael Jordan autographed Chicago Bulls leather cap Brenda had gotten her. Eddy gasped and carried on over the rare Robert Taylor biography Brenda had found on eBay for him. It was the one he was missing from his library.

Brenda was completely surprised by the beautiful autographed 11x13 photo of Bette Davis that Eddy gave her.

"Snuck it right under your nose in Fort Lauderdale." He laughed. "I didn't frame it because I thought I'd let you decide what color scheme you wanted." He winked.

It was a gorgeous, sepia-toned portrait of the starlet staring out with liquid eyes at the camera. It was boldly signed in black fountain pen and inscribed to some fan named Pearl, now long gone.

Brenda clutched it to her chest. Cubbie had given both Brenda and Tina a coupon book for meals at the Gulfbreeze good for almost their entire lifetime. Well, almost. It was the perfect gift.

Brenda stopped Tina before she ripped open the envelope. Ignoring Tina's confusion, she looked at Eddy and Cubbie. "I hope you two don't mind, but Tina and I want to exchange our gifts in private. This is our first Christmas at Malfour, and I want it to be special." She squeezed Tina's hand.

Cubbie laughed. "Hey, now, I get the hint." She got up.

"No, wait a minute, Cubbie, I didn't mean for you to leave right now," Brenda protested.

Eddy got up too. "It was a wonderful night and dinner, Brenda, Tina. It is getting late and you two have to get it on, you know." He smiled and winked again.

They both left, despite Brenda's insistence they stay longer. When Brenda shut the door behind them, Tina wrapped both her arms around her.

"C'mon back. I've got something I've been waiting to give you." She grabbed Brenda by the hand and took her back to the living room couch. They both sat back down, Brenda surprised by all the mystery Tina was spinning.

Tina reached into her pant pocket and pulled out a tiny velvet hexagonal box with a miniature bow attached to the top. A satin ribbon held the top in place.

Brenda's eyes went from the box to Tina. Judging from the box, it was jewelry. Her left hand still bothered her if she moved the fingers too far apart. The stitches were still healing, but she was able to hold the box gently in that hand and untie the ribbon with the other. Tina eyed her steadily, trying hard to suppress a smile.

Inside the box was a diamond ring. Not just an ordinary diamond. It was an engagement ring. Brenda stared at it, unable to say a word. She looked at Tina. "Is this what I think it is?"

Tina reached over and kissed her. "I want us to be forever. This is just something so you won't forget how much I love you."

Brenda fumbled in getting the ring out of the box. Tina took it from her.

"Let me help you, princess." She smiled as she slipped the ring onto Brenda's right hand. "It'll have to stay on this hand temporarily. I don't think it'll go over stitches."

Brenda stared at it, feeling the emotions pour through her system. The tears would come soon. "It's stunning, Tina." She flung herself into Tina's arms, holding on tight. She wiped her eyes, broke away from Tina and pointed at the Christmas envelope with Tina's name on it. "Open yours."

Tina smiled as she tore apart the envelope. Brenda watched her lover's face grow perplexed as she unfolded a set of papers. Tina read each paper-clipped sheet, flipping excitedly. When she read the last one, she looked at Brenda. Her eyes were open in shock, mouth moving, but nothing coming out.

"Do you like it?"

"Oh, my God. I can't believe . . ." She looked at the papers then back at Brenda. "Princess, you got me a gallery?" Her voice was a squeak.

"It's a small storefront off Howard Avenue. Great location in Hyde Park." Brenda searched her lover's face. "Is this something you want?"

Tina flung herself at Brenda, smothering her with kisses. She took hold of Brenda's good hand and pulled her up from the couch. "Let's finish celebrating in a more comfortable place."

They were wrapped in each other's arms when the phone rang.

"Don't get it." Tina's whisper was hot on Brenda's ear.

"It might be my parents." She broke from Tina's embrace.

Tina made disappointed noises as Brenda picked up the phone. It was her father. He sounded far away. Brenda's good spirits were sucked away.

"Dad, what's wrong?"

"Your mother has taken very ill. We're in New York. We had to take an emergency plane here from West Palm. She doesn't want anyone to treat her other than her doctors in New York."

"Why didn't you call and tell me what was going on? You both take off and I don't hear a word from you until now."

He paused on the other end. "I'm sorry, honey, that we didn't call. There is nothing you can do up here. All I'm doing is waiting in the hospital."

Brenda felt so helpless. Her mother had become someone she wanted to care about. The healing between them had started, just as her father hoped. Brenda didn't want to contemplate what losing her mother now might mean to her.

"Dad, should I fly up there? Please, be honest with me. Is there anything at all I can do? If not for Mom, then at least to help you out."

"Stay home, honey. The doctors are doing all they can."

Brenda struggled with the words. "How bad is she?"

He hesitated again. Brenda knew it was bad.

"She passed out at the restaurant. We were having dinner with some friends." His voice cracked.

"Dad, I can get the next flight out of Tampa to New York."

"What you can do for me, sweetheart, is make sure our belongings get shipped safely back home to Montpointe. We left in a hurry. I didn't get a chance to get everything."

"Of course. I'll do that for you. But you'll have to promise me to call me as many times a day as you want. Tell me how Mother is doing. Please."

"As soon as the doctors tell me anything, I'll be on the phone to you, sweetheart."

"I love you, Dad. Give my love to Mother and tell her Butterscotch misses her."

Brenda hung up the phone and let the tears that wanted out of her eyes fall down her cheeks. Tina was right behind her, holding on to Brenda softly. Brenda turned to her, wiping the tears off her cheeks.

"She's going to die."

Chapter 27

It should have been a memorable Christmas for Brenda. The Paula Drakes case was successfully closed. Michelle Corby survived the gunshot wound and both she and Phil, a.k.a. Jake, Brown were awaiting court dates on murder charges.

But how the hell was she supposed to have a merry holiday season? Her first Christmas at Malfour was marred by the shadows that still crawled across the walls and the cold reality of her mother's losing battle against cancer. Brenda had no strength left to fight off the apprehension that had settled in her heart.

Christmas had come and gone and the New Year's baby was ready to pop the cork off Champagne bottles everywhere. Tina had gotten a call from one of the galleries in New York. A car plowed through the gallery storefront and damaged several of her sculptures. They needed her to sign insurance papers and pick up what was left of her art. Tina left with promises of her return. South Tampa University had offered her the job and she accepted, but she had to finish off the school season at the art institute in Newark.

Brenda had moped the whole day, working on her new Pisces Zodiac Bear and bonding with Butterscotch, but it wasn't enough. She was restless. Her father called often, but she was still seriously flirting with booking a flight to New York without advance warning to her dad. If she told him, he would try to talk her out of it.

She headed out to Strange Investigations for the mail. With Cubbie gone and the case closed, Brenda had closed the office until Cubbie returned after the holidays. Picking up the mail at Strange Investigations kept her close to work, even though it was mostly junk mail.

The office felt empty without Cubbie there. Since she was already there, Brenda thought she'd call Kevin in New Jersey and see if he had any news on Paula Drakes' missing body. It was just one of those little threads Brenda didn't like to leave untied in cases.

She talked to Kevin only for a short time. He was busy as usual. The police still had no leads on the disappearance of Paula's body. They were going to leave it open but in all probability, it was as good as dead.

On the way out, Brenda stood next to Cubbie's desk and sifted through the handful of envelopes accumulated there. A letter covered in colorful, overseas stamps jumped to her attention. She looked at the scribbled return address. It was from Clifford Satterly in Spain. She remembered the heated conversation at the Fort Lauderdale autograph show.

Inside was a bundle of thick papers with a separate wafer- thin sheet. Brenda pulled it out and a check floated to the floor. She picked up the check and glanced at the amount. It was made out to her for two thousand dollars. Brenda read the short note.

Dear Miss Strange,
I would like to engage your services. I have enclosed a check for
$2,000.00 in the hopes this is enough to cover initial expenses. We spoke

briefly at the autograph show, but I was not at liberty to speak further with you about this matter.

My manuscript was stolen from me. I sent it to Hilda Moran on good faith and she is trying to steal it for herself. I have included all the paperwork proving that this manuscript was shipped and signed for by Hilda.

Please contact me when you have information to report on this case. Thank you in advance.

Clifford Satterly

Intrigued, Brenda opened the bunch of folded papers. They were copies of FedEx receipts and tracking tickets. She looked closely at the FedEx paperwork. The manuscript was shipped with the highest insurance allowed on such packages and addressed to Hilda Moran in Key Largo, Florida. The name Key Largo brought on memories of the great black-and-white vintage film with Bogie and Bacall. Brenda's parents had vacationed often in the Keys.

Hilda's signature appeared boldly on the copy of the FedEx receipt. Brenda recalled how easily Hilda had dismissed Clifford Satterly and his ranting.

Brenda tucked the check and the papers back into the envelope and stuffed it into her bag. She locked the office, her mind racing through what she remembered of the autograph show.

She got into her car and drove away from Strange Investigations. Was she ready for another case? Her mother lay deathly ill in a hospital in New York and possibly in need of her. On the other hand, a new case could shake the fog she'd been in for weeks.

She drove onto Bayshore Boulevard and crossed over the Hillsborough River Bridge on the way back to Malfour. Brenda pressed the radio on to her favorite talk radio station but only half listened to the news. Her ears suddenly picked up the words *sea monster*. She smiled as the reporter continued talking about sightings in the Tampa Bay area of a mysterious sea creature in the bay. None of the sightings could be confirmed and were being compared to sightings during the forties. The reports were being dismissed as a prank.

Brenda smiled even wider. She silently thanked Paula Drakes for her courage. She had exposed herself and risked danger in order to bring her murderer to justice.

"May you swim in peace, Paula," Brenda whispered aloud.

The palm trees along Bayshore swished high against the cloud-free blue sky, and the sun captured everything in sharp focus. It was the picture-perfect postcard except for one thing. It was cold in Tampa.

Brenda picked up her brand-new cell phone and punched in the Internet service. She found the Weather Channel and searched for Key Largo. She smiled at the temperature displayed. It was very warm.